Once you're in, there's no getting out.

The brotherhood. The Klan. They were all in it—Shad, Granddaddy, Jeremiah. Back when Shad had joined, he hadn't known Granddaddy was in, but he'd figured it out soon enough. He might have felt more at ease during his first Klan meeting if he'd known that Granddaddy was somewhere in the room. But even so, he wouldn't have joined because of him. No, he'd joined to get tough like Jeremiah. To prove himself. Grow up. Be a man. Make Mama proud. Make Daddy proud. All of those reasons, and a whole lot more. But at the time—Lord God Almighty—at the time, Shad didn't have any notion what he was getting into.

Other Books You May Enjoy

BROTHERHOOD

A. B. Westrick

PUFFIN BOOKS
An Imprint of Penguin Group (USA)

PUFFIN BOOKS
Published by the Penguin Group
Penguin Group (USA) LLC
375 Hudson Street
New York, New York 10014

USA * Canada * UK * Ireland * Australia
New Zealand * India * South Africa * China

penguin.com
A Penguin Random House Company

First published in the United States of America by Viking,
an imprint of Penguin Young Readers Group, 2013
Published by Puffin Books, an imprint of Penguin Young Readers Group, 2014

Copyright © 2013 by Anne Westrick
Map courtesy of Mike Gorman, from the National Archives in Washington, D.C.

This is a work of fiction. Names, characters, places, and incidents either
are the product of the author's imagination or are used fictitiously.

THE LIBRARY OF CONGRESS HAS CATALOGED THE VIKING EDITION AS FOLLOWS:
Westrick, Anne.
Brotherhood / Anne Westrick.
pages cm
Summary: "The year is 1867, and the South has lost the Civil War. Those on the lowest rungs,
like Shad's family, fear that the freed slaves will take the few jobs available. In this climate of
despair and fear, a group has formed. Today we know it as the KKK"—Provided by publisher.
ISBN 978-0-670-01439-2 (hardcover)
1 Reconstruction (U.S. history, 1865–1877)—Juvenile fiction.
[1. Reconstruction (U.S. history, 1865–1877)—Fiction. 2. Race relations—Fiction.
3. Prejudices—Fiction. 4. Family life—Virginia—Fiction. 5. Ku Klux Klan (19th cent.)—Fiction.
6. Richmond (Va.)—History—19th century—Fiction.] I. Title.
Pz7.W52733Bro 2013
[Fic]—dc23
2013008272

Puffin Books ISBN 978-0-14-242237-3

Printed in the United States of America

3 5 7 9 10 8 6 4 2

For Mary

BROTHERHOOD

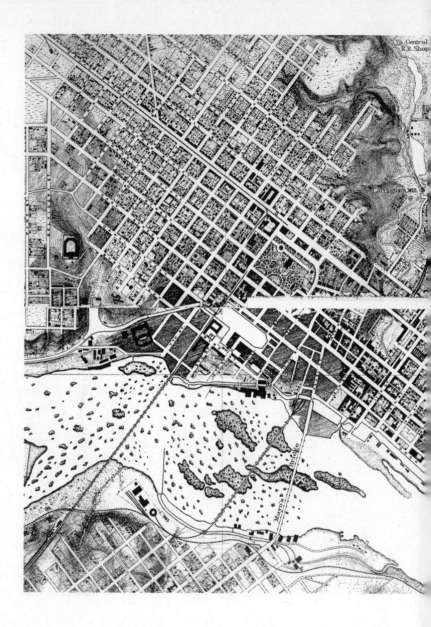

Vt. Central
R.R. Shops

Cavrington's Mill

Mayro's Bridge

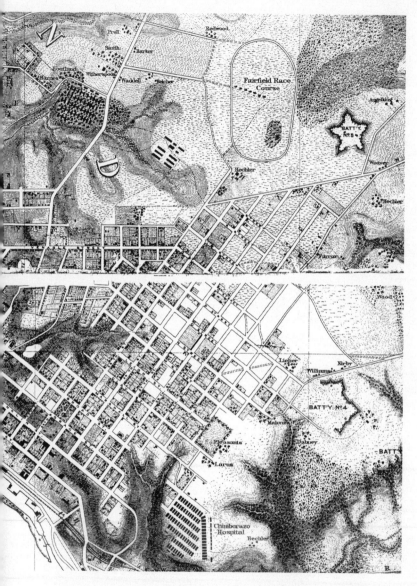

U.S. ARMY CORPS OF ENGINEERS
Map of Richmond, 1867

A Note to the Reader

IT IS SAID that we mirror the times and places in which we were born, and our journeys to adulthood are marked by moments in which we gain new understandings and the courage to change ourselves and our world. *Brotherhood* is the story of a fourteen-year-old boy whose point of view reflects his time and place—Richmond, Virginia, in 1867—but his view is one that today's readers will undoubtedly find callous and racist. My intention in writing this story was not to justify his view, but to draw readers so closely into his world that they experience his emerging capacity to question his circumstances.

—A. B. Westrick

BROTHERHOOD

1

The Posse

THE FIRST SOUND Shad heard was the squawk of a chicken. Then the thud of a fist on wood. *Bam. Bam. Bam.* The hollow walls rattled. A man's voice. "Mrs. Weaver?"

The light was early yet, and Shad glanced beside him. His older brother lay asleep there in his trousers—right there on top of the white cotton ticking. Hadn't even changed into a nightshirt. Shad nudged Jeremiah's shoulder and heard his brother grunt, but he didn't wake.

The thud came again. *Bam. Bam.* "Mrs. Weaver? Official business of the government of the United States. Open up!" The voice was flat and nasal—not Virginia-born.

Shad nudged Jeremiah harder this time, but still his brother didn't rouse. Shad rolled off the straw mattress, feet on cool dirt, and headed for the window. But at the sill, he jumped back. "Lord!"

There was a boy maybe Jeremiah's age—seventeen—maybe a tad more—blond like Jeremiah. He stood on the other side, only inches from Shad's face. Navy blue cap. Blue uniform. Brass buttons. Musket on his shoulder. He said, "Going somewhere, Mr. Weaver?"

The bedroom door flew open, and Shad spun around. Two blue-clad boys and a man stormed inside, and the man announced, "Jeremiah Weaver, you are under arrest."

From somewhere in the house, Shad heard Mama yell, "You ain't got no right!" He wanted to find her—protect her—but he felt a tug on his nightshirt. The outside boy had reached through the window and grabbed it, shouting, "He's trying to escape."

Shad balled a fist to slam in the boy's face, but the man saw him and moved fast, crossing the little room and blocking Shad's upraised arm. The outside boy yanked the nightshirt, the man shoved, and Shad fell hard, his head hitting the sill on the way down.

He heard the outside boy announce, "We got him."

"Not this one," the man said. "The other one."

Shad struggled to all fours, his head throbbing, anger

mounting. The man pushed him down again, pinning him to the floor. Shad couldn't see more than a shuffle of boots and Jeremiah's bare feet while the boys dragged his brother from the house. Then he felt a stomp on his back, crushing his ribs. Air raced from his lungs. Shad choked. Coughed. Gasped to refill his chest. Images flashed through his mind—a man stuffed in a barrel, a man flailing his arms—and for a moment, Shad thought he might vomit.

He heard horses whinny out front, and he rose in pain, holding his ribs. He rolled over the windowsill and dropped the few feet to red dirt, but by the time he circled front, the posse was galloping toward Richmond. Not two minutes there and gone, and the little white house quivered with the rumble of hooves.

"Damn Yankees!" he yelled at their backs.

He turned to see Mama, bug-eyed with fury. "Shadrach, you run into town and get your granddaddy." Her voice faltered and he feared she would cry. "You hear me, son? Tell him they done arrested Jeremiah."

"Yes, ma'am. Yes, I'll—" He reached for her.

Mama was shaking all over. When he put his arms around her bony shoulders, her tears started running, so he set his head on top of hers. His mama was small—so very small. "Yes, Mama," he whispered. "Don't you worry none. Everything's gonna be okay. I'll get him back."

But truth to tell, he didn't think everything would be okay and didn't know if he could get his brother back. All he knew for sure was that Mama needed Jeremiah. It was always "Jeremiah this," "Jeremiah that." "Jeremiah first" ever since Daddy left.

Shad stroked Mama's hair—long, thin, brown hair, going gray from worry. Then he patted Mama's shoulder and settled her into a chair. He ducked into the bedroom for his britches and burlap-sack shirt, but the simplest movements—taking off his nightshirt, bending to pull up his britches—sent pain through his innards like an arrow. "Ow!"

"You okay, baby?" called Mama.

"Fine, Mama," he lied. "I'm fine." He released his breath, long and slow, erasing the strain from his face so that Mama wouldn't add him to her list of worries. He emerged from the bedroom and kissed her on the cheek.

Then he ran.

He could see the horses way up Nine Mile Road—a straight line cut through green fields gone to weed. The sun was low behind him, and it hit him—he'd overslept. Late for lessons. Again. But no, he couldn't go for lessons today. Not today.

He ran and ran, but his sides hurt, and soon enough his thighs seized up and he couldn't keep on. His head ached. His chest. If that man roughing him up hadn't been bad enough, Shad was exhausted—he'd hardly slept last night.

Had it only been last night? That meeting of the brotherhood. Boys setting a farmhouse on fire. The smoke, the sparks, the roar of flames. It all came back and a shudder went through him. His foot hit a rut in the road and he stumbled, tripping forward, swinging his arms to keep his balance and stay upright. His ribs twisted and he cringed. His breathing came hard.

He looked up the road and couldn't see the horses anymore. He slowed. Two full years since the war had ended, but the Yankees were still beating up on Virginia.

Two full years since the surrender of the greatest general the world had ever known. Robert E. Lee.

Two full years of Yankees patrolling Richmond's streets. He hated them! And before that, four years of fighting and food shortages and hotels turned to hospitals for men blown to bits by shrapnel and cannons.

The War Between the States was supposed to have secured Virginia's right to make her own laws. South Carolina had seceded from the Union, and after a heap of argument, Virginia had seceded, too. But it had all come to naught.

Worse than naught—every Southern family had lost a boy to battle, and most lost more than one.

Daddy had dragged his feet, not wanting to fight, but he couldn't drag them forever. It was September 1862, five years ago, when he rode off on Mindy-girl to join Virginia's 62nd Cavalry Partisan Rangers regiment. Shad had watched him wave good-bye, waving his whole arm, brushing it wide and wild against a white-cloud sky, brushing so hard that for a moment Shad believed he'd brush the war away.

Now as he hustled up Nine Mile Road, Shad got tight in the throat thinking on scruffy old Mindy-girl, on Daddy telling him he had two special girls in his life—his horse and his wife. Shad squeezed his hands into fists. He picked up his pace, then slowed again. Caught his breath. What would Daddy say now if he could see the fields lying fallow? If he knew they'd arrested Jeremiah?

Only fourteen and he had to handle this without Daddy. Had to get Jeremiah back for Mama.

His eyes caught a scrap of blue cloth stuck in blackberry brambles, but he didn't stop. No, he couldn't take the time to pocket scraps this morning.

2

Twisted Wrists

SHAD TURNED TOWARD Church Hill. To get to Granddaddy's, he'd have to go south and west to Shockoe Bottom, and the very thought of the climb made his ribs throb all the more. Richmond, the city of seven hills—river city on the fall line of the James, largest city in all of Virginia—but darn those hills. Up, down, up, down— what he'd give to ride Mindy-girl again. He fingered the tender spot where his head had hit the windowsill. Lordy, life sure would be easier if his family lived in town.

He made it to Twentieth Street, then Broad—the downhill leg—and whoa! There was Rachel. She was clutching her flower-print skirts in her fine caramel hands, her brown lace-up shoes working fast. What was she doing out this early? She was supposed to be teaching, not running these gray-brick streets at dawn.

He called to her, and she looked over a shoulder.

"Shad? Oh, Lord, get away, get away."

"Rachel?" She was going the wrong way—toward the Perkinsons'. He needed to get Granddaddy. But he could take a minute here. He could see she was in a tizzy.

"I don't want to talk to you!"

"Rachel—what—?"

"I don't want anything to do with you and your family!"

Her words hit him like a slap across the face. He stuttered, "W-wait."

She looked at him, but her feet didn't stop. Her dark eyes blazed with anger. Wisps of black hair stuck out under a red calico kerchief that didn't match her dress, not at all. It wasn't like Rachel to be in town all mismatched.

Shad ran and reached for her arm. He caught her hand, and she stopped. She stopped all right. But she shook his hand away. Her eyes said, *Don't you dare!*

He pulled back and rubbed her sweat between his fingers. "Sorry. I, uh…" He winced in shame for having grabbed her. He wanted so much for her to think highly of him—to impress her. It was crazy to care what a freed slave might think. But he did care. She was … different.

He watched her chest go up and down. Watched her

breathe through her mouth. She was probably only a year older than Shad, but nearly a foot shorter and—much as he hated to admit it—a lifetime smarter.

"I hope they hang your brother," she said. "He might get away with killing a Negro, but not a white man. No, sir. That's a hanging offense."

The slap became a wallop. Shad shook his head. "What? What are you talkin' about?"

"Don't give me that know-nothing look. He said 'the Weaver boy' before he died. He said 'the Weaver boy' shoved him in a barrel. Lord, have mercy."

"Wait, wait, wait. He—who?"

"George Nelson!"

"No!"

"You ask your brother. He'll know what I'm talking about. Doc Moore sent for us to identify the body. I saw him. Saw George Nelson with my own eyes—his body laid out there. And Lord, what Miss Elizabeth will say when she hears! How am I going to tell her?"

Shad struggled to breathe. He felt winded again—his chest aching more from her words than the blow from the Yankee boot. "But—wait—"

"She's been waiting long enough. I have to go."

"You got it wrong."

"Don't give me that, Shadrach Weaver. George Nelson saw your brother. They fished him from a barrel in a pond and he said it was 'the Weaver boy,' and then he up and died. Your brother is going to pay this time. He can't get out of this one."

"No, you got it wrong," Shad said again, but the moment the words were out of his mouth, he knew he shouldn't have spoken.

He gritted his teeth and watched as the realization came over Rachel's face. Her eyes grew silver-dollar bright. Her neck stretched up and her shoulders down. Then her mouth fell open and she covered it with her hand, even as she spoke. "You were there."

Shad's tongue grew thick. He wanted to speak, but he couldn't form words.

"Get on! What do you know?"

"I—I—"

"You tell me. You tell me right now! You know what happened."

He shook his head.

"I see it in your eyes."

"Rachel—"

"Don't you *Rachel* me, Mr. Weaver. Sir!"

Maybe it was the way she said *sir*. Maybe it was the way she saw through him. Maybe it was the way Mama had shaken all over this morning. Or the way they'd taken Jeremiah when he was so fast asleep and hungover, he hadn't put up a fight. Maybe it was Rachel saying George Nelson had died.

He didn't know, but he grabbed Rachel's wrists and twisted them. He bent them into each other and heard her let out a little shriek, and he didn't let go. Through her arms he felt her weight shift and knew her knees had buckled, but still he didn't let go. Her eyes bored into him and he held her wrists and he felt strong.

He got ready for her to kick him where it hurt, knowing that if she so much as tried to kick him, he'd break her wrists. He'd snap them plumb in two.

He waited for the kick. He was ready. But she got still. She closed her mouth and her nostrils flared. Her eyes went coal black, the whites disappeared, and she winced without making a sound. Her arms were still, but he could feel the pounding of her heart through her wrists.

Then he shuddered and let go. He watched her gulp air like it was water. What had come over him? It had surprised him that he'd grabbed her wrists. He looked at his hands, wondering at himself. He was stronger than he knew, and he didn't like how he could hurt her. He hadn't meant—

She snatched up her skirts and marched off.

"Wait! Wait a minute."

She didn't wait.

He rushed to catch up. "Rachel, wait!"

She marched with a holier-than-thou air. He got alongside her and saw that one hand rubbed the wrist of the other.

"I'm sorry. Look, I'm sorry."

She kept on marching. Her eyes brimmed with tears. One tear had gone down her cheek and left behind a shiny line straight to the corner of her mouth.

He hadn't meant to hurt her. "I'm real sorry. I mean that. I'm real sorry."

"You," she started to say. Then she shook her head. "I've got nothing to say to you!"

He opened his mouth to explain—he wanted so much for her to understand—but no words came to him. He wrung his hands and stood still on the cool brick street. He'd taken too much time—he had to get Granddaddy—but he lingered a moment longer, watching her lean into the Broad Street hill, watching her flowered skirts *swish-swish* back and forth, watching until she turned toward Grace Street, watching until he couldn't see her anymore.

3

Overstepping Boundaries

SHAD HURRIED DOWN Broad, heading west, then cut across the tree-lined streets—Grace and Franklin—weaving between brick buildings and down alleys all the way to Main. The closer he got to Granddaddy's, the more he smelled the river. Or maybe it was rotting fish and vegetables. Or people dumping chamber pots in Shockoe's dirt and gray-brick streets. Two blocks farther, the canal cut along Dock Street, and beyond that, the marsh, then the James River. The stink might have come from just about anything.

At Main Street, he darted around farm carts clattering into town from New Market Road. It was only sunup, but the marketplace at Main and Seventeenth was already bustling with farmers unloading kale and onions, collards and rutabaga, turnips, parsley, and potatoes. Catty-corner to the hustle-bustle sat Granddaddy's shop, the last in a row of redbrick shops, each three stories tall with one window and a brown door at street level and two windows overhead. Granddaddy shared a wall with Hanson's Tack and Leather Goods. A white sign with blue letters over Granddaddy's door said WEAVER'S FINE TAILORING.

Shad pushed the door open and heard the familiar squeak. The little bell tinkled, and he took the wooden steps two at a time. On the second floor, his eyes caught the yellow lines of sunshine that peeked through shutter slats, drawing a slanted grid on the floor. He rounded the room to the next flight of stairs and called up. "Granddaddy?"

He heard rustling overhead. "Shad? That you? What time is it?"

"Uh, I ain't sure. It's early yet."

"I got britches from Mr. Dabney needing the pleats fixed. New hem. You see 'em on the chair there?"

"Uh, yes, sir." On an ordinary day, Shad would have run deliveries and pickups first, then taken home the simple jobs like pleats and hems. But today wasn't an ordinary day. He wanted to kick himself for touching Rachel. No, he should have kicked *her* for saying what she did about his brother! He shuddered.

He listened to Granddaddy's water hit the chamber pot. Then he heard fabric slip against fabric. The clasp of a belt buckle.

He shifted from one foot to the other, and his eyes fell on a few dresses and two men's jackets hanging on a wire rack. Granddaddy's black sewing machine with foot pedals—the one Mama hated, the one she'd said came from the devil—sat by the front window. People had been sewing clothes by hand for a thousand years, so Mama didn't see any reason to do differently now. If Shad had his say, why, he'd give his left foot for a chance at that machine. But Mama had said, "Over my dead body," and that was that.

Granddaddy came down from the third floor squinting, his feet hitting the wooden steps unevenly—*clip-thunk, clip-thunk.* Shad watched him rub his face and run his tongue over his teeth.

"Goodness," he said. "Must've overslept." He hadn't yet greased his mustache, and instead of handlebars, silvery fringe covered his mouth. He wore a white shirt with an unbuttoned black vest, and looked a mess. Shad hadn't ever seen him so rumpled.

"Sir, the Yankees arrested Jeremiah, and Mama's fit to be tied."

"Good Lord." He reached for Shad's shoulder to find his balance.

Shad braced himself to support Granddaddy, and the motion sent twinges through his gut. He tried not to show the pain. Today's emergency was all about Jeremiah, not about Shad getting roughed up by a few stupid Yankees.

"What'd they charge him with?" Granddaddy asked.

"Didn't say."

"Your mama all right?"

Shad nodded. "She sent me to fetch you."

"How'd they get him? You see 'em?"

"Yes, sir. Crack o' dawn. They came bustin' in the house and took him near sound asleep."

"Damn Yankees. They'll make up a charge to lock that boy away. They have it in for Jeremiah." Granddaddy looked up as he spoke, and Shad liked that—liked the way even his grandfather looked up to him now that he'd grown six inches over the past year.

He watched as Granddaddy paced from the brick wall on one side of the room to the white plaster on the other. He listened to the *clip-thunk* of his gait and recalled a story Granddaddy had told about an accident with a horse.

He rolled Granddaddy's words around and around

in his mind. *They'll make up a charge to lock that boy away.* He rubbed the tender spot on his head, knowing the Yankees hadn't made up the charge. If Rachel had told the truth about George Nelson fingering "the Weaver boy"—and he knew Rachel wouldn't lie—then Granddaddy was going to hear it soon enough. He might as well hear it from Shad.

"Look, Granddaddy, this is real bad. Word's out there's a dead body at Doc Moore's and—and Jeremiah did it."

"Whoa. Slow down, there. Just hold on a minute, son. A dead body?"

"Yes, sir."

"Who?"

Shad bit his tongue. He couldn't say the name because he wasn't supposed to know the name. George Nelson had never said it. Shoot. He didn't know what he knew anymore. He shrugged.

"Jiminy, Shadrach. We need to know who it was."

"Word is the man got fished from a barrel and said 'the Weaver boy' 'fore he up and died."

Shad watched Granddaddy rub his face and tried to make out what he was thinking. Then Granddaddy stomped the floor with his good leg—stomped it so hard the windowpanes rattled. "Dern it all, Shad! That wasn't supposed to happen. The brotherhood is taking things too far. They're overstepping boundaries, and they're—I don't know how to slow 'em down."

Shad nodded, and in the silence that followed, he felt blood pulse through the tender spot on his head. He watched Granddaddy fiddle with his mustache. He said, "Yes, sir—I mean, I don't know, sir."

The brotherhood. The Klan. They were all in it— Shad, Granddaddy, Jeremiah. Back when Shad had joined, he hadn't known Granddaddy was in, but he'd figured it out soon enough. He might have felt more at ease during his first Klan meeting if he'd known that Granddaddy was somewhere in the room. But even so, he wouldn't have joined because of him. No, he'd joined to get tough like Jeremiah. To prove himself. Grow up. Be a man. Make Mama proud. Make Daddy proud. All of those reasons, and a whole lot more. But at the time—Lord God Almighty—at the time, Shad didn't have any notion what he was getting into.

4

The Road to Cold Harbor

HE'D JOINED UP the third night Jeremiah had slipped out the window. Shad hadn't said anything the first time Jeremiah climbed out. Or the second. But on the third night, the bedbugs were eating him up. Shad lay full awake, itching all over—his shoulder, his leg, his side—everything itched. He scratched, but the itch kept at him. The air was sticky hot.

Light came from the moon, near full. Shad felt the mattress shift and heard the sounds of his brother pulling on a shirt and britches. The mattress shifted again as Jeremiah fetched the boot hook and tugged at his boots. Then the hook dropped to the dirt floor with a thud.

Shad's side of the bed was closest to the window, and when his brother circled around to climb out, Shad grabbed his shirt.

"Where you going?"

Jeremiah yanked the shirt free and knocked Shad back on the bed. "*Shh*. You ain't seen me."

"Course I seen you. I ain't blind."

Jeremiah snatched up something on the sill and shook his fist. Shad slipped off the mattress and stood beside him, squinting in the moonlight. He watched his brother uncurl his fingers one at a time. Jeremiah had nabbed a huge grass-hopper.

"Say that's you," said Jeremiah.

The hopper wiggled to beat all. Next thing Shad knew, Jeremiah had pulled off a leg and put it up to the moon. Now the hopper's innards were outers, and the leg was twitching with a mind of its own. Shad cringed. "Stop it!"

Jeremiah imitated him in a girlie voice. "Stop it. Stop it."

"I ain't no girl!"

"I ain't no girl," Jeremiah sang. He pulled off the other leg and shoved it in Shad's face, so close Shad's eyes blurred. Then Jeremiah put on his big-man voice and whispered so it came out like a growl, "You ain't old enough."

"Am, too. Fourteen's enough. Lemme come."

Then Shad felt something cold on his foot—something gooey—and he knew Jeremiah had dropped the hopper.

He shook his foot and the grasshopper slid off, flapping its wings against the dirt floor.

Jeremiah grabbed Shad's arm with two hands and twisted.

"Ow," cried Shad.

"Stay home. You hear me?" Jeremiah shoved him away. Then he rolled over the windowsill and took off running through the corn that wasn't corn anymore. It hadn't been corn for two years, not since the Yankees torched it.

Shad pulled on a burlap-sack shirt and the britches handed down to him when cousin Willy Johnson died. He climbed out the window, lickety-split. He wasn't going to let Jeremiah stop him. Not again. He could steal into the night like Jeremiah. He could duck behind forsythia, creep through a field, lay low, fall into a moon shadow. He could do anything his brother could do.

He saw Jeremiah get to the tree line and cut onto the road. He set a good pace, and Shad scrambled to keep up. His nose quivered with whiffs of sulfur, mole holes, and earthworm rot. Mist rose like a thin white blanket across the field, and the creeps raced up his spine. "Get off-a me, shivers. I'm-a do this."

He reached the tree line and stood there for a second,

marveling at the long shadows set off by the moon—at the brightness of the night. It was no mystery why slaves broke for free when the moon rose full up. It was no wonder Mr. Kechler used to shackle his on nights like this. No wonder so many of them got away before Lincoln freed them all. Why, the moon was so brilliant, it nearly took his breath away.

Shad rushed forward, feeling last month's dogwood and cherry blossoms grip the bottoms of his feet. He heard crickets chirping up a storm, and he prayed his brother wouldn't look back.

Don't look back, Jeremiah. Please don't look back.

Then he lost him.

Shad ducked behind a tree and peered around, scanning the road up and back, kicking himself for not following more closely. He strained to see and was about to turn back when the moonlight caught Jeremiah again. *Thank you, moon!* Shad dashed ahead.

Before he'd slid out that window, Jeremiah had tucked a bundle under his arm, and now Shad could see him marching with that bundle and a gait that said, *Don't mess with me.*

Jeremiah turned off Nine Mile Road toward town. Shad darted ahead and got to the corner. He saw Jeremiah turn on Venable Street. Not another soul in sight. Then Jeremiah took the Mechanicsville road toward Cold Harbor, and Shad ran.

Cold Harbor. The battle there had been a bloodbath. Mama's sister was a nurse at the Chimborazo hospital up Church Hill, and all the beds had filled up. They'd run out of beds, and out of floor space, and out of wagons to bring the men in. So they'd stopped bringing them in. They'd just left the boys where they'd fallen. Left them on the road. Right here—the one under Shad's feet.

Shad felt a tad queasy thinking about dead bodies, and he tried to talk himself strong. He told himself they'd had plenty of time to clean the bodies off the road. Three years since the Battle of Cold Harbor, 1864. Plenty of time for a proper burial.

Shad's head chanted, *Three years.* He kept the beat. Left foot. Three years. Right foot. Three years. He told himself to stop thinking about bodies because thinking about that sort of thing spooked a boy bad. But deciding not to think on dead bodies meant thinking on them twice as much.

Shad got the goose bumps. The talk around town about ghosts—Shad knew it was only Jeremiah running at the mouth. But it had him tight.

Left foot. Three years. Right foot. Three years. Lordy, he was walking through a graveyard with no grave markers. He looked for bodies. Left. Right. Three years.

He saw Jeremiah slip over the brow of a ridge, and he scrambled to catch up. His breathing came hard. He got over the ridge and the road stretched empty before him. Straight and empty all the way to Mechanicsville.

He'd lost him.

5

Ghosts

SHAD LOOKED AROUND. The ridge
was clear. Below him in front and in back, mist rose like
fingers from a grave. Shad shivered. How had he gotten this
far and lost Jeremiah? Shoot.

He thought he'd figured out his brother. But Jeremiah
had pulled one over on him again. He felt so . . . so stupid.

Then Shad heard something move, and he jumped
sky-high.

A twig broke.

He whirled around.

A ghost appeared from behind a tree. "Who goes there?"
Shad's heart pounded in his mouth.

The ghost was extra tall with a pointy head. He wore a
sheet that looked gray in the moonlight. Shad told himself
it was just a sheet. Just an old sheet.

The ghost said, "I am a spirit from the other world. I was killed at Cold Harbor."

Shad's knees quivered. His eyes darted left and right. Where was Jeremiah?

"Who are *you*?" said the ghost. "And where are you going?" It let out a deep, evil-sounding laugh. It pointed. "You! Who *are* you?"

Shad opened his mouth, but he had no voice. He saw another ghost come out from behind a tree. This one had a face painted on a gray sheet—a crooked, sloppy face. Shad knew these ghosts weren't real, but his heart thumped. He told himself, *Not scared. Holy moly, not scared at all.*

He heard the pointy-headed ghost laugh another deep laugh. "What brings you here?"

"I—uh—"

"The brotherhood?" asked Pointy Head.

"No!" said the other ghost. Shad sensed something in the way he said it—a jerk in his voice, or the step of his boot—something that meant Crooked Face wanted Pointy Head to shut up.

But Pointy Head didn't shut up. "Let him join the brotherhood!"

Shad looked from Crooked Face to Pointy Head. Back and forth, back and forth.

"He's a pip-squeak," said Crooked Face. "A snot-nosed pip-squeak."

Shad squinted. *Jeremiah?*

"He can learn," said Pointy Head.

"He's a crybaby," said Crooked Face.

Shad dropped his mouth open. Sure enough, that was Jeremiah under the sheet. Jeremiah calling him a crybaby. Shad wanted to punch his brother smack-dab in the nose. But where exactly was his nose?

"Speak up!" demanded Pointy Head, stomping toward him.

Shad snapped his mouth shut.

"Are you here to join the brotherhood?"

Pointy Head's dying-man voice reminded him of Jeremiah's buddy Clifton. Now Shad felt indignant. What nerve his brother and Clifton had, treating people this way—scaring the dickens out of them. "Yes, I am!" he shouted.

"Jiminy," mumbled Crooked Face.

"State your name!" croaked Pointy Head.

"Shad."

"Your full name."

"Shadrach Alfriend Weaver." He saw Crooked Face turn and kick a tree. Then he heard Pointy Head laugh.

"What do you know about the brotherhood?" demanded Pointy Head.

"Uh, well . . ."

"Speak up!"

Shad straightened, racking his brains to find the words. The truth was that he knew very little. He'd heard talk around town and had watched Jeremiah sneak out the window. He'd put two and two together, but he wasn't sure. "I know it protects people. I know brothers ride the streets at night, keeping evil away."

Pointy Head slapped him on the shoulder. "Attaboy."

Shad heard Crooked Face mumble again. "He ain't ready."

"Give him a chance."

"He don't know what he's doing."

"Sure he does. You hear him? He's got guts." Pointy Head wrapped his ghost arm around Shad. "Don't you, boy? You got guts?"

"Yes, sir," said Shad, hoping the ghost couldn't feel him tremble. When Pointy Head let go of him, Shad exhaled long and slow. He hadn't meant to hold his breath—hadn't realized he'd been holding it.

He watched Pointy Head march to a tree and pick up something. "Come over here," said Pointy Head.

A lump came up in Shad's throat like a cat's hairball. He

got an urge to run. *Stop*, he told himself. *Stop shaking. You're here. You're in.* He held his head high.

"Come here," repeated Pointy Head.

Shad knew Jeremiah didn't want him, but he wasn't going to let his brother stop him anymore. He walked toward Pointy Head.

"Turn around."

Shad turned around.

"New recruits get blindfolds. Nobody knows where the brotherhood meets till he swears allegiance." Pointy Head looped a scratchy rag over Shad's eyes and tied it behind his head. It smelled of tar. "Brother, are you ready?"

"Yes, sir."

"What?"

"Yes, sir."

"Speak up, boy! Are you ready?"

"Yes!" Shad shouted. And for a split second the crickets stopped chirping and the woods stopped rustling and everything got silent.

Then he heard Pointy Head say, "Come this way." He took Shad's arm and led him along the Mechanicsville road. The crickets started up again. Shad tried to push the lump down his throat, but it rose right back.

They walked for a piece. Shad didn't think there could be anything creepier than walking blindfolded up a road at night—blindfolded beside a brother he didn't trust. He made his hands into fists.

Shad was almost as tall as Jeremiah now. Nowhere near as strong, but almost as tall. Granddaddy had said the day might come when Shad would outgrow Jeremiah, and Shad liked that idea—that his day might come.

They turned off the road into a field. Shad heard bull-frogs and smelled wet ground. His bare feet felt the dirt get softer and colder and squishier. He felt Pointy Head's grip tighten on his upper arm, leading Shad around water, brushing up against cattails. Then they cleared the water and walked uphill.

Shad heard Jeremiah's boots stomp behind him. He thought he heard voices. They walked a tad more and now he knew he heard voices. They had to be getting near the brotherhood meeting. The voices weren't out in the open air but were muffled, like coming through a window. Pointy Head pulled Shad's arm and they stopped. Shad listened to the long, slow hoot of an owl.

"One step up," said Pointy Head.

Shad lifted his foot onto a wooden step. Pointy Head

stomped, the wood rang hollow, and Shad heard voices shush one another. Then Pointy Head pulled him through a door. Shad couldn't see anything because of the blindfold. He sensed people—warm bodies and sweat and rustling and whispering. They shoved and shuffled to make room. Shad told himself to stay strong—the ghosts were just Clifton and Jeremiah and a bunch of boys he probably knew, anyway.

Pointy Head announced, "A new member, brothers! This boy wants to join up."

"Bring him forward," said a voice.

Shad smelled Pointy Head's stale breath on his ear as he leaned in and talked low, but his words were plenty loud enough for everyone to hear. "The brotherhood will now inspect you. Keep the blindfold on."

Shad heard feet move toward him, heard them circle around. He felt something brush against his cheek and neck—a feather, maybe. He raised his shoulders to block it, but it tickled his skin—down his back, then his bare feet. He cringed as he felt a hand pull at his burlap-sack shirt, then another hand, and another. He'd never before felt anything this creepy.

Shad lifted his arms to take off the blindfold.

"Keep it on!" someone barked.

Shad dropped his arms. Then he felt someone put something down his back. The something was cold. It wiggled. It was gooey. Shad heard boys laugh, and he wriggled all over. *Get it out of my shirt!* He hopped. He danced. The wiggly thing fell to his britches. He brushed at his backside. Now the thing was in his privates.

The room howled. Shad hopped. He went up on tiptoes. Was it a worm? *Help me, Jesus.* Shad shook his britches, trying to give it room—get it to fall out. Now it was down the back of his knee. He shook his leg and didn't feel it anymore. It was out.

Then he felt it squish, cold, beneath his bare foot.

6

Brotherhood

"THAT'S ENOUGH," someone said. "Everybody settle now. The Grand Cyclops will speak."

The rustling died down. Shad trembled, suddenly hating everything about this brotherhood. He figured Jeremiah was probably the one who'd put that squishy thing down his back, and he hated to admit Jeremiah might have been right—maybe Shad was too young. Maybe he didn't belong here. He felt like such an idiot—always running after Jeremiah's shadow.

He still wore the blindfold, but even with it on, he could sense the light shift. Someone moved a lantern and the odor of kerosene rose in the room. From a crack under the blindfold, Shad glimpsed his bare feet on wooden boards. Beside them lay a squished baby bird. A baby so young it didn't have feathers yet.

"Brother," said a new voice, "you have entered the den of the most secret society on the face of the earth." The voice was rich and soft-spoken, not clipped and choppy like Granddaddy's or Mr. O'Malley's, not as deep as Clifton's. Shad felt relieved for a moment, thinking that such an educated voice wouldn't belong to the kind of person who'd put a baby bird down his shirt. This man spoke with an aura of authority and trust.

But as the man went on, Shad heard a coldness in the voice. Each word was perfect and slow-spoken. "Brother, do you solemnly desire to become a member of the society of the Ku Klux?"

Shad didn't know what a *Ku Klux* was, but he wasn't going to show his ignorance. Today he wore a blindfold and at his feet lay a squished baby bird, and he was not—no way, not ever—going to ask what a *Ku Klux* was. He said, "Yes, sir."

"We are here tonight to welcome you in," said the educated voice, and the room grew still. "State your full name for the record."

"Shadrach Alfriend Weaver."

"Now, Shadrach, answer me these questions. First, in remembrance of the unforgivable humiliation of Davis and Lee—"

"Hear, hear!" came a chorus of voices.

"Blessings to them!"

"Let's have quiet, please! Now, brother, in the solemn honor of Davis and Lee, do you commit yourself to this brotherhood and its loyal deeds?"

Shad held himself tight for a moment, thinking of President Jefferson Davis and the great General Robert E. Lee. Then he let out his breath with a shudder, resting his palms on his thighs to make them stop trembling. "Yes, sir."

"Do you promise to protect and defend the weak and the innocent, especially the widows and orphans of soldiers who gave their lives in sacrifice for our noble cause?"

Shad's thoughts raced with everything Virginia had fought for and his daddy had died for. He nodded. "Yes, sir."

"Do you promise to remain true to the Ku Klux to your dying day, and never divulge the identity of your Ku Klux brethren?"

"Yes, sir."

"I am the Grand Cyclops of this den, and I will not tolerate disloyalty to the brotherhood. If you betray the Ku Klux Klan, you will pay dearly for such betrayal. Do you understand?"

Shad squeezed his eyes shut, opened them again, and

found the blindfold still in place. He tried to reason his way through the question. If he got into an argument with Jeremiah, was that betrayal? If Jeremiah told him to splash with the water moccasins down the Chickahominy River and Shad said no, was that betrayal? He didn't like this question. "Yes, sir."

"Do you swear by the heart of your mother, by the soul of your father, and by the bones of your ancestors that you will honor this Klan from this night and forever, and do what you are bid, blindly and without question?"

Shad swallowed. "Yes, sir."

"Now, let me introduce the officers of our den. We have two Night Hawks."

Shad heard feet stomping. Applause. Whistles.

"A Grand Monk."

Again, stomping and commotion. It went on and on as the Grand Cyclops announced positions: a Grand Scribe, a Grand Exchequer, a Grand Turk, a Grand Sentinel.

"Finally, Shadrach, do you swear that you will keep secret the location of this meeting, and swear that no manner of questioning or torture will lead you to betray the Ku Klux?"

He wanted to go home. More than anything in the world, he wished that he had just stayed home. "Yes, sir."

"Place him before the royal altar and adorn his head with the regal crown."

The rustling picked up. Somebody put something soft on Shad's head. Then a hand grabbed his arm and pulled him, and he shuffled through the crowd again. Something tickled his neck—another feather, maybe—and he jerked his shoulders upward.

"Now, Shadrach," the Grand Cyclops bellowed, and the room grew quiet. "Repeat these words after me: *Oh would some power the giftie give us.*"

Shad thought the brotherhood was crazy. He had no idea what a *giftie* was, but he swallowed and said, "Oh would some power the giftie give us."

"*To see ourselves as others see us.*"

"To see ourselves as others see us."

Somebody pulled at his blindfold, and it was off. Shad saw a cracked looking glass with his own face in pieces. The soft thing on his head was made of big, honest-to-goodness donkey ears. The room howled with laughter, and he understood. He was the jackass. He was looking at this—what had the man called it—the royal altar, wearing a regal crown of donkey ears. Shad was nothing but a jackass, and these boys were having a night of fun at his expense.

Someone was holding a lantern high, and like a moth,

Shad turned toward it. The light blinded him for a spell, and he squinted. The room was chock-full of blurry white spots and ghosts—gray-white sheets stretching taller than men. Painted faces and masks.

Then they came at him, one by one, saying, "Welcome to the brotherhood." It was a blur of ghosts and handshakes and the tousling of hair and chuckling.

"Welcome, son," said a deep voice—an old man. Shad shook his hand, then the ghost backed into the crowd and another one came forward.

"Hey, hey, Jeremiah's little brother," said an extra tall one with a deep voice—Pointy Head. The ghost dropped Shad's hand and punched his shoulder lightly, then disappeared into the crowd, and Shad knew for certain that it was Clifton.

"W-w-welcome," said another ghost. His big, sweaty palm grabbed Shad's, and a smoky smell came with him. Shad couldn't believe it. Bubba? His friend hadn't told him he'd joined up. His own buddy was here—Bubba with his stupid stutter.

Then there was a ghost with only one eye. He wrapped two warm hands around one of Shad's and held them there a moment, not shaking, just holding. He said, "Welcome, son," and the voice belonged to the Grand Cyclops.

Then one squeezed Shad's hand, hurting it, twisting. It was Crooked Face. Jeremiah.

Shad yanked his hand away.

Jeremiah leaned in close so that his sheet touched Shad's forehead. He said, "Brother," with a growl, and Shad knew he was angry that Shad had followed him to the meeting. "Listen here," said Jeremiah softly. "Now you're in. And you make sure you never embarrass me or Mama or our family. You got that?"

Shad's hands went into fists.

"I asked you a question," Jeremiah whispered.

"I got it," Shad said. "I got it."

Jeremiah turned away, and Shad's eyes followed him into the shadows. Shad wanted to haul off and hit him, but more ghosts were coming at him, shaking his hand and welcoming him, and he couldn't keep stewing over Jeremiah.

Then there was a ghost who didn't say anything. He gave Shad a hug and stepped back, and because of a limp, his weight came into Shad as he tottered to find his balance. There was something about him—maybe it was the dye-setting smell or the limp—Shad wasn't sure, but somehow he knew he'd hugged that ghost a thousand times before. He knew exactly who it was.

7

Sheriff Parker

NOW SHAD WATCHED Granddaddy pace from the east wall of Weaver's Fine Tailoring to the west, and with every *clip-thunk* of his bad leg, the floorboards shook. Granddaddy punched the plaster wall beside his black devil sewing machine. Then he rubbed his fist with his other hand. "Let's get going, Shad. If they've nabbed Jeremiah, well, the first order of business is to put your mama's mind at rest—ain't that right?"

"Uh, yes, sir. Mama."

"Then let's go. We got to talk with Sheriff Parker."

Shad followed Granddaddy into Richmond proper, walking the tree-lined streets past crowds at the marketplace, past church bells chiming on top of one another, past Old Market Station. Granddaddy didn't slow at the station, and Shad knew that meant Sheriff Parker was at the other police station—the one out Marshall Street—and he braced for the walk.

They crossed Fourteenth Street—wide like Broad— and it was busy with rebuilding. Men, both colored and white, were laying bricks, pushing sand-filled wheelbarrows, mixing up mortar, carrying lumber, sawing boards. Most of the buildings that had burned in the April 1865 fire were gone now, but a few shells remained—just chimneys and rubble.

A couple of men waved to Granddaddy. He tipped his cap at them, and Shad realized what Jeremiah liked about coming here, hoping for work. It wasn't just the dollar and the meal. It was these men—this brotherhood. All this commotion. Watching a wall go up. A roof. Maybe Jeremiah got to swing a hammer here. Or learn to lay bricks. Back home in the quiet down Nine Mile Road, what did Shad and Mama do but make tiny stitches with fine little needles? No, tailoring didn't appeal to Jeremiah one bit. Never had, never would.

The walk to the Marshall Street station was a hefty one—north and west and mostly uphill. Shad had been out that way a few times, first on deliveries with Daddy and

Mindy-girl, and later alone. Weaver's Fine Tailoring had done its share of the britches-tightening business during the war, and Shad had done nearly all the deliveries.

He and Granddaddy kept to Main Street for a while, walking on and on as the numbers got smaller and smaller. They started to turn on Eighth Street but saw Yankees on patrol up that way—three of them catching a smoke, brandishing muskets on blue shoulders. He and Granddaddy kept their heads down and went on to Seventh Street and turned there, instead.

Damn Yankees. They'd put Richmond under martial law when the war ended, and their presence alone had Virginians so riled up, at times Shad half expected another war to break out. The Yankees would whistle at ladies and stare down gentlemen, gloating, *We showed you good, you stupid, bigoted Confederates*—so much so that when boys accidentally-on-purpose tripped one of them, or a Yankee's nose just happened to get in the way of a good old boy's fist ("But officer, my hand was there first. You can't blame me for his shortsightedness. Get that boy a pair of spectacles . . ."), why, cheers would go up like the Fourth of July. For a brief moment, Richmonders would feel good about themselves again.

Then the Yankees would drag the offender away and hold him overnight, and when it was Jeremiah, like it sometimes was, Mama would burst into tears. Shad would find himself explaining again how *it was good, Mama*. How Jeremiah made everyone proud.

But today, more was at stake than a punch in the gut and a night in jail, and the last thing Shad wanted was to walk by those Yankees and rile one up. He and Granddaddy continued along Seventh Street across Franklin and Grace and Broad Streets to Marshall, then west, crossing over the numbered streets until there weren't any more numbers.

After First Street the names changed to the old presidents and founding fathers. Shad's reading wasn't good enough to make out the wooden signs, but he'd memorized the names—Adams Street, Jefferson, Madison, Monroe, Patrick Henry Street. Daddy had told him all about those fine men and everything they'd done to make the nation great. Then times had changed and Yankees had set out to ruin the country—to take away rights that each state had under the Constitution—and Shad knew that no street in Richmond would ever get itself named after Abraham Lincoln.

When they got to the police station—to the funny intersection where Brook Road hit Marshall and Adams

Streets on the diagonal—there sat a two-story building made of huge cement blocks. The second-floor windows had awnings with fat red and white stripes. In front of the station stood a hitching post with a black mare that pawed the dirt.

Shad and Granddaddy went into a room with hollow-sounding wooden floors, and Shad smelled candle wax right off. He noted how high the ceiling was, how the white plaster walls held light that came through tall windows.

A voice bellowed from God knows where. "Where your shoes, boy?" Then a man came from shadows in the back—a big man with thinning hair and a black mustache. He wore dark trousers and a brown corduroy vest with a fat gold star. His face was puffy. Shad watched him spit a wad of tobacco into a can beside a wooden desk where a candle was changing shape from a stick to a puddle.

"Henry, when are you going to put this grandson of yours in shoes?" asked the sheriff. He threw back his head and laughed in a good-hearted way. Then he bent over the candle and blew it out, and Shad marveled at the pattern of wax lumps splattered all over the desk.

Granddaddy chuckled and Shad turned to see him wrap two hands around one of the sheriff's. "Good to see you, John."

"And you, Henry. And this is Shadrach, ain't that right?"

Shad smiled and shook the sheriff's hand—a mighty big hand with coarse fingers—and felt something wrong in the grip. When the sheriff pulled away, Shad saw that his hand didn't have all five fingers. It only had but four.

"John, we've got a problem," said Granddaddy. "Seems they've arrested Jeremiah."

"Damn Yankees. What is it this time?"

"Shad didn't catch the charge," said Granddaddy.

Shad felt the sheriff's eyes burrow into him, and he shifted his feet. He chose his words carefully. "They didn't say, sir. They just took him."

"Tell Sheriff Parker what you heard," said Granddaddy.

Shad shifted again, then squared his shoulders and lifted his chest to try to appear a tad taller. The lift made his bruised rib cage ache.

"Go on," said Granddaddy.

Shad nodded. "Heard tell there's a dead man at Doc Moore's, and word is that 'fore he died, he said 'the Weaver boy' did it."

"Barrel Boy," said Granddaddy.

Sheriff Parker leaned toward Granddaddy and spoke through a hand over his mouth. "He made it out of that barrel? How the hell did he get out of there alive?" He slapped a palm against the desk, and the candle wobbled. "For Pete's sake, Henry, you're a tailor and your family has the most god-awful disguises."

Shad looked from Granddaddy to the sheriff and back again. It was one thing for Granddaddy and Jeremiah—for all the Confederate families like the Weavers—to be in the Klan, but it hadn't occurred to Shad that the sheriff would be in it, too. After all, the sheriff was—well, he was *supposed* to be the law, and last night they hadn't abided by the law— not at all. The thought made Shad's eyelid twitch, and he rubbed at it to make it stop.

"Look, John, it's one thing to keep the coloreds in their place," said Granddaddy, "and it's another to kill a white man."

Shad felt his mouth go dry. He watched the sheriff pace the room. Each step of the man's boots on the hollow- sounding floor made a dust mote swirl in a neat little circle.

The sheriff stopped beside the spittoon and shot a wad of tobacco into it. *Splat.* "Henry, I don't think anybody in- tended to kill him."

Granddaddy ran a hand across his face. "Beg to differ, John."

"Now, look. Accidents happen."

"It wasn't no accident."

"Don't go there, Henry. I said 'accidents happen,' and we'll leave it at that." He began to pace again.

Granddaddy followed him across the room. *Clip-thunk, clip-thunk.* "I don't like this, John."

The sheriff stopped at a tall smoke-glass window, turned, and frowned. "If your grandsons are going to run with the Klan, they need better bedsheets."

Granddaddy kneaded the thigh of his bad leg. His gaze fell to the floor. "I'm sorry. Shad ain't had time to pull together something better. We'll get on it right away." He looked up. "But I don't want another meeting like last night."

Shad tried to swallow. He felt sick and clenched his teeth, not wanting to believe what he was hearing. He looked from Granddaddy to the sheriff, and his thoughts blurred back to the Klan meeting—to the smoky roomful of ghost disguises. He wondered who else had been under those sheets.

Sheriff Parker rubbed his temples. "Okay, boys, we need us a plan. You on foot? Tell you what. You find yourselves a bite to eat while I get O'Malley. Thelma's Restaurant ain't bad. I'll be back in an hour." The sheriff set a hat on his head, gave his trousers a tug up, and headed out the door.

He rode off on the black mare while Shad walked with Granddaddy to Thelma's—one block over at Broad Street. Shad's head had begun to throb, and as they walked, he squeezed his eyes tightly and opened them again, hoping the hurt would subside. His thoughts had splattered like candle wax. He lamented how little sleep he'd gotten last night.

They got to Broad, and there, running down the center of the street, was Richmond's new trolley, pulled by four enormous chestnut-brown horses. Shad turned to Granddaddy. "Sir, can I—would it be all right if I just waited here a spell? I heard about this trolley car, but I ain't seen it yet."

Granddaddy slapped him on the back and Shad felt the jolt from his forehead to his toes.

"Sure. It's fine, son. Fine. Wait in front of Thelma's here."

While Granddaddy went inside, Shad plopped down in the shade of a small elm tree. He set his elbows on his knees and held his head in his hands. He tried to let go of the morning—the arrest, Rachel, the sheriff, everything. He told himself to think about the trolley and let his mind rest, ease the headache.

Granddaddy brought him two heels from a warm loaf

of brown bread, then headed back into Thelma's.

"Thank you, sir," Shad called, not taking his eyes from the trolley. He ate and watched the trolley grow small in the distance. Broad Street stretched west for miles—all the way to Charlottesville, so people said. Shad knew Daddy had taken Broad Street the day he'd enlisted, and today Shad imagined him sitting on Mindy-girl, trotting along this very stretch of road.

He took a deep breath and let his belly fill and tried to forget that Daddy was gone. Forget that Jeremiah had been arrested. Forget that Mama was beside herself, sitting home, craning her neck up Nine Mile Road, waiting on Shad to bring his brother back. But the more he tried, the clearer the images became. Even George Nelson came to mind, and he shuddered. No, he wouldn't let himself think about George Nelson.

He closed his eyes so tightly that bits of light shimmered in the blackness inside his head. He opened his eyes again, then shut them, opened them. What happened to George Nelson was bad, but with Jeremiah arrested, maybe this time the Yankees would hold him longer than one night. Then no one else would get hurt—and that meant Shad wouldn't have to worry so much right now.

Why, Jeremiah being locked up gave Shad a chance to catch his breath. The more he thought about it, the deeper he could breathe, and the next thing he knew, his lungs filled so full his ribs ached again from the bruising. He put a hand to his side, but instead of wincing with the ache, he smiled. For the first time that day, he allowed a smile to settle in, to ripple all the way to the tips of his fingers and toes.

Jeremiah was locked up, and that wasn't bad news at all.

Then he felt Granddaddy pat his shoulder, and he knew it was time, and he let the smile fade.

He and Granddaddy went back to the police station and met up with Sheriff Parker and Mr. O'Malley, the man who owned the saloon a block from Granddaddy's shop. He was a big man—big as the sheriff—with reddish hair, bushy sideburns, and pale eyes, and he talked with a lisp that always made Shad wonder about Irish people and their funny accents.

"Morning, Shad," he said, and it came out *Thad*.

"Sir," said Shad with a nod.

Mr. O'Malley and Sheriff Parker looked him over, then exchanged glances.

Sheriff Parker gave the back of his neck a good rub. "Henry, we've been kicking this around, and it just don't hold water. The thing is—" He paused, looking straight at Granddaddy while pointing sideways at Shad, his arm fully extended, his finger shaking. "We know Barrel Boy saw Shadrach, not Jeremiah, and we know them Yankees don't know nothin'. They're stupid as crayfish. But the piece we don't understand is how the hell Barrel Boy knew Shadrach's name."

Shad swallowed and looked at the floor. He wanted to crawl under the desk. If he hadn't been so stupid at that brotherhood meeting, George Nelson never would have glimpsed his face.

"Sit down, Shad," said the sheriff. He pulled out the big oak chair beside the melted candle. "Now, fill us in, son. How did that pip-squeak know you?"

Shad sat. Granddaddy lifted his chin, and Shad knew what the lift meant. Granddaddy wanted him to start talking. *Go on—tell the sheriff. We're all in the brotherhood together. You can talk here.*

But Shad couldn't talk. He couldn't tell them how that pip-squeak knew him. George Nelson. How could he tell what he knew about George Nelson when it was all so tied up with Rachel? No, he didn't know how to explain anything.

8

Gin Rummy

SHAD RUBBED HIS eyes and scratched his scalp. The scratching irritated the lice, making them race through his hair, and their racing made his head itch, so he scratched all the more. Then he fingered the tender lump at the spot where his head had hit the windowsill. "Um, I'm sorry. I'm a bit light-headed today. W-what was the question?"

"You heard the sheriff," said Granddaddy with a firm tone.

Mr. O'Malley leaned in close. "How did he know you wath a Weaver?"

"Just tell us what you know, son," said Sheriff Parker.

Shad wrapped his hands so tightly around the arms of the oak chair, his knuckles ached. "Yes, sir. Well, I was up at Widow Perkinson's house to take measurements. Tailoring. She'd, uh, commissioned a dress and I needed to get the length, the waist, you know, sir?"

"Go on."

"And this man arrived. And he had a suitcase. And he, uh—he and I met. Miz Perkinson introduced me as Weaver's Fine Tailoring."

Sheriff Parker nodded. "I see. All right, then. And he had a suitcase, so he was fixin' to stay awhile?"

"Yes, sir."

"Carpetbagger," said Mr. O'Malley, sneering.

"And this was the little man with the big nose they brought to the brotherhood meeting last night?" asked Sheriff Parker.

Shad looked at the floor. He couldn't bring himself to say anything about the brotherhood meeting. He'd sworn to the Grand Cyclops he wouldn't ever say a thing outside of a Klan meeting, and now he was outside, and he couldn't bring himself to answer that question straight on.

He felt Sheriff Parker pat his back, and he sensed that the sheriff understood. "That's fine, son," he said. "But tell me, would you describe George Nelson as a short man with a big nose?"

"Yes, sir."

"And you just saw him that one day at Miz Perkinson's house?"

Shad looked at his bare feet. He scratched his head some more. He let his head bob in a motion like a nod, but not a nod, exactly. *That one day?* Yes, he'd seen him that one day, but other days, too. He couldn't begin to tell them about all the days. Lord, what a fix he was in. He hadn't ever lied to Granddaddy, but today—well, there was no way he could tell these men about all the days at the Perkinsons'. He mumbled, "Yes, sir."

"Thank you, Shad." The sheriff shoved his large hands deep into his trouser pockets and moseyed toward the windows. "Henry, you must be proud o' your grandson."

"He's a good boy, John."

"He sure is."

"But we got uth a problem now, don't we, John?" said Mr. O'Malley.

Sheriff Parker drifted back to the desk and spit into the tobacco can. He tugged on his trousers, bringing them up an inch or two, shifting the belt around at his waist, tucking in his shirt. "Well, now, O'Malley, I believe you have a fine room there in the back of the saloon. Was that back room empty last night?"

"Yeth, it wath, John. Thure wath."

"No, I don't believe so," said the sheriff, and he drew out his words long and slow and heavy. "Not. Empty. At. All. No, gentlemen, there was a card game going on in that back room last night. Right there in your saloon, O'Malley. Shad, what card games do you know how to play?"

"Sir?"

"Card games, you heard me. Or don't your mama let you play cards?"

"Uh, yes, sir, she's fine with us playing cards, long as it ain't on Sunday."

"All right, then. Last night was Thursday. Thursday night into Friday, and we were playing a mean game of— what? You tell me, Shad. What do you play?"

Shad narrowed his eyes, not understanding what the sheriff wanted.

Granddaddy spoke up. "Gin rummy. Shad and Jeremiah and me—we sometimes kick back with a little gin rummy."

"Gin rummy it was, then," said Sheriff Parker, and an enormous grin spread across his face. "And Shadrach here—he won the night. Got him a celebratory root beer. We played first to five hundred, you got that? Good job, boy. You play a mean hand of gin rummy. Let's go." He slapped Shad on the back. Hard.

Then Shad and Granddaddy and Sheriff Parker and Mr. O'Malley set off walking. Shad's ribs ached and his head hurt and his stomach churned with lies. He'd told more lies than a boy could track, and here was another one. Gin rummy.

Shad felt Granddaddy's arm circle his shoulders, then felt his mouth at his ear. "Okay, Shad, now listen up. It's best if you say nothing at all, but if them Yankees ask, well, you remember that time you scooped up the whole discard pile? We couldn't stop you playing out near every set in the deck. It was that kind of night. You got that?"

Shad nodded. "Yes, sir." But he wasn't sure what he got and what he didn't. Yes, he knew how to play gin rummy, but these men—even his very own granddaddy—were asking him to lie to the Yankees to get Jeremiah released. But if Jeremiah went free, why, *no telling* what he'd do next.

Yes, telling. Shad tried to swallow, and the lump wouldn't go down. He knew exactly what Jeremiah would do when he was free, and the thought made Shad sick. He wanted Jeremiah in jail. Forever. He couldn't stand to think what Jeremiah might do if he got out. Not *might*. What he *would* do to Rachel and Maggie and Nathaniel and Eloise and all the rest. No, he couldn't let Jeremiah hurt any of them, and especially not Rachel.

9

The S Word

RACHEL. HE'D FIRST met her more than a month ago. Maybe it had been six weeks. Maybe seven. It was after he'd pledged allegiance to the brotherhood—the very day after, as a matter of fact.

He thought back on that day—how he was headed home from Granddaddy's, carrying a bolt of fabric and wearing the same clothes he had on today—the britches that used to belong to his cousin William Johnson Alfriend Nunnally, and the burlap-sack shirt with the letters FEED AND SEED stamped across and stuck in the seams. He'd sewn the shirt himself, and even added a pocket for collecting cloth scraps.

He'd gotten to the corner of Seventeenth and Broad when he'd seen a swatch of red cloth snagged on a crack in some stones. It was a few inches' worth, and he bent over, freed the cloth, and slipped it into his pocket.

The day was hot, and he didn't relish the thought of carrying the bolt up Church Hill. He felt mighty fine about joining up with a brotherhood, but running in the night meant he was plumb short on the shut-eye. He leaned against a maple tree, collecting his strength for the haul uphill, all the while looking down Broad toward the brick building that used to be Lumpkin's jail—the site of many slave auctions. Now there were graveyards—more colored graves at the bottom of the Broad Street hill than anyone could count.

That day he saw a few Negroes milling about. Two colored girls were coming up Broad Street, each holding a sack tucked into the crook of an elbow. They had scarves wrapped around their heads, and the cloth of their scarves matched their flower-print dresses.

When they got to his corner, they stopped smack-dab in front of him. The taller of the two did a funny thing with her neck—stretching it as if to grow even taller—but her height didn't hold a candle to Shad's. She was about his age or a year older—it was hard to tell. She stood close to him—too close—and Shad felt uncomfortable. He tried to back up, but he was against a tree and couldn't enlarge the distance.

She pointed at his bolt of fabric and said, "Pray tell, why would you be carrying fine cotton prints from Atlanta?"

Shad glanced behind him, thinking she must be talking to someone else. But there was no one there. He turned back to see the other girl's eyes grow wide. Her skin was darker than her friend's, and her nose looked like an Indian's nose—like old pictures Shad had seen of Pocahontas and such. She shook her head and grabbed the arm of the too-close girl and pulled, turning her eyes to the gray-brick street. "Excuse us, sir. We need to go."

Shad breathed easier as the girls moved a few paces away. He hadn't ever heard coloreds talk so fine. He tightened his hands around the bolt and straightened his back, showing his full height. "Who told you what I got here?"

The one shook her sleeve free of the other. She laughed. "Isn't it obvious?"

He didn't like her sassy tone. He threw his free hand in the air and deepened his voice. "You're in my way. I'm tryin' to see down the street there. Get on outta my way."

But she didn't get on. She tilted her head and narrowed her eyes at the bolt of fabric. "If you please, sir, I asked about the cloth."

Now she had him flustered. He pointed at the sack she carried. "What have you got there?"

"Excuse me, sir, but where did you get a shipment from Atlanta?"

"I never said nothing 'bout Atlanta."

"Right there. The bolt says, *Pink dogwood floral, one hundred percent cotton, Frederick and Sons, Atlanta, Georgia.*"

He looked at the bolt. Sure enough, stamped on the brown-paper wrapping were letters. Lots of letters. He hadn't tried to figure them out. But this girl had him tongue-tied—she could read without pause! Shad felt his face go hot. It wasn't right that she could read better than he could. Wasn't right that she could read at all. Wasn't right that she was reaching for the bolt—that she was running her fingers along the stamped letters. Shad froze. She was nearly on his toes!

Her friend tugged again. "Come on, Rachel, come on."

"Why, Eloise, just yesterday Miss Elizabeth was saying Abigail needed a new dress." She pushed Eloise's arm away. "Where are you going with this?"

Shad didn't like the way she asked him questions. Jeremiah had told him not to talk to coloreds. He'd said the United States government was fixing to send them back to Africa. He'd said Daddy would still be alive if rich people hadn't ruined the country by hankering to get richer still and bringing slaves here so people had to fight over them. And now everybody had to live with them until they got shipped back.

Shad didn't like talking with this rich-mouthed colored girl—not one bit. But he liked his work, and he was proud of Granddaddy's shop, and he said, "Weaver's Fine Tailoring."

"So you're a tailor, then?"

Was she mocking him? Her tone wasn't like any he had ever heard. He didn't know what to make of her and her fine-lady voice. He swallowed and tried to smirk like Jeremiah. He sputtered, "You two is stealing sacks of flour."

Eloise looked down and mumbled, "My apologies, sir. Come on, Rachel."

Shad held his face stern, but on the inside he was smiling to beat all. Both of these girls had called him "sir."

"Just wait a minute, Eloise," said Rachel. She held out her sack with two hands. Held it right up to Shad's face.

He swung at the sack. But he had the bolt of cloth in his strong arm, and he swung with the other, and she was quick. She pulled the sack in. Then she held it up, and he swung again. And she pulled it in again. She laughed. She was making a game of it—holding the sack up, getting him to swing and miss. A funny little game.

Shad laughed. Then he thought he shouldn't have laughed. Shoot. He didn't know how to handle this. Jeremiah would tell him he was soft. Namby-pamby. He'd say to keep coloreds in their place.

Stupid girl, thought Shad. Who was she to play this little game with him? Who was she to speak to him with such a familiar tone? His mind raced with images of Mr. Kechler's slaves—had he met this girl at Kechler's plantation? He couldn't place her there. The Shockoe Market? He couldn't place her there, either. He didn't think he'd met her before, and yet, here she was, chatting away like they were equals. Her eyes bored into him, and he shifted his weight.

She said, "Read it."

He swung again.

She giggled and shook her head. "Read it. It's not flour. Read it."

He stopped swinging and looked at the letters. He couldn't think straight with her staring at him. He could read some, but not well. The word on the sack began with an *S.* Right there and then, he couldn't think of any *S*-words other than his name, and it wasn't his name.

"Ain't you gonna give me no clue?" He heard his voice

go high. He coughed and made it low like Clifton's. "A clue. Give me a clue!"

Her whole face went into a smile. She had the biggest, prettiest teeth he'd ever seen—every single one lined up perfectly—and in that moment, Shad envied her those teeth. His own were crooked and two on the left side had been pulled a few years back, leaving a gap the size of a peach pit. Who was she to have such fine teeth? It didn't seem fair.

"Rachel, I think it's time we go now," said Eloise.

But Rachel didn't go. She shook her head at Eloise and turned to Shad with a sad sort of look—with a sincerity that made him frown. Then she said, ever so gently, "You can't read, can you?"

"Dern fool!" The words exploded out of him. "You ain't better 'n me. You don't know what that sack says no more 'n I know what it says. Don't you go giving me no high-and-mighty attitude."

"No, sir," said Eloise. "She didn't mean anything by it."

He gripped the bolt to keep from trembling. His own words had surprised him.

"She gets a little carried away sometimes," Eloise went on. "She didn't mean to offend you, sir."

Rachel smiled. Then she laughed and her tone was

sweet—not mean or haughty—and the sound of it settled Shad's nerves. It was hard to stay angry.

He rubbed the back of his neck. He'd never met anyone like this girl. Not having a sister, he hadn't had much to do with girls, white or colored. Oh, sure, every once in a while he'd lost himself in thought over Mr. O'Malley's freckle-faced daughter, and he'd even talked with her maybe three times at Sunday school.

But he hadn't ever thought one way or another about colored girls. They were freed slaves, was all. His family had never owned one and his stomach had turned over Mr. Kechler's treatment of his, so Shad had avoided the coloreds as best he could. Between the war and Daddy dying and people up in arms over Lincoln freeing the slaves, why, there was so much so wrong that sometimes it was better not to think at all. Better just to make his deliveries and weave his foot mats and master his mending and mind his own business and let the world be.

Now, here he was in conversation with a colored girl, a conversation he didn't invite and couldn't handle. He found himself fighting an overwhelming urge to cuss and walk away.

Rachel giggled and looked at Eloise, then back at Shad, and said, "I don't know where to begin."

"Well," he said, shifting the fabric from one shoulder to the other, trying to keep control and clear his head. Maybe he could respond like Jeremiah—take charge and act like a man. "Well, how 'bout you begin by tellin' me where you're stealing sacks of flour from, 'cause I got a right mind to report you for thievery."

"Whoa, wait a minute." She smiled and waved her free hand, and he saw that the palm was light-colored, almost peach, and he knew that all coloreds' hands were like that— dark on top and light underneath—but he hadn't ever before paid it mind. Today he felt flummoxed. The conversation was turning in ways he couldn't control, and the sooner it ended, the better.

"Now look—"

"Just hold your horses," Rachel said warmly, and she pointed at the hill toward Richmond proper. "The Freedmen's Bureau is giving food to everyone who needs it." She lifted the sack and pointed to each letter. "S-U-G-A-R."

Up went the hairs on the back of Shad's neck. "I know that's an *S*. Don't you go tellin' me my letters."

She didn't miss a beat. "Sugar," she said. "Today they're giving out sugar. A few days ago it was flour. You're welcome to get in line for a sack if you need it."

Sugar. Once she'd said it, Shad knew that she was right.

It was obvious—the word was *sugar*. Why hadn't he seen it?

Rachel smiled.

"We really need to go," said Eloise.

But Rachel didn't go. She said, "How much do you charge for the dresses you sew?"

Shad looked at his bare feet, thinking about the turns this conversation had taken, about how incapable he'd been of controlling it, about how to answer her question. He squirmed, feeling that he ought to know Granddaddy's prices. But he'd never handled that part of the business.

He looked at Rachel's feet—her little brown lace-up boots. They were scuffed some, but they were nice.

His head was still down when she said, "I'll tell you what, Mr. Nincompoop. Can you remember the name? Perkinson. Mrs. Parks Randolph Perkinson, Franklin and Twenty-eighth Street, up Libby Hill."

"Don't talk to me like I'm stupid!" Lord God Almighty, he wanted to shove her down the street. "I know Widow Perkinson. Course I know Miz Perkinson."

"Well, good, then. Here. You take this sugar and sew me a lovely summer dress for Miss Abigail. Come by the house of Mrs. Perkinson and leave word how much we owe you. I'm sure one sack of sugar isn't enough. But that's all I have today."

She thrust the sack in his free arm, then grabbed Eloise by the elbow. "Miss Elizabeth will be delighted with a new dress for Abby!"

Before he could say "Jack Sprat," Rachel and Eloise were up the street and Shad was standing at the corner of Seventeenth and Broad, carrying a bolt of fabric and a sack of sugar. His mouth had gone dry. His thoughts ran in circles, trying to make sense of this colored girl, Rachel, who spoke so fine and radiated such confidence and knew her letters up, down, and sideways.

10

Brown Rabbits

WHEN SHAD GOT close to his family's little house out Nine Mile Road, he strutted with an *Ain't I something* gait because he was the one bringing home a nice sack of sugar today. For once, he had something Jeremiah didn't, and, moreover, he was Jeremiah's equal now. A Klan brother. Worthy of respect. Today Mama would thank him and see him as the man he'd become. Thinking on it made him preen like a peacock as he went through the door.

But as soon as he explained the deal to Mama, she got hot and bothered over the tailoring. She was a tiny woman with light brown eyes and a delicate frame, but there was nothing delicate about her. Mama had grown up milking cows on a farm out Creighton Road, and she still relished a good thumb-wrestle from time to time. Today she put her worn hands on bony hips and looked up at Shad, then chided him for accepting a commission without taking the measurements.

"When will you learn to think, boy? You don't dare cut the fabric until you know her height, the shoulder length, the waist. Why, the girl could be petite. She could be enormous!"

Shad smacked the side of his head with an open palm. How could he have been so stupid? Of course he should have asked, but while the girls were standing in front of him, he'd been too flustered to think.

Then Jeremiah sauntered in from the outhouse with a smirk on his face. Clearly he'd heard every word. He was tall, and on his beanpole frame, his beady brown eyes looked even smaller than Mama's—eyes too small for chiseled features—strong nose, high cheekbones, square chin. Over the past year, he'd grown a goatee in the fashion of President Jefferson Davis, and today it was in sore need of a trim.

Jeremiah elbowed Shad aside and held up a big, brown, dead rabbit he'd nabbed who-knows-where. Mama hugged him and kissed him. Shad watched her go up on tiptoes to reach his cheek. Over the top of her head, Jeremiah looked down on Shad and his smile spoke loud and clear: Jeremiah: one; Shadrach: zero.

Shad raised the sack of sugar and gave Jeremiah a nod

that said he wasn't to be outdone. A whole sack sure beat a scrawny rabbit.

Then Jeremiah stepped away from Mama, reached under his shirt, and brought out a second dead rabbit. He beamed.

Shad's face fell.

"Ooh, lordy!" said Mama with delight. "Skin them hares out back now. And save me them pelts. Don't you shred them up none."

"Yes, ma'am," said Jeremiah.

"When did you find time to hunt rabbits?" Shad demanded. "Thought you were working a day job up Fourteenth Street."

"Coloreds," he said with a snarl.

Shad squared his shoulders. "So you still ain't got no work."

"Shut up, Shad. Damn Yankees push them coloreds to the front of the pack."

Shad glanced toward Mama, hoping she'd wag a finger at Jeremiah's laziness. But Mama did no such thing. She shook her head and agreed with him. "Ain't right—all them coloreds loose on the streets."

"No, ma'am," said Jeremiah, "ain't right at all."

Shad's nostrils flared. He was a Klan brother now, as well as a blood brother, but in his own house, you'd never know it. Jeremiah this, Jeremiah that.

He knew what his brother meant about pushing the coloreds, but he doubted the Yankees had actually pushed them. Men swarmed around construction foremen, hoping for work. The ones selected were those who made the least trouble and worked the hardest—those who accepted a pittance for pay. Not hotheads like Jeremiah. Not ruffians who took to whistling "God Save the South" while they hauled bricks and lumber.

So Jeremiah hadn't gotten hired today. Or yesterday. Or the day before that. Much as Daddy and Granddaddy had tried to teach him the tailoring business, Jeremiah had never taken to needles and thread. He wanted to swing a hammer, lay a rail line. But jobs were scarce. Some were offered by carpetbaggers, and it would be a cold day in hell before Jeremiah Weaver would answer to one of *them*.

After the war, hordes of greedy carpetbaggers had flooded the South—come to make money, was all. They hadn't watched the flames lick Richmond's buildings like they were honeycomb. They hadn't fallen on their knees and prayed alongside Granddaddy. They didn't love Virginia. And worse—they'd laughed at Richmond for setting fire to her own.

The fire—Lord God Almighty, that fire! When word had come from Petersburg that General Robert E. Lee, bless his good name, couldn't hold off General Grant any longer—why, the Confederates had hightailed it to the west while Grant's army marched into Richmond from the east. To keep Grant's men from getting to the supplies along the river, Confederates had set ablaze the munitions, tobacco warehouses, and flour mills. How were they to know the fire would turn inland and burn down half of Richmond proper?

Shad would never forget the sight when, three days later, he'd convinced Mama to come see for herself. They'd walked to St. John's at the crest of Church Hill and looked out at the ruins. Such a crying shame!

In years past, they had loved that view—the beauty of Richmond laid out before them—especially at Christmas-time with lantern lights a-sparkling across Shockoe Valley and up the far hill to the capitol building. But on that day in April 1865, a sea of burned chimneys and black foundations had lain before them. Thank the Lord the capitol had been spared—Thomas Jefferson himself had designed it. And the Spotswood Hotel all the way across town at Eighth and Main still stood. But the rest was an eyesore. Block after block of chimneys and foundations and rubble, and here and there a wisp of smoke from a smoldering beam.

At least Granddaddy had been lucky—Seventeenth Street hadn't burned. But Fifteenth Street west to Ninth? Lord have mercy.

The day after the fire, when Grant's troops came marching into town, Granddaddy said it was like a column of ants with no end in sight. Said he watched from his second-floor window there in the Bottom—he didn't have the devil machine then. He sat by that window and looked down on Main Street and took in the heads and shoulders and muskets and caps of those blue troops streaming by. And he wept.

Now, two years later, Richmond was rebuilding, but progress was slow. Men who'd been wealthy before the war had nothing but burned fields and freed slaves and worthless Confederate dollars and too much pride to stand on a street corner and wait for a day job from a stupid carpetbagger.

Of course it was just like Jeremiah to say he'd tried those street corners. Tried to get a job. But what Jeremiah said and what he did—well, Shad knew those two didn't always line up.

He stiffened as Jeremiah stood in the doorframe, holding the limp rabbits aloft like trophies.

"Now, you skin them hares for me quick 'fore they stiffen up," said Mama, turning back to her iron.

But Jeremiah didn't go out right away. Instead, he approached Shad, leaned into his ear, and whispered, "You ignorant fool." Then he shoved Shad's shoulder, and Shad was so unprepared, so expecting Jeremiah to acknowledge their bond—the Klan if not blood brotherhood—so thrown off guard, that he lost his grip on the sack of sugar and it fell, breaking open on the dirt floor.

Jeremiah sauntered out the door, looking like he didn't do anything.

Shad thought to cry, "Mama, look what he did!" But he knew Jeremiah would turn and say, "What?" with his beady brown eyes so innocent-looking. And Mama would laugh.

Jeremiah always made Mama laugh.

11

Lye Soap

SHAD PICKED UP the sugar, saving what he could in a blue bowl that he covered with a plate to keep out the ants. Then he scrounged around the house for a cotton measuring strip, a scrap of paper, and a stick with a burned tip that was good for jotting numbers.

The whole way back up Church Hill, Mama's words and Jeremiah's smirk ran around inside his head. He didn't have to carry a heavy bolt of fabric this time, but even still, his legs felt heavy. He'd already done the hills twice today, going to and from Granddaddy's. What he'd give now to trade in last night's handshaking for a shove at Jeremiah and a heap of shut-eye!

When he got to Twenty-eighth and Franklin Street on the far side of Church Hill—the pretty area everyone knew as Libby Hill—he glanced up at the Perkinsons' redbrick house. Then he strolled right past it toward the overlook. He couldn't help himself—ahead at Libby Terrace was the most beautiful view in all of Richmond. Every time he made a delivery up that way, he'd steal himself a glance at the river, and every time the view would startle him. Every time felt like the first time again, and his mind couldn't stew over Mama or Jeremiah—not when he had the whole world laid out before him.

He looked east for miles down the James River, thinking it was no wonder men had settled at Richmond. This was the fall line—so full of rocks that boats couldn't travel farther inland—strategically a perfect location. Anyone— friend or foe—coming up the river would be seen long before he arrived.

Not only that, but everything was calm and beautiful here. Shad looked down the hillside with its long grasses that changed direction in the wind, shifting from green to yellow and every shade between. He took in the railroad tracks running along the river. He took in the water—how he knew it rushed along quickly, but from this distance, it seemed like blue stained glass in church windows. Three blocks away the city was all hustle-bustle with people and carriages, but here at the overlook, the world lay quiet as a napping cat.

For a long while, he relished the glory of it. Then he turned and headed to the Perkinsons'. There were a few houses along the terrace and on top of the hill, but none as fine as the Perkinsons'. Theirs stretched three stories tall and had black shutters and redbrick steps leading to a black door. Up high, little white bricks sat in a neat pattern over each window. Shad envied them those windows. As soon as he stepped away from the overlook, the river fell from his view, but from those high-up windows, he bet the Perkinsons got to see that fine river every single day.

The breeze brought the sound of piano music—quick little notes floating, tinkling, dancing, and weaving in, out, and around. Right pretty music. He walked up the wide front steps and heard the piano get louder. He fingered the door knocker—a molded brass lion's head—and thought how fancy-pants this house was.

Shad wondered if Rachel had always lived here and he'd never noticed. He'd delivered dresses and mending to the Perkinsons before, but hadn't been inside. Hadn't seen the missus. A colored woman had always answered this door. Had it been Rachel? Had he already met her and plumb not realized?

Shad lifted the knocker and let it drop twice. A *thump-thumping* started in his chest. The door opened and music came out. So did a colored face. Not Rachel. This one was tight in the cheekbones.

"Mending?" she said. She must have been the woman who always answered this door. Today his eyes met hers, and she looked straight at him—not like other coloreds who lowered their eyes. She nodded. Her chin went up to say she recognized him.

"Uh, well, not mending, exactly. I'm here to take Miss Abigail's measurements for the dress she ordered."

The woman's eyes expanded and twinkled. Her eyebrows lifted, and she seemed to hold back a smile. She set a hand on her waist and tilted her head to one side. "Is this one of Rachel's little jokes?"

Shad frowned. "Ma'am?"

She leaned into the house and snapped, "Rachel!"

The piano music stopped. Shad strained his ears over the music ending just like that. He heard the sound of shoes clicking across wooden floorboards, and he marveled at the fact that not only could that colored girl read, but she could play the piano!

Rachel appeared with a hand over her mouth. Shad saw a funny little smile start in her dark eyes and go all the way to her ears. She was no longer wearing the scarf, and her hair was plaited in rows. She said, "Well, if it isn't Mr. Nincompoop."

"What mischief are you about today?" asked the older one, and her voice was just as rich as Rachel's. For a moment, Shad imagined the two of them with their eloquent diction mingling with royalty in Queen Victoria's court. "This boy asked for Miss Abigail."

Rachel nodded. "Yes, Abigail needs a new dress."

"Well, how is he supposed to fit her when she's in Massachusetts?"

"He can estimate the size. I thought we'd surprise Abby."

Shad looked back and forth between them, and while he was trying to make sense of this little joke, a white woman appeared in the foyer. Rachel spun toward the woman, pointed at Shad, and cried, "Look what the cat left behind!"

"Watch your manners," snapped the colored woman who had answered the door.

Shad looked at the white lady, and she wrinkled her nose at him. Her ginger eyebrows rose up into curls of light reddish-brown hair. Then they came down again. Way down. She stared at Shad like he was a dead mouse. He held out the burned stick, paper, and measuring tape as if they were enough to explain everything, because sure as his feet were bare, he didn't want to open his mouth. He squirmed in the awkward silence, biting his tongue, wishing someone else would speak first.

Finally, Rachel cleared her throat. "Miss Elizabeth, this is the tailor I commissioned to sew a dress for Abigail."

Miss Elizabeth folded her arms across her chest. "I see. Well, then. Your name, young man?"

"Weaver, ma'am. Shadrach Alfriend Weaver."

"Ah, yes. Weaver's Fine Tailoring. Very good. Caroline, please take this boy to the pump. When he's washed, he's welcome inside. Rachel, would you fix us sweet tea, please?"

Then Caroline put her hand on Shad's arm and led him down the front steps and around to the well at the side of the house. She had a grip as strong as any man's, and her demeanor was pure business. She motioned for him to set aside his things and pointed to a tin pan of gray lye soap.

"You wash up there and I'll be right back. I mean to get you a shirt from Marsa Parks. The missus won't allow you in the house with . . . *that* one." She sneered at the FEED AND SEED shirt. Then she looked at his Willy Johnson britches and said, "But I suppose you'll have to keep those on."

Shad watched her walk away. Then he let out all his air. He liked his FEED AND SEED shirt—he'd sewn it himself. But he took it off, rolled it into a ball, and set it by the front steps.

He worked the pump, filled a large tin bucket, and stuck his head into the cold water. He scrubbed his hair and under his arms, a few little chest hairs, and what he could reach on his back. He got good and clean. It was the first washing he'd had that week. The water wasn't simply cold—it was ice-cold and brought out the goose bumps, so he jumped up and down in the sun to dry off and warm up.

When Shad had finished, his head itched like the dickens. Lye soap always killed some of the lice but never got them all. He scratched for a spell, then balled his fists to keep from scratching. If he left them alone, they'd calm down. He didn't want lice getting loose in a house as fine as the Perkinsons'.

When Caroline came back, she carried a clean white shirt with buttons. A silk shirt—silk! With double stitching along the collar and cuffs—not from Weaver's Fine Tailoring. Shad marveled at the touch of it—the sheen, the drape.

"Uh, no, ma'am. I can't accept this."

But Caroline jerked her hands away, refusing to take it back. "A tailor will appreciate it, and the missus will be happy for you to have it."

"*Have* it? You mean, *keep* it? Uh, no, I—I couldn't."

"Wear it for now," she snapped.

Shad swallowed as he slipped it on. Silk was such a magical fabric—cool on hot days and warm in the cold. As much as Granddaddy would have liked shipments of silk, they were hard to come by. He'd turned to cotton because it was inexpensive and readily available, and times were times. Weaver's Fine Tailoring took what it could get.

Inside the house again, the white lady said, "My, what a difference a bath makes." She smiled, and he guessed she was maybe the age of his mama, but it was hard to tell. Mama had lost three teeth and her skin had wrinkled, so she appeared older than she was. But this lady hadn't wrinkled yet. One of her lovely teeth sat crooked, but the rest sat just plain perfect.

She had pulled her hair into a bun, low at the back of her neck, with all manner of wisps curling free so that when she stood near the window and the sunlight caught her head, a halo appeared. Her skin was white with freckles, and she wore a blue dress with buttons all the way up the front. He found her right pretty.

"Caroline, you made a good choice with that shirt. Thank you. Young man, you may retain it. It's a little large on you, but you have some growth coming yet. I imagine it will look fine in a few years."

"Uh, thank you, ma'am."

The colored woman cleared her throat and Shad glanced her way. Her face said, *Told you so,* and he smiled.

"I'd like your grandfather to notice this stitching," said the white woman, pointing to the collar. "Let me know what he thinks." Shad nodded and something in her manner told him the shirt itself—not the stitches—was the thing that mattered. She wanted his grandfather to know that she still had silk in her possession. She was doing fine despite the war.

"Thank you, ma'am," he said again.

"The name is Perkinson. Mrs. Parks Randolph Perkinson. Miss Elizabeth to you."

"Miz Elizabeth, yes, ma'am. Thank you, Miz Elizabeth."

"You're quite welcome. And this is Caroline," she said, nodding toward the colored woman. Then she nodded toward Rachel, who was setting out glasses of sweet tea. "And Rachel. You and Rachel have met, of course."

"Yes, ma'am."

Shad saw Rachel straighten and fold her arms across her chest. Her eyes caught his, and she tilted her head to one side. She mumbled, "*S* is for *sugar.*"

12

The Tortoise and the Hare

"WHAT WAS THAT, Rachel?" Miss Elizabeth asked.

"Nothing, ma'am."

Shad furrowed his brow, but something about this Rachel girl made a grin come up, and he had to look away. He took in the fine furniture, the European rug with tassels on the edges, lush upholstery fabric on the settee, heavy draperies—everything in shades of crimson and royal blue. He settled his eyes on the sweet tea, waiting for an invitation to drink it.

"Well, let's get on with it," Miss Elizabeth said. "Rachel and Abigail are close enough in size. If you tailor the dress for Rachel, it will fit Abigail fine. Go ahead and take the measurements."

Shad took a deep breath and nodded. He went down on one knee, set the paper and writing stick on the rug, and tucked one end of the measuring strip under his bare foot. Then he stood, stretching the strip to the top of Rachel's shoulder. He heard her make the tiniest huff of impatience as she squared her shoulders, lifted her chin, and set her gaze toward the front window.

Shad made a note on his paper. Without even needing to be asked, Rachel lifted her arms straight out, turning her body into the letter *T.* Shad felt beads of sweat burst upon his head. He gritted his teeth, leaned forward with the measuring strip, and ran it around Rachel's waist as fast as he could, trying not to touch her. His thumb noted the measurement, and he dropped to the floor to check the strip and jot the number on his paper.

"You're better with numbers than letters, aren't you?" Rachel's words surprised him, and he jerked the stick, turning a six into a squiggle. She giggled. "Maybe not."

There was a knock at the door. A funny knock. *Rat-a-tat-tat.* Then *tat-tat-tat, ta-ta-ta-ta-TAT!*

"Goodness," Miss Elizabeth said, and Shad saw her nod in Caroline's direction. "I'm so sorry, Mr. Weaver. Just a moment and let us see who our visitor is."

Shad waited while Caroline hurried to the foyer. He glanced at Rachel, then away, thinking it best not to engage her right now. He didn't know what to make of her—how to read her, how to converse with her. Caroline reappeared, announcing, "Mr. George Nelson, ma'am."

Miss Elizabeth looked surprised. She stood abruptly, smoothing the front of her dress, brushing hair from her face. She said, "Oh, well then, let him in." When the man came through the front hall, Shad saw Miss Elizabeth's eyes nearly burst from her head. Then she clenched her jaw tightly as if to hold back a laugh.

He turned to see George Nelson bow with a flourish. He was a funny-looking little man with a big nose. Shad thought he was probably the littlest man he'd ever seen, but his nose was the biggest ever. It was even larger than his glasses. Mama used to tell a story about a leprechaun, and of course, Shad hadn't seen one, but today the word *leprechaun* popped right into his head.

George Nelson wore a green three-corner hat and dusty gray-green waistcoat. He set down a bulging leather suitcase tied shut with lengths of twine. Knots in the twine stuck out like burrs on wool socks, and threads peeked from two seams in the suitcase. Right away Shad thought to pocket the loose threads, and he fingered the silk shirt around the seams, looking for a pocket. But the shirt didn't seem to have any pockets at all.

Miss Elizabeth's hand went to her mouth and she coughed. Shad didn't know if George Nelson saw her pretty green eyes flash, but Shad saw them clear as day. Sure as his measuring strip was long, that lady was laughing on the inside, but she was doing a fine job of not showing it. She said, "I wasn't expecting you until tomorrow."

"Madam, what a charming door knocker." George Nelson's voice was high like wind whistling through the reeds.

"Yes, well," she said, and glanced at Shad. He thought she was going to introduce him, but before she did, George Nelson hopped on one foot.

"May I have another go at it?" Then he was gone and Shad heard the door open and *rat-a-tat-tat, tat-a-tat, tat-a-tat-a-tat-a-tat.*

"Goodness," said Miss Elizabeth again.

The door banged in its frame and George Nelson hopped back into the room. He made circles in the air with his arms and bowed again. "At your service, ma'am."

Miss Elizabeth cleared her throat. "Yes, well, lovely, thank you." She raised her arm toward the coloreds. "I'd like you to meet Caroline. And this is Rachel."

Shad's hands went into fists around the measuring strip

and paper. She'd introduced the coloreds *first*. Before *him*. Why, it was downright ugly to introduce coloreds first, or even to introduce them at all. He didn't know what to make of such a lapse. If she could defy conventional manners, so could he! He snatched up a crystal glass of sweet tea.

Miss Elizabeth smiled. "Ah, yes—the tea. I was so caught up in the dress measurements that I forgot—oh, Mr. Nelson, this is Shadrach Weaver of Weaver's Fine Tailoring. And Shadrach, Mr. Nelson has come to Richmond to teach—"

"Wonderful!" George Nelson darted to Shad's side, reaching out a hand. The top of his head came to Shad's shoulder.

Shad fumbled with everything he was carrying—the sweet tea in one hand, the measuring strip, paper, and stick in the other. He didn't have a hand free to shake, and for a split second he froze. Then he set down the tea, but the wetness on the side of the glass had made his hand cold and damp, so he dried it by wiping it on the front of the silk shirt, and along the way, Shad felt everyone's eyes upon him. His throat grew thick.

"We *hear* he's quite the tailor," said Rachel with a flip of her head.

Shad felt his cheeks flush. He shook George Nelson's hand and noted how soft it was—how it belonged to a man who'd never plowed a field.

"That's enough, Rachel," said Miss Elizabeth. "Caroline, would you please put Mr. Nelson's things in the spare room? And the cot—have you set up the cot for him?"

"Certainly, ma'am."

Rachel said, "I'll get more tea." Then she followed Caroline, and Shad heard the two of them chatter all the way down the back hall.

Miss Elizabeth settled into the wooden armchair, nodded at George Nelson, and gestured toward the settee covered in beautiful fabric—a thick crimson brocade.

George Nelson plopped down, crossing one thigh over the other, then placed both hands on his top knee. He nodded in Shad's direction. "Is Shadrach one of your own pupils, Mrs. Perkinson?" But before she could answer, his eyes caught the bookcase that sat beside an upright maple piano with chipped ivory keys. He jumped up, dashed to the dark-bound books, and ran his fingers along the spines.

"Uh, no, he's not. He's with a tailoring shop."

While Shad watched George Nelson slide one book out and back, then another and another, he adjusted his weight from his right leg to the left. He didn't know what was appropriate here. Should he sit or remain standing? Comment or keep quiet? He decided on the second of both choices and stood, feeling awkward, but not minding the fact that they paid no attention to him.

They talked and talked, and after a while Shad grew tired of standing. He inched his way to the settee where he sipped the delicious tea and felt his tongue tingle. His eyes went back and forth from George Nelson's enormous nose to the case of books. Lord, what his daddy would have given for a collection like that!

Daddy loved books. He used to read stories to Jeremiah and Shad, and his favorite was one about the emperor's new clothes. Well, of course that would be the Weaver family's favorite because in that one, the sly tailor tricks the emperor. But there were other wonderful stories, too. Shad's thoughts drifted back to one particular night when Daddy had read them a story, then said, "Here, Shad. It's your turn. You read to me now."

How old was he then? Nine, maybe? He'd taken Daddy's book and held it like Miss Jenny had taught them to hold the Bible—held it with respect and awe and thankfulness. He'd opened it to "The Emperor's New Clothes," and read the whole story out loud. But truth to tell, Shad hadn't *read* one lick. He'd heard the story so many times, he'd memorized every word. He'd *recited* that story. Daddy had beamed and slapped him on the back, and Shad had felt proud that Daddy was proud of him.

Then Daddy had flipped to another page, and said, "Now read me this one, Shad. 'The Tortoise and the Hare.'"

Shad's eyes found the first line, but the letters blurred into a fog right there on the page. He squinted and, sure enough, some of the letters straightened out. But he didn't have the story memorized. It was hard. He began, "Once upon a time," and it was downhill after that. Some of the words made sense, and some didn't. Shad's tongue tripped and fumbled over the lines. He put a finger under each word to slow down the letters and get them to make sense.

After a spell, Jeremiah said, "Ignoramus."

Then Daddy said, "Now, now. That's okay, Shad. It's bedtime. You boys need some shut-eye." Daddy took the book and the candle and patted Jeremiah and Shad on their heads and headed out of the bedroom.

Jeremiah said, "You are so stupid."

And Shad said, "Shut up," but he knew Jeremiah was right. And Daddy knew it, too. And after that day, Shad had never let Daddy put that book into his lap again. He got Daddy to read "The Tortoise and the Hare" to him, and he knew he was even slower than a tortoise because he couldn't ever keep up with so many letters.

"Schooling," George Nelson said as he wagged a finger at Shad, and his voice and his finger jolted Shad out of the memory. "No one should cross the threshold from youth to manhood without reading Shakespeare!" His words seemed to come through little black hairs that protruded from each nostril.

"Shakespeare might be a tad too advanced for Mr. Weaver," said Miss Elizabeth.

"Why, Mrs. Perkinson, I've got the alphabet and every level from there to Hegel. I've got primers and I've got philosophy. There are methods to teaching. What methods do you use?"

But before Miss Elizabeth could open her mouth, George Nelson spun clear around on one foot, making a funny little circle and throwing his hands into the air for balance. He dashed away, crying, "Caroline! Where is my bag? Caroline!"

Shad watched him go, and it seemed like all the air blew right out of the room with him, leaving behind only the word *methods*. Shad had never before heard such a thing—*methods to teaching*.

Miss Elizabeth giggled, mumbling, "Goodness." Then a twitch went through her—top to bottom—and she collected herself, straightening her back and lifting her head. "Well, Shadrach, I have to tell you that on paper, Mr. Nelson's credentials are quite stunning. Impeccable, really. But in person?" She closed her eyes for a moment and settled her hands in her lap.

"Of course, that's neither here nor there." Abruptly, she changed the subject, thrusting both wrists toward him and showing off the cuffs. "Your grandfather tailored this dress perfectly, don't you think?"

Shad nodded. "He does good work, ma'am. Yes, he does."

"And, of course, you're apprenticing under him."

Shad squirmed on the settee. "Uh, well, no ma'am, not exactly."

"And why ever not?"

"Well, Granddaddy done taught me a lot, but I ain't no firstborn, ma'am. My brother—he has rights to the shop."

Miss Elizabeth cringed. Her arms tightened against

her body, shoulders rose up, jaw stiffened. Shad tightened, too. He'd long tried to convince Mama and Granddaddy that he was worthy of the shop, that he was putting his heart and soul into learning the trade. Jeremiah clearly didn't want it, and Shad had argued for his own position.

But papers were papers. Before enlisting, Daddy had written his last will and testament, giving Jeremiah his half of the shop. Granddaddy and Jeremiah owned it now. Or, more accurately put, they shared the debt. And every time anyone reminded Jeremiah of his financial obligation, he cursed the inheritance laws with two fists. Could no one in the South start afresh?

Miss Elizabeth cleared her throat. "I *am not* the first-born. Can you say that correctly for me? I *am* not."

Shad frowned. "Uh, yes, ma'am. I *am* not no firstborn."

"Oh, my." She jerked her head in a funny way and leaned toward Shad, forehead creased like a field before planting. "Shad, the double negative—well, son, there are rules of grammar."

"I ain't never had no formal lessons, ma'am. Only Sunday school."

"I *haven't ever* had formal lessons."

"Uh, I haven't. Ever. Had. Formal lessons."

"Yes. Yes, that's better. Thank you. And certainly, Sunday school is a start. A good start."

Shad beamed, remembering how happy Miss Jenny had been when he recited "Blessed are the meek." Then his face dimmed at the memory of her putting him in the corner with a dunce cap while Jeremiah and the others snickered. There was something about letters—Shad didn't know what it was exactly. He could recite parts of the Bible, but ask him to sit down and read it, and he'd need most of a day to figure out half a page.

"I can read some, ma'am. It's just that I'm slow. But with proper instruction—*maybe a new method*—maybe I could catch on. Do you reckon Mr. Nelson might-could take me on as one of his students?"

"Well, I don't know, Shadrach."

"I'd be willing to do chores in exchange. Tailoring. Deliveries. Choppin' wood. I'd work hard at it."

"I'm not sure that—"

"A lesson just once a week, ma'am? Perhaps?"

"Listen, Shadrach, you're clearly not ready for Shakespeare. Now, I tutor at the intermediate level, but my slate is full, and the tuition is steeper than your family could afford. The only other option here would be with the beginners, and I can't imagine that your mother would approve of your sitting with Rachel and the little ones. Why, I doubt Rachel would want you, anyway."

Sitting with Rachel? Had he heard Miss Elizabeth right? Shad stopped breathing. A white-fuzz sound filled his ears.

"Rachel has her own school, you know." She leaned toward him. "Did you know that?"

13

A Burst Bubble

SHAD FELT SWEAT break under his arms. He'd heard about colored schools, but he couldn't imagine that a white woman who thought herself a member of polite society would ever so much as mention them. "No, ma'am. No, I don't know nothing 'bout no colored school."

Miss Elizabeth paused, looking pained. She coughed a little cough. "Why, yes, Shadrach. She and Eloise run it together, and it's—well, they have a time of it. Her students can't always pay. They're the youngest ones. And sometimes they arrive hungry. I must say, we're all grateful for support from the Freedmen's Bureau. Those staples provide a breakfast each morning. They run their school from my shed—well, here, I'll show you."

Shad stood when she did, and walked with her to the

back window, opposite the river. He followed her gaze out over a green lawn that sloped away from the house and was almost entirely enclosed by a tall holly hedge. Miss Elizabeth pointed to a large, whitewashed woodshed. In relation to her fine house, Shad could see why she'd called it a shed. But to Shad, it wasn't a shed at all. It was nearly the size of his family's little house out Nine Mile Road.

The shed sat beside the entrance to an icehouse or cold cellar. Along the other side of the backyard, Shad saw a vegetable garden and a hut that might have been a henhouse, and beyond that, the privy.

"Rachel and Eloise have eight regular pupils who arrive each morning at dawn and are gone by midmorning to tend to their own household chores. Then the girls go into town for advanced lessons at the building that will soon become Richmond's first Colored Normal School. I'm quite excited about it."

Shad nodded as if he understood, but truth to tell, he felt a tad dizzy. He gripped the sill to keep his balance. "I see," he said, but he didn't see. Rachel and Eloise—they were *teachers*. Like Miss Jenny. But they were coloreds. Who was it who'd told him colored folk were animals? Like mules and plow horses. Like cows you bred and traded and sold. It was illegal to teach them reading and writing—or, at least, it used to be illegal. And now—well, did Miss Elizabeth mean that Rachel might teach him something? A colored girl. Teach *him*? No, that wasn't right at all.

"Shad," she said, "I brought Mr. Nelson here to help with the establishment of a colored school, not to tutor white children."

Shad felt like he might need to run to that privy. Something was wrong here, and it made his head throb like a bee sting.

Then Shad heard the rhythm of feet skipping on wooden floorboards, and George Nelson burst into the room. He waved a fistful of papers in one hand and a large piece of slate in the other. "I found her! Got some materials right here."

George Nelson plopped onto the settee and it creaked from the shock. He patted the cushion beside him, motioning for Shad to sit.

Shad told his innards to calm down. *Just settle a spell, now.* And he slipped from Miss Elizabeth's side to join George Nelson on the settee.

From the corner of Shad's eye, he saw a weariness come over Miss Elizabeth. He heard a whoosh of air, and looked up to see her chest collapse and her shoulders round in. "Mr. Nelson, I was just explaining to Mr. Weaver that I hadn't brought you here to teach white children."

"But Mrs. Perkinson, with all due respect, white or colored—they all need to learn."

"Well, here in Richmond, well—"

George Nelson shoved the slate into Shad's lap. "What shall we start with, Mr. Weaver?"

Shad felt the strength of Miss Elizabeth's eyes locked on George Nelson, and he wondered if he ought to get up and leave. He wanted lessons—yes, he did—but right at that particular moment, the house didn't sit right with him. Schools for coloreds. Lordy. And besides that, Miss Elizabeth and George Nelson clearly had something to work out—something that wasn't Shad's business. But right then and there, his bottom was on the settee and he felt a tremendous need to keep sitting. He wanted very much to stay and calm his innards.

Miss Elizabeth tapped a foot. "I'm not sure you heard me, Mr. Nelson."

"Yes, go on," he said.

Shad watched George Nelson finger his papers without looking up. Then Shad glanced at Miss Elizabeth and saw a shadow cross her face. She folded her arms over her chest and stood there, pondering George Nelson while he fussed with the papers.

After a time she threw her hands in the air and said, "Oh, good heavens. Fine. Just for today, sir. Fine."

George Nelson waved the back of his hand absent-mindedly and continued to sort through his papers while Miss Elizabeth marched from the room. Shad listened to the *click-clack* of her shoes all the way down the back hall.

George Nelson leaned forward. "My apologies in advance, Mr. Weaver. When we start at the beginning, I call it an *assessment*. Helps a teacher know what a pupil needs. Here." He pressed a piece of gray chalk against the slate—a flat gray rock, smooth on the top and bottom, jagged around the edges, with a ridge running crooked through the middle. He wrote a sentence. "Read that for me. Easy, right?"

Shad shifted his bottom on the settee, feeling torn between Miss Elizabeth's drama and Mr. Nelson's eagerness. He squinted and tried to figure out the words. They reminded him of Sunday school. "*God*," he said.

"Yes, yes! But of course. And the rest of it?"

"Uh. *God is* . . . uh, *God saw that it was good.*"

Mr. Nelson frowned. "You put more words into it than

I've got there, Shad. Okay, here. Try another one." He wrote a new sentence.

Shad let out all his air. The letters blurred together. "*The dad*—no, *the bab*—no, *the*—"

"Fascinating!" proclaimed George Nelson. "I had another student who flipped the *b*'s and *d*'s. Here. Don't you see how this is a *b*?" He wrote a letter on the slate. "And this is a *d*?" He took off his green jacket and rolled up the sleeves of his white shirt. Shad watched him tap the tips of his fingers in quick little pats. "Come, come, now. Try again."

Shad stared at the slate. He didn't see clearly how one letter was a *b* and the other a *d*. He sighed. George Nelson reminded him why Sunday school was so hard.

"My, my, my. All righty, let's start somewhere else. What is this?" George Nelson wrote, W-E-A-V-E-R.

"Well, that's my name, sir. I know my name."

"Wonderful! Of course. See? Just checking. Very good."

When Miss Elizabeth and Rachel returned with more sweet tea, George Nelson stood, and Shad stood alongside him, towering long and lanky over them all. George Nelson announced, "A fascinating problem. I've encountered this once before, and I do believe he can overcome it, but it's not routine. Not at all. You've started me off with a bit of a challenge."

"And do you like a challenge, Mr. Nelson?" Miss Elizabeth asked.

"Oh, yes. Most definitely, ma'am."

"Welcome to Richmond, sir."

"Good, good. All good."

Rachel leaned toward them with the tray of sweet tea, and Shad waited for George Nelson to go first. Then Shad took a fresh glass, too. He'd already finished the first one.

"I've just spoken with Rachel about this matter," said Miss Elizabeth, "and my preference would be for you to guide her in this challenge, Mr. Nelson. She teaches the beginners while I handle intermediate-level students. I brought you here to instruct at the advanced level—to teach the teachers, as it were."

"Ah, I see," said George Nelson. "Well, this sort of reading problem is rather complex, dear."

Rachel picked up a glass of tea and took a sip, and Shad clenched his teeth. He had never known coloreds to drink while in the same room as whites. But this Rachel girl— she up and had herself a glass of sweet tea. And Miss Elizabeth smiled. Shad felt his eyes nearly burst from his face. He blinked repeatedly to settle them down.

"No two students exactly alike," George Nelson was saying. "You have to figure out which letters the pupil is flipping. Find the patterns, then help the pupil see what he's doing wrong."

"Rachel is quite the teacher," said Miss Elizabeth, raising her shoulders a full inch and puffing up her chest. She walked to Rachel and patted her shoulder. "I'm sure she could handle it as long as—well, let's talk about arrangements, shall we?"

Miss Elizabeth turned to Shad. "Rachel and I spoke about the matter of your requesting private instruction. It would not be private. She simply doesn't have time in her schedule for that. But if you were amenable to sitting quietly in her classroom, she would have no problem as long as your presence is not disruptive. Do you understand?"

Him? Sitting in *her* classroom? That *shed* out back? His mouth dropped open.

"We begin lessons at dawn, Mr. Weaver," said Rachel. "And I would need a day to discuss the arrangement with Eloise, of course, and to prepare my students for your arrival, so you may not start tomorrow, which is, let's see . . . Friday. No, not Friday, and not Saturday because we don't do Saturday lessons. Monday would be fine. And of course, there's the matter of compensation. Each of my students makes a contribution, and each is different, depending on his family's situation. In your case—"

She talked quickly, and Shad had trouble taking it all in. He held up a hand the way Miss Jenny had insisted that students signal a question.

Rachel smiled. "Hard of hearing, too, are you? Allow me to slow it down." She leaned into each word. "Having. Trouble. Imagining. The. Arrangement. Sir?"

"I—uh, I don't know," said Shad.

Rachel rolled her eyes. "Well, that makes two of us."

"It was my suggestion," Miss Elizabeth explained.

"It will only work if you're willing to provide something for my students," said Rachel, setting one hand on a hip. "Teach them to sew, perhaps. You learn reading and they learn tailoring. My students need skills, Mr. Weaver. Letters will expand their horizons, and tailoring will put food in their bellies."

George Nelson darted to the piano, shouting, "A song to celebrate the institution of education!" His fingers flew across the keyboard.

Rachel set down her glass and clapped to the beat.

Miss Elizabeth's eyes twinkled.

Shad looked from one to the other to George Nelson. He had walked into another world! He glanced down at his mismatched clothes—the fine silk shirt that belonged to Mr. Parks Randolph Perkinson, and the tattered britches of

Willy Johnson's with a rip becoming a hole over his knee. His clothes said it all. He didn't belong in this house.

But he liked it here. He liked funny George Nelson, and he wanted lessons. Daddy had always wanted him to master reading. But if Miss Elizabeth was saying that the only option was Rachel's school, well—Shad couldn't imagine how that might work. He couldn't sit for instruction from a colored girl. But he liked how George Nelson would guide Rachel—would teach the teachers. If the lessons would be George Nelson's, tailored for Shad, coming from Rachel, well, then, yes. That might work. The girl would deliver the lessons, was all.

"I want to read better, yes, thank you. I do. And yes, I can teach tailoring. But I—would you—well, if it's all right, well, I couldn't no way tell Mama I was learning reading from no colored."

George Nelson abruptly stopped playing. Music hung unfinished in the air like residue from a burst soap bubble.

Rachel's nostrils flared.

Miss Elizabeth closed her eyes and pinched the skin at the top of her freckled nose. She spoke slowly. "No, of course not." She opened her eyes and walked to the front window overlooking the hill. "Richmond has such a long way to go. You know, Shadrach, in Paris people would think nothing of a highly educated Negress teaching white children. The education matters, not the color of the skin. But here in Virginia—no, I'm sorry, I struggle to understand the ways of Virginia."

George Nelson stood and Shad turned toward him. The little man raised his arms to the ceiling, circled them like blades of a windmill, and bowed. "I am here to right the wrongs."

"Well, now, Mr. Nelson," said Rachel, and Shad marveled at the confidence in her voice, at the way she looked at Mr. Nelson sideways. "Something tells me you're full of book learning, but you'd best be wary, or you won't last a day in this town."

"Come now. Come, come, come," he said.

"Here at Libby Hill," Rachel went on, "Miss Elizabeth affords us freedom from the conventions of Richmond. We study music and Shakespeare and philosophy. But on the streets of this town, well, let's just say we 'do as the Romans do.' If you were to encounter me at market, Mr. Nelson, you would encounter an ignorant Negress."

George Nelson's face shriveled like a raisin. "Is that really your public persona?" he asked. "Are you saying that you cannot be true to yourself?"

"Myself," said Rachel, laughing. "Ha! Who am I, Mr.

Nelson? Those who survive in Richmond reinvent themselves as circumstances dictate."

"I see," said George Nelson, frowning and stroking
his chin.

"Mr. Weaver," said Rachel, "if you keep your mouth
open like that, a bug is likely to fly right inside and set up
shop."

14

Yankee-Lovers

WHEN SHAD GOT home with the measurements for Abigail's dress, his head was still working to make sense of everything he'd witnessed. He carried a package in one arm, and his FEED AND SEED shirt in a ball under the other.

The moment Mama saw him, she reached for the finely tailored shirt. "Miz Perkinson give you this?" She rubbed the fabric between her fingers and huffed. "Silk."

Shad swallowed. He wanted to kick himself for not thinking to change shirts. "Uh ... yes'm."

"And you accepted it?" Mama showed the whites of her eyes. "What were you thinkin'? You want to be beholden to Miz Perkinson?"

"Well, I told her I couldn't take it. I said *no*! But she insisted, Mama. She wanted me to show Granddaddy the double stitching. See, here—look at the cuff."

Mama rolled her eyes. "That lady's always putting on airs. She's a Yankee-lover, Shad. She tell you that?"

"Well, no, ma'am."

"The only reason we do her tailoring is how good she pays. You got to keep your distance from that one." Mama took the package and opened it, and her little brown eyes twinkled. Flour, salt, cornmeal, dried peas, sorghum molasses, and salt pork. Mama beamed from ear to ear, showing the gaps from three missing teeth—one on top, two on the bottom. "You got them measurements?"

"Yes, ma'am."

She pried the wax off the molasses jar and stuck the tip of a finger into it. Then she set the finger in her mouth and sucked like a nursing baby. Shad watched her eyes close and saw a calm come over her. The hollow in her cheeks grew deep, and wrinkles formed like needles around her lips.

When she opened her eyes again, they were busy. "And Miz Perkinson sent along mending, I see. Awful fine payment for one dress and a little mending."

"Well, and I chopped some wood for her, and ran a delivery into town."

"Delivery?"

Shad swallowed a lump in his throat. He coughed. "I

asked for lessons, Mama. Readin' lessons." There, he'd said it.

He watched Mama frown, and her mouth went so crooked, he'd have thought a fishhook was caught in one cheek. She took a big breath and let it all out. Then she tilted her head and peered at him. Sideways. She seemed to be pondering everything he'd said, and yet she seemed far, far away.

"I know you think the world of Miss Jenny, but Mama, she ain't learned me to read good. In her class, I memorize Bible verses, is all. And you know Miss Elizabeth does tutoring up there. So today I got up my nerve and asked. She's willing to give me schoolin' for extra work."

"Schoolin'?" A look of pity came over Mama's face—a look she reserved for wounded animals, for horses injured so bad that a shot to the head was a blessing.

Shad tightened. He knew that look—knew how much he hated it. He didn't want to hear again how disappointed she was in him.

"Aw, baby, come on now, Shad."

He stood behind a ladder-backed chair and set both hands on the top rung. Mama wanted to protect him from another day in a corner with a dunce cap. But he didn't want her protection. "Mama, I—"

"Some is meant for schooling and some not. Your tailoring is coming along fine."

"Look, Mama—"

She reached for his arm. "I'm proud of you—ain't I told you that? I'm proud how Sunday school learned you good, and you got your Bible memorized, and that's all you need, baby."

"Well, I—"

"Now, I ain't ever learned my letters, and you can't, neither, and baby—it's okay. You gonna be okay without that book learning."

"But, Mama—"

"Daddy was the reader in the family, wasn't he? Daddy and Jeremiah—Lord, how the two of them can read! *Could* read. Daddy *could*." She stammered and Shad saw a shadow cross her face. All of a sudden, Mama was so close to tears, Shad found himself twisting up on the inside, preparing to ease her into a chair. He hated how hard everything had become for Mama since Daddy died. Hated how he hadn't been able to make it better for her.

Shad held his breath and waited for the shadow to pass—waited for Mama to have a moment there—for air to move again before he refilled his lungs. "With all due respect, Mama, I think I can do it."

She shook her head. "Each of us, Shad—the good Lord meant each of us for something in this world, and He ain't meant you for schooling. How I hate to see you run after something you ain't meant to have, baby."

Shad's gaze fell to Mama's bare feet—she always went barefoot in the house. He wondered how old he'd been when Mama had given up on him. When had she first seen him as a simpleton? He thought maybe he should drop this talk like he'd dropped it so many times before. But today was different. Today he straightened and planted his feet firmly.

"Let me try, Mama. I'll get good schooling at Miz Elizabeth's, and I've handled everything myself, so you don't need to worry about it one bit. I ain't gonna let it get in the way of tailoring. I'm gonna do short lessons at dawn at Miz Elizabeth's, then do a chore or two for her—whatever she needs—and she agreed on chores being my tuition since she knows we can't pay. And after lessons, I'll stop by the shop, in case you need something from Granddaddy, and I'll run our deliveries like always."

Mama shook her head. "I don't know, baby."

He cringed. "Look, Mama—"

"Don't *look* me."

He dropped his gaze to the floor and rubbed a hand

across the back of his neck. "I'm sorry, Mama. I'm tired. I need me a little shut-eye before dinner."

"Shut-eye? That's sloth, pure and simple. It's midafternoon. You sick? Don't tell me you comin' down with something."

Shad shook his head. He stood there, exhausted from lack of sleep, not wanting Mama to pick up on anything he was up to—the lie over the real arrangements at the Perkinsons', running with the Klan at night. He didn't want to talk with Mama anymore, and couldn't find a way to explain himself.

"Mama, I just need me a moment, okay?" He put two hands in the air and retreated to the bedroom. He fell onto the straw mattress and let his body fold in on itself. His ears shut down. His eyes shut down. He got a breath and then a bigger breath and his whole body shuddered, and he curled into a ball. He was so very tired. So much had happened over the past day and night that he couldn't begin to sort it all out. He was changing in so many ways—growing up, becoming a man, making decisions for himself. But to Mama, he was a simpleton—always had been, always would be. A simple, stupid boy.

15

Letters

SHAD HEARD Granddaddy laugh, and the sound seemed far away. He opened his eyes. The light was low.

"Shad!" Jeremiah called. The bedroom door banged open. "Shad! Supper. Get your butt to the table, boy. Mama's made a feast."

Shad rubbed his face. The skin on his cheek had mashed like the folds in the cotton ticking. The silk shirt had wrinkled to beat all.

He got up, his posture slack, mind dulled by sleep. He went to the outhouse, then stopped at the well and splashed up. When the cold water hit his cheeks, it startled him—as unexpected as a dam break—releasing his thoughts like a flood. The Klan—joining up last night—the Perkinsons, the colored girls, that shed where coloreds got lessons, the eagerness of George Nelson, Mama's disappointment in him. It all flooded his head and weighed him down, damp and heavy.

He slumped into a chair at the table. The day was fading, but enough light came through the window that they didn't need a candle. Not yet. No use wasting a candle.

Granddaddy bowed his head and Shad followed. "Come, Lord Jesus, our guest to be, and bless these gifts bestowed by Thee. Amen." Shad noticed that Granddaddy had waxed his silvery mustache to a perfect handlebar, and shaved his chin clean. He still smelled of shaving lather.

Shad glanced at Jeremiah, loudly slurping the rabbit stew. Jeremiah sat sideways at the table because his long legs didn't fit underneath anymore. His back was rounded, and he leaned in, splaying his elbows wide, his dirty straw hair sticking every which way, his straggly goatee masking his chin.

Shad set his eyes on his own bowl—a white ceramic one, chipped along the edge. He felt the slap of Granddaddy's hand on his shoulder and jerked his head up.

"You okay, son?" asked Granddaddy.

"Fine, sir. I'm fine."

Granddaddy fingered the silk. "Mighty nice tailoring, but too big for you, boy. Where'd you get this shirt?"

"Pass the parsnips there, please," said Mama, a little louder than usual. Her eyes caught Shad's and something told him not to point out the fine double stitching in the collar and cuffs. Mama went on, "And thank you for bringing the parsnips. Lordy me, we ain't eaten this good in months. Pass 'em over to Shad, there."

Shad squirmed and lifted a spoon. He blew across the stew, trying to remember what was true and what wasn't. "Miz Elizabeth, sir."

Granddaddy fingered the shirt a tad longer. Then he shoved a forkful of parsnips into his mouth. The bags under his eyes sank lower than usual today, and Shad knew it was because they'd run with the Klan. They were all tired. Shad could hardly believe he'd joined last night. It seemed like a month had passed between then and now.

Jeremiah leaned toward Shad to feel the shirt, too. "What's with the shirt? You getting all fancy, grown-up, ain't you?"

Shad swallowed. "Well, Miz Elizabeth made me wash at her well and put this on 'fore she let me in the house. I 'spect I smelled ripe."

Jeremiah hooted, and Shad let a smile come up on his face.

"Didn't you wash up this morning?" Mama asked.

"No, ma'am."

"Lord have mercy."

Jeremiah whistled. "Ignoramus."

"Shut up."

"Now, boys," said Granddaddy, leaning back in his chair. "Now, now, now."

For a while, the family ate without talking. Mama had made the stew thick with flour and peas and a little bit of molasses—not a lot, but enough to flavor it up just fine. Shad slurped the last of his and pushed away from the table—the farther from everyone's scrutiny, the better. He took up the work he'd yet to finish—the new pleats he was setting in Mr. Hanson's trousers—and settled into the chair by the front window.

Mama stood and lit the kerosene lamp, then set it beside Shad. When she went to stack the dirty bowls, Granddaddy said, "Adeline, it's been a long day." He patted the cane seat of her chair. "Leave those dishes be. We'll tend to 'em later. Come set a spell." He pulled out his pipe and a pouch of tobacco.

From the corner of his eye, Shad saw the edges of Mama's mouth rise. First smile on her face all day. She put the bowls on the cookstove and sat down, letting out a big old tired sigh like letting go of the whole day. "All righty. I'm-a put my feet up."

Granddaddy lit a match and sucked the flame into the bowl. Up came the sweet smell of tobacco with a hint of cherry. "Jeremiah, how's that construction job going?"

"Coloreds," mumbled Jeremiah.

"Come again, boy."

Shad rolled his eyes. Jeremiah's story was always the same.

"Granddaddy, sir—look, I tried. Me and Clifton, we stood in that pack and we craned our necks, and I know that foreman saw us, no question. But he up and pointed at a handful of coloreds, and that was that."

Mama shook her head. "My boy is strong as any colored boy. It ain't right."

"Damn Yankees," said Jeremiah.

Granddaddy lifted his eyebrows and tilted his head—a posture that Shad understood to mean there was nothing Granddaddy could do about it. But it meant something else, too—that Granddaddy was disappointed Jeremiah hadn't come to work at Weaver's Fine Tailoring. "High time y'all moved to my shop."

Good Lord, Shad thought. *Here it comes.* Ever since word of Daddy's death, Granddaddy had urged Jeremiah to apprentice and Mama to move to town. But Jeremiah didn't want a label of *tailor* tacked onto his forehead, and Mama didn't want to move.

Not only had Mama never taken to the hustle-bustle of the city on account of growing up on a farm, but she laid on another reason, and she laid it on thick. She claimed that out Nine Mile Road, she felt Daddy in the walls and saw him in the fields.

Long before the war, Daddy had arranged to rent these two acres and the little house, and he'd paid rent every month until the day he'd enlisted and ridden off on Mindy-girl. Ever since that day, Mr. Kechler had let the Weavers live on his property without asking for a dime. And ever since, Mama swore Daddy was still living in this little white house, and she couldn't bear to leave him behind.

On some days she out and out refused to believe that he'd died. She'd say she needed to wait for him—that he was going to walk through the front door and join them for supper.

It happened sometimes—happened that men who were long thought dead plumb up and appeared on doorsteps. And they weren't ghosts! Men returned in the flesh, saying the news had been mistaken. They appeared without their horses or muskets or anything. They returned looking like skeletons because of how hard the journey back home had been. But at least they came home.

Shad sometimes felt the same way Mama did—sometimes felt a sadness that seemed more than he could bear. Tonight he glanced at the door, waiting. If he wished it hard enough, would Daddy come home? He sighed. No, he had to stop fooling himself. They'd gotten a letter and Jeremiah had sat Mama down in a chair and read it out loud. Then they'd all cried. Even Jeremiah.

He and Jeremiah and Granddaddy didn't have it in them to set Mama straight, to tell her again and again, *He ain't here, Mama. He done died at Gettysburg.* No sense making her cry.

Tonight Jeremiah pushed his chair from the table and it scraped a new ridge in the dirt floor. He stood and pulled on his goatee and planted his feet wide. "Due respect, sir, but we been over this before."

Mama shifted and the cane chair creaked. "Let's not get into that. Now, Shadrach, tell 'em what you told me today."

Shad froze. It was one thing to change the subject and another to put him on the spot.

Jeremiah wheeled around and plopped back into his chair, his knees pointing at Shad like mounted shotguns. "What did I miss?"

"Shad's taking on something he probably shouldn't," said Mama.

Shad pushed his needle through the trousers and kept his eyes low.

"Fill us in here, Shad. We're family," said Granddaddy.

"Uh," said Shad, "well, see, turns out maybe I got a problem with my letters."

"Well, ain't that news," said Jeremiah with a scoff.

"No, I mean—it's different. Like maybe I flip 'em around or something."

"Letters? You want to talk *letters*?" Jeremiah tipped his chair onto its back legs and laughed. "Oh, I got letters for you."

Granddaddy grunted, and Shad lifted his head in time to see his eyes go slant. "Not now, son."

Jeremiah smirked. "Come on, Granddaddy, sir. We got us some good letters."

Granddaddy shook his head and Shad could tell he was fixing to say something, but Jeremiah beat him to the punch.

"K-K-K," said Jeremiah proudly. "Ku Klux Klan."

"Oh, you good ol' boys," said Mama.

"K-K-K, Shad. Them's all the letters you ever need to know."

Granddaddy coughed. He got up, marched to the window, and sent a wad of spit into the breeze.

Shad straightened, feeling proud to be part of the brotherhood. But he felt tight inside. Mama was sitting right there. Jeremiah wasn't supposed to say anything outside of KKK meetings. He'd best keep the subject off the Klan. "Well, I asked for lessons today. Readin' lessons in exchange for chores."

Granddaddy raised his eyebrows. "You don't say?"

"From that Yankee-lover?" asked Jeremiah.

Mama shook her head. "I done tried to explain to him this afternoon—how ain't nothin' good to come of it."

Jeremiah pointed at Shad. "You gonna do chores and get nothin' in return. You can't read."

Shad bit the inside of his lip. Lord, everybody was tired and on edge. He watched Granddaddy's fingers tighten around his pipe. He raised one shoulder. "No harm in trying."

Mama tapped her fingers on the pine table. "I don't

know. Them Perkinsons—I don't want Shad up there more than he has to. Deliveries is enough. They're Yankee-born, and breeding don't hold a candle to blood. That Perkinson family money come from Massachusetts."

Granddaddy cleared his throat. "Well, Adeline, you got to give Parks Perkinson credit. He died for the Confederacy."

"He's still Yankee."

"Let it go, Adeline. If Miz Elizabeth wants to spend her family money on our business, and if Shad wants to try a new teacher, it's all good."

"I don't want to be beholden to her."

"And you ain't," said Granddaddy. "You ain't."

"What's she doing giving a silk shirt to my boy?"

"Now, Adeline, she don't need them fine shirts no more."

Jeremiah stood and crossed his arms over his chest, and all eyes turned to him. With authority, he said, "What Mama is saying is that Miz Perkinson looks down on us, and Mama don't want no more of it."

Mama set her shoulders back and folded her hands in her lap. "You said it right. Thank you, son."

"I tell you," Jeremiah went on, "every time I see one of

them bluecoats, it's all I can do to keep from reaching for my knife."

"Amen, son. Ain't I taught you never to kick a boy when he's down? Well, that's exactly what them Yankees are doing to us right now. They got us down. Licked us good. And now they're taxing the living daylights out of us. What in God's good name are we supposed to pay with? They done burned everything."

Jeremiah pointed a finger at Granddaddy. "They say we're one country again, proud to be united, but it ain't true. Them Yankees hate us bad."

Granddaddy sighed so loudly, Shad reckoned an incoming storm wouldn't have drowned him out. Granddaddy ran his tongue around his lips and rubbed a hand through his hair. "Business is business, and they got a good account with us."

"Now we ain't hurtin' that account," said Mama. "We're just saying."

Granddaddy's gaze fell to the floor. "I'm mighty tired. I'd best be heading back to Shockoe 'fore pitch-dark." He moseyed away from the window and set his chair square to the table. "Thank you for dinner, Adeline. Good to see you, boys."

Then Mama set one hand in the crook of his elbow and her other hand patted his arm, and she walked him out the door. They stood for a spell and their voices got low. Jeremiah grunted, then shuffled off to bed.

Shad craned his neck to overhear the conversation out front, but he couldn't catch any of it. He was too tired. He'd gotten some shut-eye before dinner, but with his belly full now, he felt his eyelids grow heavy. Too much had happened in too short a time, and too much lay on his mind. He couldn't afford to jumble his thoughts and slip and say something he shouldn't. Best to rest up. No telling when the brotherhood would call another meeting.

He set aside Mr. Hanson's trousers and headed to the outhouse, and by the time he got back, he could hear Jeremiah snoring on his side of the straw mattress. It sure had been a long, long day.

16

Devil on His Shoulder

CRACK OF DAWN Monday morning, Nine Mile Road and most of the low-lying areas lay under a white fog blanket. As Shad headed up Church Hill, he marveled at the way the fog disappeared quick as hot breath on a cold day. The air at Libby Hill was crystal clear, and he watched the sky turn from white to pink, orange, and blue, all in a matter of minutes.

Shad had decided that a tailoring lesson called for a finely tailored shirt, so he'd put on the silk one. He'd slipped from the house a few minutes behind Jeremiah and before Mama had a chance to comment on the shirt. He didn't want either of them breathing down his neck this morning.

He went up Twenty-eighth Street and down the alley that separated the backyards of the houses on Franklin and Grace Streets. He carried a sack of tailoring supplies—scraps of cotton, a spool of thread, four sewing needles. And on his shoulder, he carried a devil, buzzing like a mosquito, saying, "You're gonna get caught." He slapped around his ears but couldn't make the buzzing stop.

Lordy, if someone saw him take the alley instead of the front door, he didn't have one cotton-picking notion how he'd explain it. *Lesson with Miss Elizabeth*, he'd say. And they'd know full well—it was only coloreds who went in through the back. He'd have to give this lie more thought.

Shad was standing at the door to the shed behind the Perkinson house, waiting, when he saw a little black face peek through the opening in the holly hedge. Then the face disappeared. A moment later, another face peeked through. It disappeared, too.

Shad felt regret for a moment, thinking he should forget the whole arrangement. It had been crazy of him to think it might work. It wasn't right—him being at the shed. He held his arms in tight, not wanting to touch anything. *Get over it, Shad*, he told himself. He shook his head, rattling it this way and that, reminding himself that he was here to learn to read, but darn if that devil didn't grab on to his shoulder and knot up his muscles good and tight.

Then he saw Eloise march through the opening in the hedge. He couldn't see any little ones, but he was near certain they were behind her. Her skirt jerked from side to side, and she smiled. Quietly, she said, "Good morning. Miss Rachel tells us you're teaching basic sewing today."

"Uh, yes'm. That's right."

She set a hand on Shad's arm and he flinched. "Don't worry. The hedge is too high for neighbors to see you."

He ground his teeth. Was it obvious that he was nervous as all get-out? He heard a door creak and turned to see Rachel slip down Miss Elizabeth's back steps—a good six or seven whitewashed wooden steps from the door into the yard. He looked from Eloise to Rachel and back again, and whispered, "You came up the alley. Don't you live here?"

"No, sir. What gave you that idea? I live just around the corner."

Shad blinked. Just because he'd met the girls together didn't mean they lived in the same house. What a fool he was! In a split second he'd lost his credibility. How would these children respect him when he asked stupid questions like that?

To learn from him, they'd need to respect him, but he knew no model to demand respect other than intimidation.

He didn't have it in him to bark the way Mr. Kechler barked at his slaves. Didn't have it in him to hit anybody or bully them the way Jeremiah bullied him. His head spun.

Then he heard children giggle. A little one dared to peek from behind Eloise's skirt. "Is that the tailor?"

Then another peeked out. And another. And another. One was so bold as to march forward and offer his hand. Shad shook it. The boy was the tallest of the children, his skin only as dark as finished maple. His eyes flickered brightly with a cleverness that took Shad in quickly. He was barefoot and wore a burlap sack not so different from Shad's FEED AND SEED shirt.

"I'm Nathaniel," he said, "and Miss Rachel tells me I'm to make sure you know the alphabet. All twenty-six letters. And if'n you don't, I'm-a teach you."

"Ah, you've already met Nathaniel," said Rachel, coming up behind the boy and rubbing her open palm against his head. "And I see you've brought some things. Shall we begin with the tailoring lesson?"

"Uh, yes'm," Shad mumbled, and right away he wanted to kick himself. His answer should have been something bold. *Of course!* Or *Certainly!* Not a mumble.

He watched as the children filed into the shed behind

Eloise. Two, four, six, eight of them. Rachel gestured for him to follow the last one—Nathaniel—and Shad ducked through the doorway to keep from hitting his head. Rachel came in last and closed the door.

Inside Shad smelled fresh-cut pine and laid his eyes on a rough-hewn table. Three long, low benches looked worse for wear—some rotting sections, a faint mildewy scent. He took a place on a bench by the east window, hoping the light there would be good enough for sewing.

"Would you rather we do this outside?" asked Rachel. "Beautiful day."

Shad shook his head. No, even with the tall hedges, he couldn't risk being seen.

The littlest girl went up on tiptoes and down again. Up, down, up, down, her patched calico skirt swaying, her thumb in her mouth. Then she pulled the thumb free and announced, "He's scared, Miss Rachel. Ain't he?"

"*Isn't*, Maggie. *Ain't* isn't proper English. Say *isn't*."

Maggie looked at Shad, her mouth suddenly down, her eyes wet. She reached for Eloise's skirt, pulled in close, and stuck the thumb back in her mouth, never taking her eyes off Shad.

Good Lord, he thought. He'd have liked a skirt to hide

behind, too. He hoped Maggie couldn't see the way his hands quivered. Hoped he could settle himself before he launched into the tailoring lesson.

He straightened his back and squared his shoulders. The children formed a circle around him. His tongue felt thick.

Another girl asked, "What's your name?"

He opened his mouth to answer, but Rachel held up a hand, cutting him off. "Kitty, no names this morning. We have a special arrangement with this tailor, and it's best if you not learn his real name. You may call him Mr. . . ." She paused, frowning in search of possibilities. Then her face brightened. "*Lourdaud.* It's French. Please say it for me once. *Lourdaud.*"

"Lourdaud," the children recited.

Shad looked at the floor. Rachel was protecting him. He felt overwhelmed with stupidity and, at the same time, incredibly grateful.

When he brought his head up, the children were staring, waiting for him to begin. Rachel stood behind them so they couldn't see what Shad saw—couldn't see her wink.

Rachel winked at him!

It was the tiniest of movements, barely perceptible,

and for a split second, he didn't quite believe he'd seen it. A tingle went through him, head to toe. He could have sworn she was laughing at him.

Then, abruptly, her look shifted and seemed to say, *You can do this.* This time when the devil buzzed so loudly he thought his eardrums would burst, he didn't try to shake the buzz away. It wasn't right—his smiling at her winking. But that smile just came on up with a mind of its own.

She nodded and raised her eyebrows—an expression that begged him to get on with it. *Begin the lesson!*

In that moment he'd have given anything to possess her sense of authority. How could a freed slave stand so strong and think so highly of herself while he struggled to find the slightest bit of confidence?

He took a deep breath and reached into his sack for the cloth and needles. Scanning the eager faces, he said, "Raise your hand if you've ever used a needle like one of these."

Two hours later, Shad's taste buds were singing on Rachel's butter-sweet biscuits, and the lesson was going well. Very well. The children were taking turns, and one—Kitty—had gotten the feel of the needle quickly. She had run many fine stitches, in a straight line. The others would need more practice. Lots more. But it was a start.

Shad saw Rachel come up behind Nathaniel and set her hands on his shoulders. He was probably the oldest of the children—nine or ten, Shad thought—and Rachel clearly relied on him to set an example. She'd ask him to read something aloud to the group, or fetch biscuits from the kitchen, or walk Maggie to the privy and check it first for snakes.

Rachel announced, "Time to stop. What do you say to our guest?"

"Thank you, Mr. Lourdaud," came a chorus of voices.

Shad waited for her to say it was his turn now—reading lessons.

"Set the sewing supplies here," she said. "And look around before you go. Leave the schoolroom spotless, please."

Nathaniel rose immediately and the others followed suit, scurrying about, picking threads off the dirt floor, brushing off the benches. Shad frowned and pointed a finger at his chest.

"Tomorrow, Mr. . . . *Lourdaud*. First thing tomorrow, letters."

"I want to sew," said Maggie.

"Reading tomorrow," said Rachel firmly. "Now, get along or you'll be late for chores."

"Mr. Lourdaud's angry with you, Miss Rachel."

Shad rolled his eyes. Earlier the child had announced that Shad was scared. And now angry. He glared at her, and she cowered behind Rachel.

"He'll get over it," said Rachel.

Shad opened his mouth, ready to argue his case, but Nathaniel had appeared beside Maggie, and his eyes bored into Shad. His hands formed fists. He was maybe two-thirds Shad's height, but his stance said he was fixing for a fight.

For heaven's sake, back off, boy, Shad thought. Clearly, Nathaniel wanted to protect Maggie and Rachel. But Shad hadn't planned to hurt them. The boy was overreacting.

Nathaniel's mouth curled in a near snarl, and Shad half expected him to show his teeth like a mistreated dog. If the boy came at him, Shad would flatten him in a second. Even the thought that Nathaniel might come at him—it was crazy. He was colored. Surely he knew his place.

"Now, now," said Rachel. "No one is angry. We're simply out of time for today." Then she patted Nathaniel's back. "I'm counting on you, young man. The alphabet for Mr. Lourdaud tomorrow, yes?"

The boy released his fists and nodded. "Yes, ma'am."

Shad breathed deeply. Why, watching Rachel work the room was a lesson in itself. She turned to him, and he couldn't help but smile.

"I hope you planned to leave the tailoring supplies here. These needles are extras the school might keep, yes?" And without giving him time to answer, she said, "Thank you so much. The school appreciates your generosity. Now, off with you! All of you. Eloise and I have our own appointments today. We'll see you tomorrow bright and early." And she brushed everyone out the door.

Shad shielded his eyes from the sun. Children ran off in twos and threes, disappearing through the opening in the hedge. A chicken cooed from the henhouse.

Nathaniel paused, waiting and watching as the others got away, safe and sound. He made sure to be the last to leave—the last but for Shad. Nathaniel's eyes seemed to read Shad through and through. He took in every twitch of Shad's fingers, every bead of sweat down his cheeks.

Now that Shad thought about it, that colored boy had been sizing him up all morning. Shad hadn't paid any mind to his tailoring. Was that his problem—that Kitty had outsewn him and Shad had praised her and not him? He had no idea. No, he couldn't read Nathaniel at all.

17

Whiskey

AFTER LESSONS, SHAD dallied along shop windows in Church Hill and took his good time getting home. Let Mama think he was running errands to pay for Miss Elizabeth's tutoring. It would give him more time to get his story straight—to think on how tutoring might have gone if he'd actually gotten tutoring—the front room, the crimson settee, the hardwood floors, and Miss Elizabeth's high expectations. He wouldn't grow beholden to a Yankee-lover, because he'd stay on top of errands. Never a debt owed.

Yes, he thought, *I can do this*. And one day, once he'd learned to read, he'd convince Jeremiah to give him his share of the Weaver's Fine Tailoring business. When the time came, he'd be ready. Yes, it was all going well.

Later that night—Monday, May 20—even more went well. Shad had a real good night with the Klan—his second brotherhood meeting. He brought along a coarse piece of muslin for his disguise. He'd cut two eyeholes in it, and that was good enough. Lots of the KKK boys had long ghost costumes, but some only had hoods or masks or whatnot like Shad—enough to cover their faces, and that was the point.

Two new fellows joined up, and the brotherhood put them through the same crazy ceremony they'd put Shad through—the giftie business and the donkey ears on their heads. Shad felt good being on the other side, already a brother and all.

Shad didn't know the new boys. Bubba said they'd come from Highland Springs, just up the road a piece. How they'd found the Klan meeting, Shad didn't know. But they seemed like fine fellows, a bit older than Jeremiah and Clifton. The fact that they were older meant they'd made it through the war and back again. They might have been twenty, or at the most thirty, and it struck Shad how he rarely saw boys who were twenty- or thirtysomething. All the boys of a certain age had gone away to fight for freedom from Northern aggression, and for the most part, they'd never come back.

After the two new boys got initiated, one of them launched into singing "Dixie." He just up and started singing, and Shad saw the Grand Cyclops raise a hand to stop him. Shad sensed the Cyclops wanted to keep from riling up the meeting or taking attention away from himself, or some such thing. But then the Cyclops lowered his hand, giving permission to everybody, and darn if Shad didn't lose himself in that chorus—the part that went "In Dixie land I'll take my stand, to live and die in Dixie." He lost himself thinking about his daddy. How his daddy died for Dixie. But he didn't get to die *in* Dixie. He died far, far away.

Next thing Shad knew, he missed his daddy bad. He wished Daddy could have joined the Klan, too. He thought Daddy would've hankered for this group. After all, the most important part was taking care of Mama—it was protecting Confederate widows. Daddy would have been proud of Shad for joining, and thinking about it made Shad feel awful proud of himself.

When they emptied out of the meeting, the moon was near full. Tonight Bubba and Shad had a job to do—a job the Grand Cyclops had explained to them before the proper meeting began. Someone had overheard a freedman gathering support for a colored candidate for city council. The

Cyclops wanted Shad and Bubba to have a little fun with that man's family—just spook them a tad. Jeremiah and Clifton would show them which house.

They were supposed to pretend to be dead bodies risen from the Cold Harbor battlefield because they hadn't been buried proper. One of the Klansmen had given Bubba an animal bladder—a large one that maybe had come from a goat. Bubba held the bladder under his sheet, waiting to fill it. Really, the whole thing was silly—just boys being silly.

Truth to tell, Shad felt tight over the plan, but he wasn't going to say anything. He walked beside Bubba, following Jeremiah and Clifton. The Mechanicsville road stretched long and straight in front of them. Bubba wore a sheet over gray wool trousers and work boots. He smelled of smoke and grease. He was the luckiest boy Shad knew—lucky because his daddy came home from the war and got his job back. He got Bubba a job, too. Together they worked all day at Tredegar Iron, feeding scraps into massive ovens and reshaping heavy molten lumps into fence posts and gates and railroad ties.

Bubba was stocky and strong—fourteen like Shad, but shorter and a real workhorse. Years ago they'd made fast friends in Miss Jenny's dunce-cap corner—Shad, the problem reader, and Bubba, the stutterer. Tonight as they walked together up the Mechanicsville road, Shad was glad for the friendship—glad that since he'd agreed to do this crazy spook-a-family business, at least he'd have Bubba by his side.

Up ahead, all of a sudden, Jeremiah and Clifton stopped in the road and tossed off their sheets. Shad and Bubba stopped, too. Jeremiah pulled a flask from his britches, took a swig, and offered it to Bubba.

"N-n-naw," said Bubba. "N-not now."

"Pete's sake, Bubba," said Clifton. He grabbed the flask from Jeremiah and took a swallow. He rattled his head. Then he laughed and shouted, "Whooo, yeah!"

Shad watched Bubba shake his ghost head. Then Clifton offered Shad the flask, and Shad thought, *Me?* He pulled the muslin cloth off his head and reached for the flask. Yes, him. He was a Klan brother now—one of the boys.

He leaned into the bottle, and the whiskey smell made his eyes smart.

He heard Bubba mumble, "No, no," and he said, "It's okay, Bubba." Shad closed his eyes and took a huge swallow.

Fire! Wet fire. He threw his head sideways. He spit and coughed and his tongue went numb.

Bubba slapped him on the back and Shad doubled over.

He felt Jeremiah snatch the flask away and heard his brother laugh and laugh. Then Bubba seemed to be all-out trembling, and it came to Shad that he was laughing, too.

"It ain't funny!" Shad yelled.

Bubba hooted to beat all. "Aw, Sh-Shad, you g-got to s-s-see yourself."

Shad shrugged his arm away and marched up the road. He took deep gulps of air, swallowing the dank bog smell, the sweet chestnut. He watched fireflies drift around him. Creepers rubbed their wings together in all manner of racket. A strong feeling hit him—he could lift an ox. This prank they were doing tonight—it was nothing.

"Where's this house?" Shad yelled.

"Keep it down," barked Jeremiah. He and Clifton stopped for Bubba and Shad to catch up. "It ain't far. Just down that way."

They turned off the Mechanicsville road onto one that went downhill and around a bend to the train tracks. Past the tracks lay a field with so much mist rising up, it looked like steam. Past the field Shad could make out a few shacks in the moonlit dark. Old slave quarters.

They climbed over the tracks and Jeremiah stopped. "Here," he said, handing Shad his ghost costume. "You can't go in there with that stupid little cloth."

"Yeah, okay. Thanks." He traded his cloth for Jeremiah's sheet. It surprised him that Jeremiah had even thought twice about the cloth. Him offering to switch disguises—it wasn't like Jeremiah to be considerate.

Shad threw the sheet over his head and twisted it around until he found the eyeholes. The sheet fell past his knees. Sure enough, now he looked like a ghost ought to look.

"I don't want nobody messing this up, you hear?" said Jeremiah. "I got to report back to the Cyclops."

"Go to the first house there," said Clifton. "The one closest to us. You got that? And if they come out with rocks or clubs or whatever, you hightail it back over here, okay?"

Shad nodded. Rocks or clubs—he could handle them, no problem. It was something how he didn't feel his innards twisting up anymore. That whiskey sure was something. "You ready, Bubba?"

"R-r-ready."

"Let's go."

They ran to the shack and Shad knocked slowly and firmly on the door. *Thud. Thud. Thud.* The wooden door was half rotten, and it gave a little with each knock. Shad heard rustling in the house and he knocked again. *Thud. Thud.*

"Who dere?" a man's voice called.

Bubba kicked the door and it flew open. Even through the disguise, Shad caught the smell of fried onions and fish. *Whooee,* he thought, *these coloreds ate a fine supper a few hours ago.*

"Help us," Shad said deeply, making his voice quiver. "They done killed us at Cold Harbor and we is real thirsty. So thirsty. Help us, brother. Won't you give us a drink?"

He heard the shuffle of feet. Then more feet. A child's voice. "What is it, Daddy?"

Under his sheet, Shad put a hand over the smile on his face. *Don't laugh,* he told himself, squeezing his cheeks. He tightened his jaw and said, "Thirsty. Thirsty."

He heard the hushed tones of a man's voice telling the child, "Get back to bed."

"But Daddy, he's thirsty."

"Lord," said another voice—a woman. "Fetch a bucket of water, boy."

Shad moaned. He groaned. "Thirsty. Thirsty." He stepped forward into the shack, looking for weapons like Clifton had told him to. But at first he couldn't see a thing. Then a boy came through the back with a stick on fire, holding it up for light, not wielding it like a weapon. Shad didn't see any weapons.

The family cowered together, gasping at Bubba and Shad in their awful sheets. *Stupid coloreds.* It was obvious he and Bubba were only boys having a little fun. Shad counted four of them—a man, a woman, and two children. Then another boy came in, lugging a bucket, and the father put his hand on the boy's shoulder.

"Thirsty," Shad said in his ghostliest voice. No matter how he tried, he couldn't get the smile off his face. It occurred to him that whoever came up with the idea of KKK boys wearing old sheets—he was brilliant. This was too funny. The family couldn't see his face. And after that swig of whiskey, Shad wasn't even telling a lie. He was thirsty as could be.

As planned, Bubba said nothing because he had the stutter that could give him away. He groaned and shuffled, tottering off-balance with one outstretched hand, and Shad knew that his other hand was holding tight to that goat bladder.

The father took the bucket from the boy, set it on the packed dirt in the center of the little room, and backed up, arms outstretched to shield the family behind him.

Bubba groaned and Shad picked up the bucket. Darn if it wasn't so heavy the wire handle cut into his palm. He mumbled, "Thirsty," and set it down again. Then he stooped low and wrapped his arms around the bucket. He lifted it—cold, wet metal—and leaned backward to get it high enough for Bubba to draw the water through a ryegrass straw and into the goat bladder. Bubba sucked on the straw to start the flow, then made happy moaning noises as the water ran from the bucket through the mouth hole in Bubba's sheet to the hidden bladder.

One of the children whispered, "He's drinking the whole bucket, Daddy!"

"Hush, chile."

Shad thanked the Lord that the bucket grew lighter as the bladder filled. Slippery as that bladder might be, Bubba was so strong, he could probably carry three buckets' worth without breaking a sweat. Bubba kept on moaning, and the eyes of that colored family grew wider and wider. Shad bit his tongue to keep from bursting out laughing.

When the bucket was almost empty, Bubba turned toward the door, and the ryegrass straw fell to the floor. Bubba leaned backward under the weight of the hidden bladder. He'd done such a good job of shuffling in that his shuffling out didn't look any different.

Shad tilted the bucket to the hole in the sheet where his

mouth was and took a real drink. The water tasted fresh and cool after the whiskey. Some of the water splashed down the front of his sheet, but he didn't pay it any mind. He set down the empty bucket and groaned. "Thank you. The spirits of Cold Harbor thank you kindly."

Then he and Bubba were out the door and across the field. Bubba waddled with the weight of the bladder, and both of them laughed without making a sound. Shad heard the door of the shack creak shut.

Once they reached the train tracks, Bubba turned the bladder upside down and emptied it. Jeremiah slapped Bubba's back, and Clifton slapped Shad's, and they headed uphill, around the bend, through the trees toward the Mechanicsville road.

"I tell you, Jeremiah," said Clifton, "you got to be proud of your little brother now!"

Jeremiah grunted. "Gimme back my sheet. Aw, Shad— you got it wet."

Shad pulled off the sheet, but he didn't apologize. He laughed. He was full of himself tonight. What a crazy group this KKK was.

Bubba started telling about the stupid coloreds in that little shack, and even with his stutter, or maybe because of it, the story went from scary funny to laugh-out-loud funny. He told about the children asking questions and the parents hushing them, and him leaning over backward trying to keep that bladder from slipping to the ground and bursting open. By the time they hit Venable Street, even Jeremiah had to hold his belly because all four of them were aching from sidesplitting guffaws.

18

Yankees on Patrol

WHEN SHAD WOKE Tuesday morning, the sun was already up and the other side of the bed empty. He jumped from the straw mattress like a fire had been set beneath him. Lessons! He'd overslept. Darn those KKK boys and their funny pranks.

He darted past Mama's frown and the word *cornbread* on her lips. No time for breakfast. He ran to the outhouse, splashed at the well, then dashed up Nine Mile Road and Twenty-eighth Street. By the time he ducked into the shed behind the Perkinson house, his FEED AND SEED shirt was soaked through with sweat. His brow dripped like hot butter.

The children looked up from their lessons with all manner of expression—surprise, confusion, alarm, and even relief that he'd returned. Their tailoring teacher hadn't decided to quit.

"You're late," said Rachel from the west window. She'd been leaning over Kitty's slate, and she straightened at the sight of him.

"I'm sorry. I—I'll set out from home sooner." He wiped his brow against the sleeve of his shirt, and when he felt the coarse fabric on his face, he realized that he'd put on the wrong shirt. He had planned to wear the fine white one to distinguish himself. But in his haste this morning—Lord, he wanted to kick himself.

Rachel clucked her tongue.

Maggie hopped up with the biscuit basket—one biscuit remained—and approached him, holding the basket aloft.

"Now, Maggie," said Rachel, "if Nathaniel were late, would you reward him with a biscuit?"

Maggie hung her head.

"Tell Mr. . . . *Lourdaud* our rule about breakfast."

Maggie shook her head and shifted the basket into the crook of one arm in order to free the other. Then she stuffed a thumb into her mouth. Children shifted their bottoms on pine planks. They twiddled fingers and kneaded the dirt floor with their toes.

A bead of sweat dripped down Shad's face, and he wiped it against his other sleeve. His chest heaved as he labored to catch his breath. He lifted both palms. "I said I was sorry."

"Oh, I'm sure you are," said Rachel. "But it's hardly cause for reward. Maggie?"

The little girl slowly pulled the thumb from her mouth and set the basket on the pine plank. "You late. No breakfast."

Rachel pointed to the bench beside her—the one nearest the west window. "You and Nathaniel here. And since Nathaniel is your tutor this morning, I believe he deserves the extra biscuit. Kitty—let's have you and Matthew over here . . ."

She went on directing children to move around the shed, freeing up a space for Shad to sit beside Nathaniel, but the noise inside Shad's head was so loud, he couldn't hear her anymore. Rachel had humiliated him in front of the children. She'd awarded his biscuit to Nathaniel.

His hands became fists. He dragged his feet toward the bench, but in his mind he was returning to Miss Jenny's corner, and his face flushed red. Children laughed and pointed fingers at him, and Miss Jenny set a dunce cap on his head.

Then a hand gripped his elbow and he jerked, raising

his arm to wallop the offender, when he saw it was Eloise. She was holding out a slate, and Nathaniel stood behind her with lumps of gray chalk.

Shad blinked. Eloise? He blinked again. The sweet smell of honeysuckle drifted through the west window and the memories of Miss Jenny's Sunday school class faded. He looked around. No one was laughing or pointing. The colored children had turned toward their own slates.

For a moment he watched their little hands form letters and words and sentences. Then he sat where Rachel had directed and saw Nathaniel pop the last biscuit in his mouth. The boy stood over him, and Shad got the distinct feeling that Nathaniel liked that position—liked towering over Shad, looking down, knowing he possessed knowledge Shad did not.

A sense of confusion washed over Shad, and he doubted the arrangements he'd made. Tailoring in exchange for lessons—what on earth had he been thinking? The lessons were supposed to come from George Nelson by way of Rachel. But here was a colored boy fixing to tutor him. A little boy! It wasn't right at all.

He started to stand—to go—but felt a hand on his shoulder, patting him gently, easing his shame. "Only the first lesson or two," Rachel said, as if she'd read his thoughts. "Nathaniel can help Mr. Nelson and me understand exactly where you are in terms of reading. Then we'll decide on the appropriate level of instruction."

Her eyes twinkled and he couldn't read her expression. He watched her wipe her hand against her apron, wiping away the sweat from his FEED AND SEED shirt.

"Eloise, would you mind getting Mr. Lourdaud some water from the well? He's awfully overheated this morning."

After Tuesday lessons, Shad walked alone down Twenty-eighth Street, and if any of the residents of Church Hill had seen him, they'd surely have noticed the swagger in his step. Rachel had smiled when Nathaniel gave his report: Mr. Lourdaud knew all of his letters!

Shad had beamed. Truth to tell, he knew his alphabet fine. Especially when the letters were presented in the same order as the ABC song—the one with a "Twinkle, Twinkle, Little Star" tune. He'd had no problem identifying the letters as Nathaniel wrote them, uppercase and lower. He'd memorized his letters years ago. Now, if Nathaniel had presented them out of order with the upper- and lowercases mixed up, the report might have taken a different turn. But today, he was a star pupil in Miss Rachel's classroom, and for Shad, it was all that mattered.

As he walked toward Granddaddy's shop, hungry but happy, Shad worked out a way to wake on time. Without a rooster to signal dawn and with church bells too faint out Nine Mile Road to rouse him, he'd have to ask Mama for help. Most mornings by the time Shad arose, Mama had already said prayers and stoked the cook fire and put in a few stitches by lantern light. If he asked her to wake him, she'd expect him to join her for prayers. Ugh. He supposed he could do that—supposed getting to Libby Hill on time was worth a few amens.

He was working out the details in his head when he crossed Grace Street and saw ahead of him, at the corner of Twenty-eighth and Broad Streets . . . Jeremiah. So much for his brother getting a day job.

Shad dragged his feet, trying to remember what he'd said and not said. Lessons from Miss Elizabeth. Doing a chore such as chopping wood. That chore would be his fallback if ever he needed to account for his time. *Lord,* he thought, stoking a lie was a chore in itself. He picked up his pace.

Jeremiah was wearing the boots he'd gotten from Mr. Hanson last year. They were fine boots—fitted for him alone—much better than the blister-rubbing things Mama had scrounged up over the years. Shad knew his own boot-wearing days would be coming soon since his feet had stopped growing, but for now, he was happy to go barefoot. Happy not to rub blisters.

Jeremiah held a large red clay pot that was sprouting long, thin leaves. As Shad got closer, he could see tall stalks with green buds between the leaves.

"Hey, there," called Shad.

Jeremiah ignored him. He was staring down Broad Street toward St. John's Church, and when Shad reached the intersection, he saw why. Darn if there weren't Yankees on patrol down that way. They were stopped only ten or fifteen paces off, their backs toward Jeremiah. One was having a smoke.

Shad froze. Those Yankees didn't belong in Richmond and they knew it. Ever since the war had ended, they'd been skulking around in their blue uniforms, watching towns-folk skitter like mice from a tomcat. Look at that. Today people were coming along Broad and crossing to the far side so as not to brush elbows with those blue boys.

Nobody wanted to give them an excuse to use their muskets.

Jeremiah shifted his grip on the pot.

Shad whispered, "Easy, now."

Jeremiah lifted his shoulders and puffed up his chest, and without even looking at Shad, shoved the flowerpot in his face. Shad wrapped both arms around it, and its weight surprised him. He leaned for balance, bent his knees, took a step back. The greens tickled his nose and he sneezed.

The Yankees looked their way.

Shoot, thought Shad. Rule number one with Yankees on patrol was "Don't draw attention." One of them lifted his chin and snickered.

Jeremiah's hands went into fists. He didn't check for his knife, but Shad knew he was thinking on it—knew he kept it in his boots.

The snickering Yankee made his chest big, too. His eyes locked on Jeremiah's. He coughed. He and Jeremiah squinted at each other, and people on foot made a wide circle around them. A carriage stopped in the middle of the gray-brick road, and Broad Street got quiet as curfew.

The Yankee let go of his smoke and moved a hand to his musket. Tobacco paper hung at his lip.

Shad braced himself. "Don't start nothing."

Seconds passed. Maybe a whole minute. Jeremiah stared, unmoving, not even so much as blinking. People peered from second-story windows. They hid behind bushes. They watched from safe distances. Shad knew Jeremiah thought they were a bunch of cowards. But they were an audience. He loved an audience.

Then Jeremiah shouted, "Beautiful day for a stroll in a *free* society, ain't it, gentlemen? Won't you join us?"

The crowd cheered. Jeremiah smiled, waving his hand and nodding his head as if to say thank you to the people. *It was nothing.* Pure bravado.

The carriage driver cracked a whip and his horse jolted forward. People emerged from alleyways between houses and went on with their errands.

The Yankees shifted their feet. One pulled off his cap to scratch at stringy yellow hair. The squinting one took a drag on his smoke.

Jeremiah laughed and strode down Twenty-eighth Street, his head high. Then he called over his shoulder to Shad. "Hurry up!"

"I ain't your pack mule." The long leaves tickled Shad's face and he sneezed again.

Jeremiah stopped, and when Shad reached him, he took

the pot and hoisted it up on one shoulder. "Mama's gonna love these daylilies."

"Where'd you get 'em?"

But Jeremiah didn't answer. He strutted toward home, whistling "Oh! Susanna" and leaning toward the sun as if its only purpose in the sky was to shine on him alone.

Shad headed for Granddaddy's, all the while thinking it was just like Jeremiah to stand up to those Yankees. Just like him to work some deal and come home with flowers for Mama. Only seventeen and so bold, so cocksure of himself. He made everything look so easy.

19

Stitching Seams

ON WEDNESDAY morning, Shad arrived at the shed on time, dressed in the white silk shirt and his Willy Johnson britches, breakfast in his belly, a sack of fabric scraps in hand, and Mama's amens behind him. From the east window, he showed the children differences in types of fabric—how the fronts and backs were the same on some, but how for others, the colors were brighter on one side, the weave of the grain prettier or the sheen shinier. He had swatches of print cotton and plain linen, and had even found a small swatch of velvet for them to pass around.

"This is called the nap of the fabric," he said, running a hand up and down a four-inch square of dark green velvet. "See how it looks different when I hold it this way . . . then this way?" He let the sun catch the nap, and the children marveled at the hue—how the green seemed to change before their eyes.

"If you get lucky enough that someone hires you to sew a fine set of velvet draperies, you have to line up the fabric just so. You can't have one panel face up and one down, or that person ain't gonna pay you 'cause it'll look like you used two different bolts of velvet when it was the exact same, only one panel was upside down."

"*Isn't*, Mr. Lourdaud," said Rachel.

He stopped with his hand in the air. Her interruption made him lose the train of his speech. "Beg pardon?"

"*Isn't*. You said 'ain't,' but 'ain't' *isn't* a word."

He lowered his hand and tilted his head. Very slowly, he said it again. "Beg pardon?"

"It's slang, Mr. Lourdaud."

He frowned. Rachel was sitting behind the children, and when all of them turned their heads toward her, she threw her hands in the air. "Oh, my, *I'm* sorry. Forgive me, Mr. Lourdaud, I've interrupted your lesson, and I didn't mean to do that. Continue. Please continue. We can talk about it later."

The children turned back toward Shad, but now he felt flustered. Doubts over the whole tailoring-reading lesson arrangement rushed into his head. He fingered the swatches of fabric, trying to pick up where he'd left off, finding himself more confused than humiliated. Had he come here to learn fine-lady speak? No, not at all. He wanted to read, but he didn't need to learn how to put on airs. *Isn't* versus *ain't*—they were simply patterns of speech. He hadn't asked her to correct his speech! She was turning their arrangement into something it wasn't.

"Can I feel the velvet?" Maggie held her little hand toward his, and her question brought Shad out of his confusion.

"Uh, oh, yes, here. Pass this around. And this one."

He paused while the children fingered the fabrics, and when he raised his head, there was Rachel letting out a little puff of air. An enormous smile came up on her face and she lifted her shoulders in apology. Then she stood. "Thank you so much, Mr. Lourdaud, for showing the children these fabrics today. Will they be practicing their stitching this morning, or should we move on to reading lessons?"

"Oh, stitching please, Miss Rachel," cried Kitty. "Please."

Rachel raised her eyebrows at Shad.

He swallowed. The way his role shifted in this classroom kept him always on his toes. "Yes," he said, "I think they should practice their stitching."

"Perfect," said Rachel.

Shad fumbled through his sack of scraps—he'd brought a burlap one filled with leftover pieces of dress fabrics—and gave each child two pieces of matching cotton prints. Then he instructed them to hold the fabric right sides together and stitch a straight line up the middle. "A straight line makes a seam," he said.

For the rest of the morning, they took to the task, sharing the four needles, taking turns threading them and stitching. Rachel, Eloise, and Shad helped the children, and when each had finished sewing, Shad would get the child to fold the fabric open along the seam.

For some, the results were like magic—the colorful side of fabric came up, the raw seam on the back side down. A boy named Thomas hadn't put right sides together before stitching, so his looked funny. Matthew had decided to stitch a curved line instead of straight, and his fabric didn't open correctly. Maggie got hers to work and was so pleased with herself that she twirled in a circle. "Look, Miss Rachel! Look what I made!"

Shad winced at the uneven stitches but didn't point them out. Practice and time would get them straight. For now, delight was spreading around the shed, and Shad reveled in being their hero for a day.

"You got an iron here?" asked Shad.

"Well, it's inside," said Rachel, gesturing toward the back of the Perkinson house.

"My mama's got her an iron," said Maggie. "I can press 'em!"

"You got to press 'em with the back side up, you got that?" said Shad. "Right side down, damp cloth on top, and hold it like this, see? That way you get the seam open."

"Yes, sir!" said Maggie, filling the word *sir* with so much pride, Shad laughed.

Never in his dreams had he thought he'd enjoy teaching colored children! And the fact that Maggie's mama would iron their practice pieces? Perfect. Every tailor knew the wonders of an iron—how pressing masked the imperfections. Weaver's Fine Tailoring never delivered a finished piece without the magic of an iron on it first. But the children's pieces—well, he couldn't take them to his own house for ironing. Scraps with crooked and uneven stitches? When he was seven or eight, sure. But not at fourteen. He'd never be able to explain them to Mama.

Today he was mighty happy that Maggie's mama would take on the task of ironing. By the end of Wednesday's lesson, he was mighty happy all the way around.

On Thursday morning when it was time for reading lessons again, Shad's doubts returned. Rachel divided the children into groups, putting Shad and Nathaniel at the west window to review the sounds that letters made. As Nathaniel wrote letters on their slate and Shad softly made the sounds— *ah, ay, buh, cuh*—he grew aware of each group's quiet conversation. Rachel had pulled aside one boy, Gabriel, and Shad overheard her asking him why he'd been absent the past two days.

The boy mumbled something.

Rachel said, "What sort of spooks?"

Shad's ears perked up. He straightened his spine.

"They come in the night, saying they was thirsty, and oh, Miss Rachel—it was awful."

Fuzz started in Shad's ears.

"Did they hurt you?" Rachel asked.

"No, ma'am," said Gabriel. "They—they—Lord, Miss Rachel, you should've seen how much they drunk. And I was too scared to leave the house. Just too scared."

Nathaniel rapped his knuckles on the slate. "You got to pay attention, Mr. Lourdaud."

"I—oh, I'm sorry. Right. Yes. *D*. The letter *d* what makes the sound *duh*." His breath came hard. *Settle*, he told himself. *Settle*. That little boy—Gabriel—he'd been one of the children in the shack near the train tracks. The one with the stick on fire. Or, no—maybe he was the one who had carried the bucket inside.

Shad's palms grew damp. Suddenly he was aware of the stench of his own underarms, and he pulled his arms tight to his sides.

"You okay, Mr. Lourdaud?" asked Nathaniel.

Shad heard Rachel's voice. "Everything all right over there?"

"Y-yes, fine," Shad said. "Uh, hungrier than I thought this morning." Shad tapped a finger to his forehead. "A tad light-headed yet. Uh, we're fine."

Then the door opened and who should appear but George Nelson in his gray-green waistcoat. Every pair of eyes turned his way, and he bowed. "Delightful, delightful!" He tapped his fingertips together and beamed. "I'm thrilled to see such dedicated students."

Rachel stood and did introductions around the room, making a point to stress the name Mr. Lourdaud for George Nelson's benefit, raising her brows to make sure he caught the ruse. The little man's eyes widened on hearing the name, and he made a funny face. He blinked and stared at Shad, and Shad shrugged.

Then Rachel said, "Children, Mr. Nelson is going to be

my teacher at the Colored Normal School. Mine and Miss Eloise's. And if you study hard and excel at your lessons, in a few years you'll be attending the Colored Normal School, too."

"Excellent! Excellent. Thank you, Miss Rachel." George Nelson bowed again. "Well, now, *Lourdaud.* Uh, quite creative, I must say." He nodded at Shad. "Now, if you don't mind, I have about thirty minutes before Mrs. Perkinson and I must attend to other matters. May I sit with these two boys for a bit?"

"Yes, sir. Why, of course. Nathaniel, scoot over there, would you, please?"

Nathaniel moved closer to Shad, and George Nelson plopped onto the bench. Nathaniel's thigh touched Shad's—the boy's brown trousers against Shad's Willy Johnson britches—and both of them tightened all over.

"What have we here, boys?" asked George Nelson.

Shad opened his mouth to answer, but Nathaniel beat him to it. "He knows his letters fine, sir, and now we're working on the sounds the letters make."

Shad's hands went into fists. He couldn't think straight this morning. It wasn't right for a colored boy to talk before he talked. What were Rachel and Eloise teaching these children? If they didn't learn their place, well, then, what good was their learning?

Shad frowned. He didn't belong in this shed. Right, wrong, heads, tails—everything here was topsy-turvy. Did any of them even understand the risks he took to be here? Did they appreciate the dangers he faced? Good Lord, if his Klan brothers learned he was here, giving these children tailoring supplies and lessons, why, the Klan would have a field day with all of them.

Shad's thoughts raced so fast, he had to close his eyes. *Settle*, he told himself, but the devil on his shoulder buzzed loud enough to wake the dawn. After a spell he felt a poke, poke, poke on his forearm, and he opened his eyes. Nathaniel was trying to get his attention.

"Mr. Lourdaud? Look at the slate here. Mr. Nelson wrote all these words for you. We're doing words now, not letters."

Shad glanced at the slate, then around the room. Nathaniel had slid far enough from him that their thighs weren't touching anymore. George Nelson had gotten up from their bench and was sitting by Eloise now, checking on the math lesson.

"This one, Mr. Lourdaud," Nathaniel said. "Start with this one. Can you read it?"

Shad took a deep breath and let his air out, and the buzzing in his ears lifted like morning fog. There were words on the slate in front of him. His reading lesson. He needed to pay attention and stop worrying about the Klan. Darn that brotherhood, messing him up this morning so he couldn't get his letters straight. Letters. He was here to learn and he wanted this learning more than he wanted that brotherhood. Well, no, maybe the same as he wanted them. Reading and brotherhood—was it too much to ask for both?

Shad looked at the slate. *"Tat,"* he said.

"And this one?" prompted Nathaniel.

Shad narrowed his eyes. *"Tab.* No. *Tap.* That's *tap,* isn't it?"

"You had it right the first time. See, that's a *b,* not a *p.*"

Shad slouched and all his breath whooshed out the window. "Okay," he said. "And the next one—that's *tad,* right? It's *tad,* not *tap.*"

"Good," said Nathaniel. "Now you got it. Try the next set."

"Ban and *pan."*

"Uh-oh. The other way around, Mr. Lourdaud. Come on now, sir. You're guessing instead of reading. Here, take it slow."

Guessing. Humph. It wasn't right for this boy to correct him. Shad wanted to haul off and punch Nathaniel. He wanted—shoot. He rubbed at his temples. Reading was so hard.

"Do the next one," said Nathaniel.

Shad studied the letters. He tilted his head. His brain wanted to blur the letters into the same form—any form—*b, d, p.* He narrowed his eyes and stared at the line going up on the right edge of one circle and down on the left edge of another. He strained to remember which was which, to separate them in his brain and not let them blur together. Such little details to track! He knew they had to be different, or George Nelson wouldn't have written them side by side.

He concentrated. The first was a *d* and the second a *p.* He thought of the sound that a *d* made, and the sound of a *p.* Slowly, he said, "*Mad* and *map.*"

"Right! Now you got it, Mr. Lourdaud."

Shad shifted on the bench. He noticed his clenched hands, knuckles bleached with tension, and he made himself release them, finger by finger. He set his palms flat on his knees, rubbing his open hands against his Willy Johnson britches. He took a breath, and a damp pine scent came with it.

Then Shad felt eyes on him, and the feeling made him raise his head slowly. He turned. There was George Nelson, sitting with Eloise's group but watching Nathaniel and Shad. Darn if that little man hadn't figured out exactly which letters Shad flipped around. That leprechaun had designed this lesson for him alone. For *him*.

Shad's eyes caught George Nelson's and held them for a second. It was nothing short of crazy—two white people in a shed full of coloreds. Shad looked for something that would tell him that he and George Nelson shared the same thought—anything—a glimmer of understanding between two white people. But no, they didn't see eye to eye. George Nelson's face told Shad that he didn't think this shed business was crazy in the least. It was his work. His calling. Lordy, if Jeremiah only knew, he'd—Shad blinked the thought away.

He watched George Nelson turn back to Eloise's math lesson, but just before he turned, Mr. Nelson brought the tips of his fingers together, making dull tapping noises, and his smile grew even bigger than his enormous nose.

20

Bending Low

THAT THURSDAY night the Klan held another meeting, and it was crowded but slow. No new recruits. No crazy business. Boys wanted to sing some more, and the Grand Cyclops gave permission for the likes of "Dixie" and "Camptown Races." There was a lot of talk about the dern Freedmen's Bureau, the dern coloreds thinking too highly of themselves—that sort of thing. Dern this and dern that.

After a song, one of the ghosts waved a hand high and commenced to thanking boys for their good work in protecting Confederate widows. Normally that sort of talk came from the Grand Cyclops, but tonight the voice was more rough than educated. It sounded familiar, but Shad was with Bubba in the back of the room, only half listening, and didn't take it in.

A smoky odor wafted around Bubba, and Shad wondered how Bubba would ever get the stench of those Tredegar furnaces out of his clothes. Would vinegar take it out?
Baking soda, maybe. Lord, that smoke came on thick.

Bubba elbowed him. "Who's t-t-talkin'?"

Shad went up on tiptoes and narrowed his eyes through
the slits in his coarse muslin piece.

"Y'all done good," the ghost was saying, "and you should
be proud o' yourselves." He turned, and Shad glimpsed the
painted face on the gray sheet. Crooked Face. Shad scoffed.

Bubba elbowed him again.

Shad came down, leaning into Bubba's ear. "Jeremiah."

Bubba nodded. "A-awful g-g-good sp-speaker."

Shad rolled his eyes, thankful no one could see his face.

"You l-l-lucky he's your b-b-brother."

"Lucky?" Shad whispered. "Naw. He picks on me all
the time."

"Wish I had m-me a b-b-brother like him."

Shad took a deep breath. Now Jeremiah was talking
about the value of brotherhood, of boys supporting one another. His voice was strong and clear. "It's been real hard for
my family ever since my daddy died, and I know every one
of you boys lost somebody, too, and I just want to tell y'all
how much you mean to me and my family."

"Hear! Hear!" ghosts shouted.

Jeremiah went on. "If it wasn't for this fine brotherhood and all you fine men, I don't know how I'd get along."

"Amen, brother."

"'Preciate it. That's all from me."

The crowd broke into applause. Bubba whistled and Shad clapped his hands high over his head. Leave it to Jeremiah—he always knew the perfect thing to say.

When the meeting ended, everybody spilled out feeling right brotherly and proud. Shad, Bubba, Jeremiah, and Clifton left together, pulling off their disguises once they got a quarter mile up the road. The night was humid. An occasional bat swooped by them, picking off mosquitoes. Then an animal scurried by and Shad jumped. Skunk? Woodchuck? Possum? Too dark to tell. *A bad omen*, he thought, but he didn't want the others to see him get the creeps, so he marched forward, swinging his arms, his hands fisted in fake confidence.

Shad got to thinking about Jeremiah's traps snaring critters for supper, and that was a fine thought. But not skunks. Jeremiah had caught one once, and the house had stunk for a month after. Stunk worse than Bubba. But possum and woodchuck? Shad smiled. Possum was fatty, and woodchuck—tough as tough could get. But when Mama simmered it real long and slow, woodchuck made for darn good eating, especially with collards and cabbage. Better on day two or three than fresh-caught.

Thinking on supper, Shad rubbed his FEED AND SEED shirt and patted his tummy. Stew thoughts could get a boy hungry right fast. He was looking forward to getting back and rummaging for leftovers. Then he'd get some shut-eye and wake to Mama baking up spoon bread. Yum.

By the time they got to Venable Street, Shad was lost in thoughts on good eating. He started to turn left toward home, but Jeremiah said, "Hey, let's have us some fun. Come on."

Clifton laughed and picked up his pace.

Bubba shrugged. "Yeah, o-o-okay."

Shad hesitated. His version of fun and Jeremiah's never lined up. He didn't want to scare the likes of Gabriel anymore. Didn't want to run into any of the children he'd teach tomorrow morning. But explaining his qualms was worse than swallowing them. He let out his breath and turned with the boys.

They headed downhill. Shad slipped on his muslin cloth again, and it trapped his breath, warm and wet in front of his face.

Venable Street led them to the north side of Shockoe

Valley, the low-lying Seventeenth Street with its mishmash of houses—freedmen's homes—a few brick, mostly wood. Living along Seventeenth were carpenters, masons, tanners, farmhands, ironworkers, and the like. Shad never ran deliveries to this area, and he didn't know it well, but he wasn't so ignorant as to think a group of white boys could get by without being noticed. Clearly, Jeremiah had the same thought, and he stopped to put on his disguise.

"Let's just go for a stroll, that's all," said Jeremiah. "No nothing. Let's just walk, okay, boys?"

So they walked. Shad in his FEED AND SEED shirt with the muslin cloth over his face, and Bubba with only a mask, too. Jeremiah and Clifton wore their dunce caps covered in gray sheets with faces painted high.

They walked. And walked. If any of the freedmen could see the shadowy figures, they never let on, never stirred. Shad thought it wasn't so bad—this walking. They could walk Seventeenth Street if they wanted to. Walk and listen to the racket of the night insects—their own cadence, steady as a heartbeat.

When they got to Broad Street, Jeremiah stopped, and Shad felt relieved that they'd done nothing but walk. Nothing had happened.

Uphill to the west stretched Richmond proper, where

gas streetlamps twinkled, making their own starlight. Here at the bottom of the hill near the old slave graveyards, there were no streetlamps. No candles. No one with a lantern or torch. Just creepers chirping the night away and bullfrogs calling from the lowest spot of all—the place where Sixteenth Street should have been, but a creek trickled instead.

It was more swampland than creek—easy soil for burying bodies. Shad figured those bodies would stay buried right fine—at least they would as long as the James River didn't flood. Problem was that sometimes she flooded right much. And then what? Did all those slave bones wash up from the deep? Why, in a flood the James would send water right up the creek. Shad frowned. Or no, he thought, the water would come down the creek. Either way, that water would lift those bodies to the surface. Thinking on it made him shiver.

"Come on," whispered Jeremiah, and Shad jumped.

"Ha! Look at Shadrach, boys. Scaredy-cat!"

Shad swung at him and Jeremiah darted away, laughing.

"C-c-come on," said Bubba, pulling Shad by the arm, patting him, settling him.

"Let's sing real low," said Jeremiah. "*I'm coming, I'm com-*

ing, for my head is bending low ... You know that one? 'Old Black Joe.' Real low now, like we're dying while we're walking. Like dragging ourselves to our graves."

Clifton laughed. "Yeah. That's good."

Bubba shook his head. "I c-c-can't sing."

"It's okay, Bubba. You just come along," said Jeremiah, slapping him on the back.

"Look—" Shad began.

"You don't want to sing," snapped Jeremiah. "Is that what you're gonna tell me?"

"No, I just—"

"Okay, sure—I hear you. Hey, fellows, Shad don't want to sing. You know what he wants to do instead?" Shad was shaking his head, but Jeremiah was already pulling off his own sheet. "Here, put this on."

"No, listen," Shad said, and his voice cracked. It pained him to think how scared Gabriel had been—so scared he'd missed two days of school. "I ain't gonna spook no more colored families, you hear me? Don't you go sending me into one of them houses. I ain't going."

"Sure, sure, sure," said Jeremiah in a dismissive tone. "No, we ain't going into no houses. You know what we got tonight?" Jeremiah shoved his face into Shad's. Then

Clifton's. Then Bubba's. Shad rolled his eyes. His brother could be awfully dramatic. "*Bones!*"

Clifton bent over, laughing so hard he had to hold himself up, hands on knees.

Shad let out a huff of air to signal how stupid he thought this was. But on the inside, he squirmed like the dickens.

Jeremiah threw his sheet over Shad and twisted it around. "Eyeholes. Where are the eyeholes?"

"Jeremiah," said Shad, "why don't *you* spook these people tonight? Why do I have to do it?"

"You're an embarrassment," said Jeremiah. "You got to get *tough*. Get a little gumption in you, boy. Come on, now. We ain't gonna do nothing hard tonight. This'll give you a little gumption."

Jeremiah had gotten his sheet over Shad's head, and now the fabric covered Shad head to toe.

"Here's what you gonna do," said Jeremiah. "Pretty soon, them coloreds what work the Spotswood Hotel will be heading home for the night, and they're gonna come down the hill and turn up Seventeenth here. And you're gonna greet them, Shad. That's all. Just a 'Welcome home, gentlemen.'"

"What the—?"

"Now, don't worry. Clifton and Bubba and me, we're gonna hide right over yonder. You know, if there's too many of us, them coloreds won't get close. But if there's four or five of them and only one of you, they won't pay you no mind."

"Look, Jeremiah—"

"No, no, no! *Shh*. They're comin' already. Now you just ask one of them to shake your hand, you got that? Just a handshake and a 'good evening.'" Then Jeremiah thrust something hard and smooth into Shad's hand. "And when one of them reaches out his hand to shake yours, you just put this out and let him shake this instead of your hand. You got that?"

Then Jeremiah and the boys dashed off, leaving Shad alone in the dark on the northwest corner of Seventeenth and Broad.

Shad strained to see through the cutout eyeholes. The intersection was wide, and he knew that on the southwest corner sat an enormous maple tree—the tree he'd leaned against the day he'd met Rachel. He knew it was there—knew this intersection well—but not in the dark. No, it wasn't the same in the shadows, with him covered in a gray sheet with a—what was this thing in his hand?

He felt the object. Smooth and hard. He moved his

hand along it. One end was clearly broken off and rough—something fabric would snag on. At the other end, the stick branched out, thinning into bumps, into—

Shad froze. Holy moly. It was a *hand*! The bones of a hand! Where did Jeremiah get these things? It was awful. A skeleton's hand right there in his own. He wanted to drop it, but instead his grip tightened. All of him tightened. His breath got short. *Dern you, Jeremiah.*

He turned, thinking to throw the skeleton hand across the intersection, but he sensed people coming. The coloreds who worked the Spotswood—just as Jeremiah had said—there they were, walking toward him. A group. It was hard to tell how many in the dark, especially with lights twinkling up the Richmond hill behind them.

The closer the men got to Shad, the slower their footsteps. He heard caution in their feet, heard the pitch of their voices drop from easy to hushed. They'd seen him, and they were working out what to do, whether to approach, how wide of a berth to give him.

Shad swallowed. Blood pulsed in his ears. He strained to see through the eyeholes.

One of the men stood apart from the rest, looming large. He was even taller than Shad. Muscular. Strong.

Shad bent his knees, found his balance, lowered his

chest, made his voice deep as he could. "Ah, sir. Good evening, good sir. Won't you shake my hand?"

He sensed the group of men easing past him, past the one of their own who had stopped—the big fellow who could take Shad down with a pinkie finger if he dared try. Shad braced for a wallop. He held out his sleeve for the handshake.

Shad hoped Jeremiah and Clifton and Bubba hadn't gone any farther than the maple tree. *Here it comes*, he thought, expecting the freedman to knock him over, expecting Jeremiah to rush to his rescue, expecting—he wasn't at all sure what would happen.

The big man reached forward to shake his hand.

Shad extended the bones.

The colored man wrapped his fingers around the skeleton hand. "Lord!" he cried. He let go and took two steps backward.

The group of freedmen took off—gone in less than a second, running north up Seventeenth Street.

Then Jeremiah and Clifton and Bubba were beside Shad, hooting and laughing like there was no tomorrow. Shad found his breath again. Under the sheet, he wiped sweat from his forehead.

He thrust the skeleton hand at Jeremiah. "Take that

stupid thing!" He glanced up Seventeenth Street, straining to see the colored men, but it was too dark to see much of anything at all.

"Now are you boys ready to sing?" Jeremiah baited them. "Let's go."

He grabbed Shad's arm and the four of them headed up Seventeenth—Shad and Clifton in sheets, Jeremiah and Bubba with muslin cloths over their faces. On a normal day, Shad's route home from that intersection would have been Broad Street east to Twentieth, then around to Venable and out Nine Mile, but nothing was normal about that day— that night. They didn't belong on the north side of Seventeenth Street, but no one who lived there dared tell them so.

Jeremiah started singing, and Shad's throat was so tight, at first he couldn't join in. Shad tripped and jerked as Jeremiah pulled him along. The street curved slightly to the left, following the creek bed, and as they passed shadow after shadow of little houses, Jeremiah's voice began to crack and he let go of Shad's arm. His saunter shifted from swagger to shuffle, his posture from bully to ... *What?* Shad squinted. Jeremiah's arms had gone limp. They swayed willy-nilly.

His brother was trying to look like a dead body risen

from a grave. The very sight made a smile come up on Shad's face. His good-for-nothing brother had a skill, after all. Acting. Why, he ought to go to the theater.

He ain't scary, thought Shad. *He's silly!* Shad chuckled and rounded his shoulders, leaning forward, swaying, and his voice came back to him. *"I'm coming, I'm coming, for my head is bending low ..."* He tried to look like a dead body, too, but the effect was so comical—so ridiculous—he felt plumb stupid making this spectacle of himself. He was glad for the sheet that covered him head to toe. Lord, the Klan was one crazy group!

All the way to Venable Street, they sang low and strong. Jeremiah rattled that skeleton hand to beat all, and under his sheet, Shad couldn't wipe the smile from his face.

21

Chickens

IN THE WEEKS after the skeleton hand in-
cident, Shad's life settled into a routine. Tailoring lessons
one day, reading the next, deliveries late mornings, and his
own tailoring tasks most afternoons—setting sleeves and
pockets, basting linings, pinning drapery hooks. Occasion-
ally, the Klan called a meeting, and Shad came to like it best
when he'd get in a song or two and a pat on the back, then
head home early. No mischief. Just brotherhood and plenty
of shut-eye so he could keep up with lessons and chores.

At the Perkinsons' shed, Rachel was now instructing
him, and they focused on four-letter words. He was start-
ing to recognize the traps—the letters that flipped—and
he slowed when he hit a word with a *b* or *p* or *d*. He would
think through the options each word presented and narrow

his eyes until his brain figured out which letter was which. Sometimes the context of a sentence helped him find the meaning. Sometimes he even got through a few sentences before making a mistake.

Soon he hoped to read like Nathaniel could. Why, that boy had his own copy of a magazine called *All the Year Round* by Charles Dickens. His own copy! Mr. Nelson had given it to him. And every day while Shad fretted over the position of letters in the smallest of words, that boy would help Matthew or Gabriel with his letters. Then, in the last bit of lesson time, he'd sit by the window, engrossed in his magazine. Oh, how Shad envied him. Then he'd kick himself for getting caught up in his envy. There was no easy way to settle into lessons in that shed.

On tailoring days, the children progressed from simple seams to simple sacks. Shad taught them to clip corners before turning their pieces right side out. He showed them how to create a casing for a drawstring. Then it was practice, practice, practice so that the topstitching along the casing was straight as could be. They spent one full day on the drawstring itself, braiding it from strips cut on the bias.

At home one afternoon, Shad took a break from his own work to steal away with the brown wrapping from a bolt of fabric. He sat on his bed and ran his fingers across the letters until he understood each word: *pink dogwood floral, one hundred percent cotton, Frederick & Sons, Atlanta, Georgia*. He beamed. His progress was slow, but it was progress nonetheless.

On Monday morning, June 10, when Shad had finished another lesson on four-letter words—*beep, deep, heed, heap*— he went to Granddaddy's shop to pick up the lace trim Mama needed to finish Miss Abigail's dress. The farmer's market was closed Mondays, so Main Street was quiet. Shad pushed open the door to Weaver's Fine Tailoring, and it squeaked. The little bell tinkled.

Granddaddy came *clip-thunk* down the wooden stairs. Halfway down, he saw Shad and stopped. "You've taken to that silk shirt, eh, son?"

Shad smiled. "Yes, sir."

He turned and *clip-thunked* back up, and Shad followed. Granddaddy wore his same old black vest and white shirt with the sleeves rolled up. He had lodged a piece of gray chalk over one ear.

"Shadrach, when are you and your mama and Jeremiah gonna move into town?"

"Yes, sir," Shad said. "I mean, no, sir, you know Mama don't like town." Did they have to go over this yet again? There was a new odor in the shop today. It smelled tight like vinegar. A dye-setting smell. A new fabric smell the dust and moths hadn't dulled yet.

"Jeremiah ready to apprentice?" Granddaddy nodded at the black devil machine.

"No, sir." Shad breathed out long and slow and shook his head because this chitchat was a favorite of Granddaddy's. Shad would always answer no, and Granddaddy would say, *S'pose I need to discuss the matter with your mama.*

"S'pose I need to discuss the matter with your mama."

"Yes, sir."

Not a hint that anything had happened over the past month. Not a hint that Shad had joined the Klan—that he and Granddaddy were now brothers in a sense. Not a hint that the Klan had sent Bubba and Shad to spook a family, or that they'd pulled the prank with the skeleton bones. Shad knew the boys talked—knew Klan members kept abreast of all the shenanigans going on—but if Granddaddy was on top of these things, he didn't show it. His questions were routine, and so were Shad's answers.

No, Jeremiah didn't want to apprentice. Not now, not ever. Shad could run gathers and set pleats and hem-stitch without anybody seeing the thread line. But he wasn't the firstborn. It was one thing to be an assistant and another to own a shop. All the big expectations swirled around Jeremiah, and the scraps fell to Shad.

Scraps. Granddaddy's wooden floor was littered with scraps. Thread, cuttings, trim. Shad scurried around and picked up the bits.

Granddaddy chuckled. "Didn't you notice?" He pointed to the sign that said FIFTY CENTS, but the space on the plaster wall beside it was empty. "Sold one of your foot mats this morning."

Shad looked at the cracked white wall beside the FIFTY CENTS sign. Something had changed, after all. And something about that sale struck him as odd. He'd braided that mat from thread and cloth bits, and it had been hanging for months without anyone caring two cents about it. "Who bought it?"

"Bertram Dabney. Said he could use him a mat at the door. Not only that, he left you all two chickens. Got 'em in a crate out back."

Granddaddy dropped a few coins in Shad's hand.

"Thank you, sir." Shad went to slip the coins in his pocket when he remembered the silk shirt didn't have a pocket. Humph. He wondered about Mr. Dabney—about the fact that he probably didn't need a foot mat today any more than he'd needed it last week or last year. And chickens? What had brought on such generosity?

Then he knew. Or thought he knew. Mr. Dabney had to be KKK, and the Klan was committed to taking care of its own. Whooee. It made Shad think of Daddy—how proud Daddy would be. How happy he'd be that his family was getting along okay without him. A brotherhood. Chickens. The Weaver family was going to be fine, thanks to the Klan.

Granddaddy slipped some lace trim into a little cloth sack for Mama, and Shad slipped the coins and the scraps of cloth bits into the sack. "Thank you, Granddaddy." He headed downstairs where a brown mouse skittered across the floor planks and disappeared into a hole smack-dab in the middle of the front room.

Downstairs Granddaddy had a woodstove for cooking, a pine table and cupboards for foodstuffs, and a set of cane chairs. But he didn't keep much downstairs because of the river flooding sometimes. If he could, he'd move his shop up Church Hill, away from the river. But it would be a long time before he'd be able to pay back that fellow who'd loaned him money for the devil machine. No, Shad didn't think he'd manage to move uphill anytime soon. Anything worth keeping, Granddaddy kept upstairs.

Shad went around back and peeked through the slats of the little wooden crate. Two scruffy red-brown chickens tilted their little heads to look at him. Then one of them squawked and Shad jumped. Ha! It scared him. Funny chicken. That bird had personality. He'd have to come up with good names for them. He squatted beside the crate.

"You gonna give us some eggs?" he asked the chickens nicely.

One of them said, "Peep."

"Peep to you," said Shad. The other one stuck a beak through the slats. Shad lifted the crate and the chicken poked his hand. "Okay, that's it. Poke and Peep. How's that for names?"

Poke kept on poking at him through the slats, and he had to shift the crate around to keep his hands from getting pecked at. He set the crate on his shoulder and headed out past the empty market stalls. He felt like a rich man—silk shirt, coins in his pocket, a crate of chickens, membership in a fine brotherhood. *Look at me now, Daddy,* he thought. *Just open up them eyes from heaven, and look at me now.*

The wind brought the sweet smell of searing butter

and fried fish, and Shad knew someone in the Bottom was cooking a fine midmorning breakfast. At O'Malley's hitching post at Seventeenth and Grace, two horses were tethered together—a copper mare and a black gelding with a bushy brown mane. Shad looked at the wooden sign over O'Malley's saloon door. It had been a long time since Shad had enjoyed a nice root beer, and today his mouth watered up just thinking on it. He had money on him today—first time in months. High time he treated himself to a root beer.

He pushed open the door and looked for a spot that wasn't sticky so he could set down the crate. The floor was always sticky in O'Malley's. The tables were sticky and the air was smoky. Today the place was almost empty. Two old men sat on tall wooden stools at the bar. They wore coarse woolen vests, and one man's vest was coming apart at the side seam. It wouldn't take but a few quick stitches to fix, but Shad knew it wasn't his place to tell a man his clothes needed mending.

Mr. O'Malley smiled from behind the bar. "Well, fancy that," he said, and it came out "fanthy that." "All in the family! How you been, Thadrach? What can I do for you?"

"Hello, Mr. O'Malley." Shad set down the crate and the sack of lace trim under the front window. The chickens squawked. Stuck on the floor was a black shoelace, and he peeled it up and shoved it in the sack. Then he pulled a penny from the sack and went to the bar. He sat on a stool at the end, away from the men, and set the penny on the counter. "Root beer, sir."

"Glad you're keeping it clean," said Mr. O'Malley, raising his arm high over the thick glass mug so the root beer splashed and a big white froth came up on top. He slid the wet mug toward Shad and shoved the penny at him, too. "It'th on me today, boy."

"Oh. Uh, thank you, sir." They shared a look, and something in O'Malley's eyes told Shad that he was probably Klan, too. Shad wondered how long this special treatment would last.

Shad put his mouth to the mug and the white froth foamed and tickled his nose, making a mustache on his lip. The sassafras root stung his throat, and he liked it. He'd have his own mustache someday soon—a real one.

Then he heard voices start up. Angry voices. He looked around but saw no other people. Hairs on the back of his neck straightened. His skin grew tight.

Shoot. When Mr. O'Malley had said "all in the family," Shad hadn't thought anything of it. But now he understood—Jeremiah was in the back room.

The voices got louder. They came from behind a musty brown curtain at the far end of the bar. Shad heard the sound of wood scraping along floorboards. Chairs moving. Feet scuffling. A thud. He couldn't see anything, but he knew Jeremiah had just thrown someone against a wall. He plumb knew it.

"Come on, fellath," said Mr. O'Malley. Shad watched him go to the curtain, but before he got there, a shiny-headed man fell through.

The man bumped into a square table and sent two wooden chairs helter-skelter.

Jeremiah burst in, yelling, "And don't you show your face to me again!" He came full-on toward the man, and Shad saw the glint of something in his hand. Jeremiah had pulled a knife.

The man scrambled out the front door. The two old men downed their drinks and eased off their stools. "Good day," one said to Mr. O'Malley without taking his eyes off Jeremiah. They left, patting their vest fronts and trousers, checking for coins, tobacco, a pocket watch maybe.

Jeremiah folded the knife and slipped it in his boot. He nodded with a real satisfied smile. Then his eyes caught Shad's and the smile went to a scowl.

"What the hell you doin' here?"

Shad didn't answer. Didn't move. Didn't breathe. He looked at Jeremiah straight on and waited.

"I asked you a question, Shad." Jeremiah walked toward the bar with his legs wide, each boot stomping on the sticky floor. He walked like he owned the place. He wrapped one huge hand around Shad's mug, took it to his mouth, and guzzled half the root beer. Then he slammed the mug down, wiped his mouth on his white shirt, and narrowed his eyes.

Shad's hands went into fists. He wanted to pound his brother but didn't dare. Jeremiah would bloody his nose in a second. Then he saw Clifton saunter through the back curtain. Shad felt his day go from bad to worse. He clenched his teeth.

The last few times Shad had seen him, Clifton had been under a sheet or swigging whiskey in the dark. Today, there he was—skinny, blond, with a bulging Adam's apple. He was eighteen—a year older than Jeremiah, and a year meaner. He looked sickly with his deep-set blue eyes and too-white skin with red pimples. But he wasn't a weakling. Thin as a flint and strong as an oak, he was the fastest runner Shad knew. Shad hated thinking on all the times Clifton had treated him like a hog, chasing him down and wrestling Shad's arms behind him.

Shad said, "I thought you was working today."

"Yeah, well, that shows what you don't know," said Jeremiah.

"How we supposed to work with all them coloreds out there, huh?" said Clifton in his too-deep voice. He plopped down on the stool beside Shad. He grabbed the mug and drained the rest of the root beer in a gulp. "Don't gotta pay them coloreds nothing and they keep on laying bricks."

"Ain't right," said Jeremiah.

"No, ain't right at all."

From the corner of an eye, Shad saw Mr. O'Malley pick up the wooden chairs. He put them back at the square table and stood, watching and listening.

Jeremiah sat and put an elbow on the bar. He and Clifton stared at Shad. It was only midmorning and Shad was sure they'd been drinking already.

Clifton hit the side of Shad's head with an open palm and smiled his crooked son-of-a-gun smile—one Shad took to mean, *Hey, Klan brother.* Then Clifton burped loud enough to call the cows home. "So, Shad," he said, "tell me something. Rumor floating around—there's a school for coloreds up Libby Hill."

Shad's fingers gripped the edge of the bar. He froze.

"You go up Perkinsons' for tutoring, right? That's what Jeremiah tells me."

"Yeah," Shad said, not looking at either of them. "Yeah."

"They got a school or not?"

Shad shrugged. "Miz Perkinson—she does tutoring in the house there—the, uh, front sittin' room."

Jeremiah punched Shad's arm. "Everybody knows she tutors, Shad. It ain't what Clifton's asking. You heard him."

"Get off-a me. I don't know."

Clifton leaned in so close, his nose touched Shad's nose. He smelled rank. "Next time you go up there, you look around. You got that?"

Shad leaned back. "Yeah, sure."

"You keep your ears to the ground, Shad," Clifton went on, "and if you hear anything about a Negro school up there, you let us know."

Shad slipped off the stool. "Yeah, sure. Okay."

"We don't need no Negro schools."

22

Cat and Mouse

SHAD GRABBED the packet of lace and the crate of chickens, and the hens started squawking like Shad wanted to squawk. Geez, he needed to get away from these boys.

"Whoa!" shouted Jeremiah. "What you got there?"

"Uh—chickens. Mr. Dabney done give us two chickens. I'm taking 'em to Mama."

"Well, I'll be!" said Jeremiah. "Dabney, eh?"

"Yeah, Mr. Dabney."

Jeremiah hopped off the stool. "Come on, Clifton. Let's go. Listen, Shad, we'll run by Kechler's. See if he can spare some scrap wood. Whooee. We gonna build us a little chicken coop and get us some eggs."

The three of them ducked out of O'Malley's together. Inside the light had been dim, but outside was blistering bright, and Shad squinted. The horses that had been hitched out front were gone now.

They headed to Broad Street, and Shad paused by the maple tree. At this spot in Shockoe Valley, hills sloped up in three directions, and behind him the ground angled down to the river. He thought of the night he'd stood on the far side with skeleton bones in his hand. He tried to shake it off, but a glance toward Richmond proper brought back memories of shapes and shadows—of the colored men walking home from the Spotswood. Of the fear in the man's voice when he'd yelled, "Lord!"

Shad rubbed his forehead against his sleeve. There had been a time when he'd marveled at how grand Richmond was, how enormous. But today it struck him how small the town was. How very, very small.

"Come on. What you waitin' for?" called Jeremiah.

Shad turned and shuffled behind Jeremiah and Clifton, up Broad Street toward Church Hill, then around the Twentieth Street hill to Venable. The whole way, he was cranked up, tight as a jack-in-the-box. He didn't breathe easy again until Jeremiah and Clifton turned in the direction of Kechler's—toward the Fairfield Race Course. Shad kept on out Nine Mile Road.

"Whooee" over chickens? His head spun. "Whooee" was right. He'd have to think things through. As long as he was anywhere near Jeremiah, he'd need to keep his mind blank as could be so his face wouldn't show a thing. He had to be extra careful.

How had they learned about the school? Shoot, there wasn't anything secret in this town anymore. If Jeremiah and Clifton learned not only that there was a school, but that Shad was teaching there—teaching the coloreds to tailor—he shuddered. He couldn't think about it.

Every day his reading was getting better. He wasn't guessing anymore. No more memorizing and reciting what he'd heard. No more embarrassment like that time Daddy realized Shad couldn't read a lick. His reading was slow, but at least he was reading.

Someday soon Shad would pick up Daddy's book and open to any story he wanted. He'd read it out loud for his Daddy up in heaven. He wasn't stupid. Shad knew he wasn't stupid, but—did Daddy know? Could Daddy look down on him and see him read?

He didn't want anybody messing this up. He didn't want any Klan brothers getting wind of something at the Perkinsons'. He needed reading lessons more than anything else—even more than the chickens on his shoulder.

It seemed like everything had gotten awfully compli-
cated in only one month's time. Between the Klan and the
school, Shad figured the only way he'd handle all of it was
to say as little as possible. No telling who knew what in this
town. He had better keep his mouth shut as best he could.

On Tuesday, June 11, at the crack of dawn, Shad didn't take
the alley. He knocked lightly at the Perkinsons' front door,
without touching the fancy-pants brass knocker.

The heavy black door inched open and Caroline peeked
out. "Mr. Weaver? Why, you're supposed to be around back.
They've started already."

The smell of bacon and fried eggs caught Shad's nose
and made his whole body smile. He leaned in and whispered, "Caroline, it ain't right—uh—I can't let nobody see
me down the alley. Please? Can I please come through the
house? I'll go straight through—front to back—no questions."

Caroline looked him up and down and raised her eyebrows. She made an odd face, then opened the door all
the way.

"Thank you, ma'am."

Caroline pointed down the back hall, and Shad scurried through and past the kitchen, pausing for the briefest of moments to eye the bacon popping in a clear puddle of grease in a large, black cast-iron skillet. What he'd give for a piece of hot bacon melting on his tongue! But no, he darted out the back, down the steps to the yard, and into the shed.

"Ah, Mr. Lourdaud has arrived," said Rachel with a smirk. "What's the excuse for your tardiness this time?" Without waiting for an answer, she launched into a nursery rhyme and raised one hand, inviting the children to chime in. A chorus of singsong voices pummeled Shad willy-nilly.

It's raining, it's pouring,

The old man is snoring.

He went to bed and bumped his head,

And couldn't get up in the morning.

Rachel tapped one finger on her chin. "Is that it, Mr. Lourdaud? Bumped your head?"

Shad's eyes caught hers and held them there, strong and steady. The children were giggling, but he kept his mouth flat. "I needed to come through the front this morning.

And—and every morning. And I'll need to go back out through the main house, too."

Rachel put hands on hips, narrowing her eyes, puckering her mouth. "What happened?"

"Nothing," he said a little too quickly. He scanned the children's faces, and when his eyes caught Maggie's, he wanted to hide. He turned back to Rachel. "It's a matter of . . . of propriety. Uh . . . appropriateness." His choice of words surprised even him, and he scratched at his scalp. He sounded like Rachel. Like Miss Elizabeth!

Rachel gave him a sideways look.

Eloise pointed at the burlap sack Shad carried.

"Uh, yes," he said. "Pockets today." He gestured toward the east window and moved in that direction, his presence commanding the room. *The Tailoring Teacher has arrived!* "I already showed you topstitching, and you'll need that skill to set your pockets. Today I'll show you blind stitching. But don't think blind stitches can be any less straight just because no one will see them. Blind don't mean crooked, you hear me?"

The children nodded, swarming around him, hanging on his every word. Through the lesson, Rachel stood by the west window, arms crossed, jaw tight. Shad had the distinct impression she could see through him—read through him—somehow read his mind. She knew something was wrong, but he couldn't tell her a thing. *Wouldn't* tell her a thing.

His running with the Klan—that was the other Shad. The Shad who was learning to stand up to his brother, make his mother proud, protect widows, grow up, be a man. That Shad wasn't this one—the Tailoring Teacher and struggling student. No, they weren't the same at all, and he'd do everything he could to keep them apart.

That afternoon, the sky was fixing to rain. Shad had stopped by Weaver's Fine Tailoring and run a delivery to Doc Moore in Richmond proper. Now he was headed up Broad when someone called to him from the alley between Eighteenth and Nineteenth Streets. He glanced that way and was surprised to see little Maggie leaning over a picket gate. The gate led to a grassy patch behind a big, white two-story built a hundred years ago as a plantation house. Shad knew the house—such a fine one with three chimneys. He'd always liked the way the front sat diagonal to the corner at Nineteenth and Grace.

"Mr. Lourdaud!" Maggie waved.

And lookee there—behind her stood Rachel. Shad wanted to wave, but he stopped himself. Broad Street was full of people. The market, two blocks over, was always slow on a Tuesday—there would be double this many people on the streets by Friday—but the market was open nonetheless, and business was steady. People were coming from the farmers' stalls. He heard a horse whinny. Carriage wheels clattered up the brick street. Church bells clanged the top of the hour.

No, Shad didn't want a conversation with any colored girls. He looked at his feet, pretending he hadn't heard Maggie. Let her think the bells had drowned her out. He picked up his pace.

"Sir! A moment, please, sir."

Shad slowed. *Sir.* This voice was older—not Maggie's. It had come from Rachel, and she'd called him *sir*. What was it she'd said to George Nelson—that on the streets of town he'd encounter "an ignorant Negress"? Well, here she was, calling to Shad proper for all the world to see. He had to pay her mind. He'd treat her like an ignorant Negress—that's what he'd do.

Shad stopped and raised his chin as if to ask what she could possibly want. He didn't let his face show any sign that he knew her. No telling who might be Klan. Why, half a block behind him was a farmer with a bin of something—kale and collards—on his shoulder. Across the street Shad saw the blacksmith—what was his name?—carrying two horseshoes, one in each hand, and waving to a man in a black suit and stovepipe hat. Beyond him three ladies in spring bonnets walked with woven reed baskets that looked to be full of greens.

"Sir," Rachel said again, and she slipped through the gate into the alley. She hurried to Broad Street, stopped a polite distance from Shad, and lowered her voice. "Maggie and her mama made you some corn bread. Just something to thank you for lessons." Then darn if she didn't bend her knees quickly—the littlest bob of a curtsy—and put a funny smirk on her face. She whispered, "Mr. Lourdaud, *sir*," in an awfully slow and pointed manner.

Shad wanted to roll his eyes. He wanted to call her a nincompoop—to smile, to laugh! But instead he bit the inside of a cheek and said quietly, "She can give it me in the morning, Rachel. Not here."

"But it's hot. Fresh from the oven. She saw you and wanted you to have it. Isn't that sweet?"

Shad glanced toward the farmhouse. "She live there?"

Rachel nodded. "Maggie's mama is the cook and

laundress. Well, actually, she handles everything there but the tailoring, and one day Maggie hopes to handle that piece, thanks to you."

Then Shad saw Maggie jump up and down, waving wildly with one hand and holding a bundle in the other arm. She beamed to beat all, and even though Shad sensed that it wasn't a good idea—that he shouldn't pay this little girl mind—he strolled down the alley to the gate. Maggie pointed to her dress, thrusting her flat chest upward so that the green gingham bodice came first.

Shad smiled. Lookee there—right in the middle of the bodice was a pocket. "Did you sew that yourself?"

"Yes, sir. All by myself."

The pocket was a mess of crooked stitches and puckered lines. For the pocket to lie flat on the bodice, she'd need to rip it out, reset it, restitch it, and take a hot iron to it. But today Shad wasn't about to tell her that she'd sewn it wrong. He said, "I'm proud of you."

Maggie up and glowed from the top of her little head to the tip of her chinny-chin-chin. Ha! The fairy-tale words popped into Shad's head and the next thing he knew, he was glowing, too. He reached over the gate and took the cloth bundle. "Thank you, Maggie."

Then Maggie dashed to the brick outbuilding and Shad strutted through the alley, back to Broad Street. Rachel walked a few paces behind him, and when they got to Broad, she said, "Thank you. That's all, Shad. I just wanted to say thank you."

He nodded, sensing she wanted so much more than "thank you." She wanted a better explanation for his tardiness, for his insisting on coming and going through the house. But he was learning to keep his mouth shut.

He started up Church Hill.

Rachel said, "We'll see you in the morning."

Shad didn't look back. He walked away, but with each step a sense of worry grew inside him. After four or five steps, the worry turned to dread. It was more than a sense of uneasiness over keeping information from her. Something told him to look back, and he slowed. He glanced over a shoulder, expecting the worrisome feeling to go away when he saw that everything was fine.

But everything was not fine.

A figure was coming fast up the alley from Grace Street. Shoot! It was Jeremiah, tugging on his goatee. Then Shad saw him slam a fist into an open palm. Again and again, *whack, whack.* He walked with such a tall and menacing manner, it was as if he owned the block. He made it to the gate before Rachel did, and set his feet solid, smack-dab in her path.

Shad froze. He wanted to run Jeremiah off, but his feet wouldn't let him. He stood glued to the gray-brick street, his eyes on Rachel.

She stopped in front of Jeremiah. She had to stop. There wasn't any way for her to go forward without running into him. She couldn't get through the gate without going around him. She kept her head down and took a step to one side.

Jeremiah stepped to the side.

She stepped the other way.

Jeremiah blocked her again.

She moved right. Left. It didn't matter which way she tried—he was there, blocking her path. Cat and mouse.

Shad felt fury rise from the inside out. If Jeremiah so much as touched her, Shad would—

"Miss Rachel?" little Maggie called.

Jeremiah turned and Rachel took the moment to dart around him, making it through the gate before he blocked her again.

Jeremiah threw his head back and laughed.

Rachel ran to Maggie. Then she stood in the grassy stretch, the brick outbuilding framing her proud black figure, and she stared at Jeremiah. She held her head high.

Shad felt his chest rise way up and fall with a whoosh of air. He saw the farmer wave to Jeremiah, and watched his brother saunter away from the gate.

A bead of sweat ran down the side of Shad's face and dripped onto the warm cloth in his hands. More than anything, he wanted to apologize. He wanted to tell Rachel how sorry he was that his brother ran these streets. He wanted to hug little Maggie and thank her for thanking him.

But Shad couldn't say or do anything. Not here. Not now. Satisfied that the moment had passed, he headed up Church Hill. Dern that brother of his!

He stewed all the way home, trying to figure what he'd say when Jeremiah asked why a little colored girl had baked him some mighty fine corn bread.

He could eat the corn bread on the way. Hide the evidence. He peeled back the cloth and bit into the buttery corner—crisp on the edge and soft inside, still hot. He took one bite, then another, and another. It was mouthwatering good. But it was too much for one person. He couldn't finish it between here and home.

Shad thought to give it to the birds, befriend a stray dog...

But no. After years of scraping by, sometimes whole

days with nothing to eat, he had to give this corn bread to Mama. He would add one more lie to his list. The corn bread—it came from Doc Moore as a thank-you for Mama's beautiful tailoring—that extra special embroidery that she'd done on his collar and pocket. *Doc Moore said, "Thank you, kindly."*

Oh, and Mama—Shad was just so sorry—he couldn't help himself. He'd had to nibble a tad on the edge as he walked home. Jeremiah said the bread came from a colored girl? Pshaw. Jeremiah didn't know what he was talking about. Making things up, he was.

23

The Best of All Possible Worlds

AT SUPPER THAT night, Mama said, "What's got you boys worked up? You two ain't said one word to each other in the past hour."

Shad looked at his plate and didn't reply. Neither did Jeremiah.

After supper Shad helped Mama wash the dishes. Then he headed to the coop to check on Peep and Poke.

Yesterday, Jeremiah and Clifton had gotten scrap wood and wire from Mr. Kechler and built a little coop—nothing fancy. The roof wasn't even as high as Shad's waist. It was a small wooden house with a board on top that Shad could easily lift at egg-gathering time. The chickens could exit the house on one side—the side where the boys had stretched a large piece of wire mesh. They'd lashed the mesh to stakes in the ground. It gave the chickens plenty of yard without letting them get away, and it kept out the raccoons and such.

Shad liked Peep and Poke a lot. He liked to watch them strut about. Listen to them cluck and coo. They were settling in well—not laying eggs yet, but once they got good and comfortable, Shad knew they'd start laying, and the family would have real breakfasts again.

Today, not two seconds into the yard, Shad heard the kitchen door open. Jeremiah was plumb on his heels. Smirking and walking with a swagger, he whistled. "You're getting to be quite the liar."

Shad gritted his teeth, waiting for Jeremiah to knock him one.

But he didn't. Instead, Jeremiah crossed his arms over his chest. "I'm impressed, little brother." Jeremiah whistled again, this time louder than the first. "Very impressed. I think you're growing up."

Jeremiah seemed to be waiting for Shad to say something, but Shad kept his mouth shut. He didn't know how much Jeremiah had seen of him and Maggie and Rachel.

"Keeping a secret is a sign of maturity," Jeremiah said, drawing out the word *maturity* as if to make fun of Shad, as if to suggest Shad was too stupid to understand a four-syllable word. Then he marched at Shad, and Shad flinched, raising an arm to block the punch. But no punch came. Instead,

Jeremiah patted his back. Shad didn't know what to make of it.

Jeremiah leaned toward him and talked quietly. "You worked a deal with a colored and got us some nice corn bread tonight. Heh, heh, my little brother is proving to be slicker than I thought."

Shad kept his guard up. He didn't smell whiskey on Jeremiah, and Clifton wasn't here for him to show off to, so Shad was having a time of it—trying to read him. Jeremiah's posture was pure bully, but at the same time, darn if he wasn't paying Shad a compliment. Darn if Shad didn't feel a wee bit of pride rise up inside. Part of him didn't ever want anything to do with his brother and part of him had been hankering after Jeremiah ever since he could crawl.

Then Jeremiah said, "I guess you just wanna talk with colored girls."

"I do not." Shad's hands went into fists.

"Is that it, Shad? You got a thing for colored girls?"

"Shut up."

Jeremiah laughed and danced around Shad with his fists up. "Oh, yeah? Is that it?"

Peep flapped her wings and squawked.

"Get out of here, Jeremiah."

He laughed and laughed. "Wanna fight about it? Put

them dukes up. Put 'em up. Fight like a man."

"Go away."

"Put 'em up. Come on, put 'em up."

Poke and Peep squawked, and Jeremiah danced in close. Shad swatted at him and missed. He laid one into Shad's cheek, but not hard. Jeremiah was all playful tonight. He tilted his head sideways. Shad swung at him and Jeremiah caught his wrist and pulled him so hard and fast, Shad's chest smashed into his. Jeremiah grabbed Shad's other wrist and held his arms behind him. He squeezed him into his stinking wet armpit.

"Stop it, Jeremiah!"

"Stop it, stop it," he sang. Then he twisted Shad's arm.

"Ow!"

Jeremiah let go and clapped at the chickens. They squawked. He walked toward the house, then suddenly turned. He was on Shad again, pinching his arms behind his back and breathing hot air down his neck. "Let me tell you something, and don't you forget it."

"Ow—"

"Don't you never shame our family, you hear me?"

"What?"

"I don't know what you got going on, little brother. But I'm gonna find out."

"Stop—"

"And you better make sure that whatever it is, it don't embarrass me or Mama or our family."

"Geez—I—"

"You understand?"

Shad tried to shake loose.

"Say it. Tell me you understand."

Shad coughed. Jeremiah held his arms crooked, pinched up behind him. Shad coughed again. "Yeah. Yeah, I understand."

Jeremiah let him go with a shove and he bumped against the wire and the coop rattled and the chickens squawked full-out.

Then Jeremiah was gone and Shad's knees were knocking so bad, he had to sit a spell. His arms throbbed. His chest hurt. He plopped down, and darn if he didn't land lickety-squat in chicken shit.

Wednesday at dawn, when Caroline opened the front door and stepped aside for Shad to slip through the house and down the back stairs to the shed, Shad's feet held fast to the brick step.

"Caroline," he whispered, "I can't do lessons in the shed

no more. Mama's almost finished Abigail's dress, and I'll deliver it next week. And here—this here cloth belongs to Maggie and her mama. Would you give it back and tell her thank you for me?"

He turned to go and heard Caroline say, "Wait. Just you wait there a minute, Mr. Weaver. Don't you leave, now."

Shad listened to the door slide into its frame, and he stood there as the sun rose beyond a clump of pines to the east. With the light behind them, the straight black tree trunks loomed over him like bars on a prison cell. He felt trapped. He needed to get away—far, far away.

He couldn't see the river from the steps, and even though she'd asked him to wait, he couldn't keep himself at the door. Just couldn't. He slipped down the steps, across Franklin Street to the hill, taking in the fresh smell of the water and pine and wet earth. He started toward the terrace where the view was best—where he might watch the morning sun touch down on the river—but when he heard the Perkinsons' door open, he stopped and listened.

He didn't look to see who it was, but he hoped it was Rachel. He heard footsteps—light ones—down to the street. The footsteps stopped. He still didn't turn around. He thought he shouldn't have waited—he should have gone.

He had come to return a cloth and deliver a message, was all. There was nothing more to do or say. Shad was finished here. It was plumb too dangerous.

But still, he didn't go. He lingered, waited, feeling drawn to this place. He breathed deeply and turned, ready to say no, he couldn't do lessons anymore, and the words caught in his throat.

Miss Elizabeth stood in the middle of the street. She was halfway between him and the house, her arms crossed, her hands running up and down from elbows to shoulders and back again, rubbing away the morning chill. Dew glistened on the azaleas and rhododendron that lined the house behind her. The way the sun hit the bushes just so, slanting horizontal across the hill, the dew glistened like a good dream. The azalea blooms had fallen away over a month ago, and the rhododendron were finished now, their big pink petals drooping brown.

"Mr. Weaver, I was just having coffee and toast with Mr. Nelson. Please join us, won't you?"

"Ma'am, I—"

"I insist."

She said it so firmly that he shuffled behind her. He brushed dust from his Willy Johnson britches, took the wide brick steps in a leap, and trod softly across Miss Elizabeth's clean wooden floorboards. His feet were bare. Now that he'd stopped growing, soon Mr. Hanson would fit him for his first real pair of boots. In exchange, Shad would sweep Mr. Hanson's floors, run a few errands, and do whatever the man needed. If Mr. Hanson was Klan—and he probably was—he wouldn't ask for more than a week's worth of chores for a pair of boots. Brotherhood was enough.

Shad nodded at George Nelson, sitting there on the crimson brocade settee. George Nelson jumped up and offered his soft handshake. "Ah, Mr. Weaver! How is our student this morning?"

"Just fine, sir."

Miss Elizabeth gestured for Shad to sit, and he slipped onto the settee beside George Nelson. Caroline came with a tray of toast and coffee, cream and sugar. One whiff of coffee and Shad closed his eyes to savor the smell. Then he picked up the silver spoon, added two heaping spoonfuls of sugar, and filled the pretty china cup to the brim with cream.

He took the first sip slowly and felt the heat touch every inch of his innards. It lined his throat, soothed his chest, and eased his belly. The taste brought a gleam to his eyes.

Delicious. *How good these people have it*, he thought. How he wished they'd let him take lessons here in the sitting room, not from coloreds in a shed out back.

"Ah, Mr. Weaver," said George Nelson, beaming, "your expression brings to mind Voltaire. What a joy it will be for me—for *me*, mind you—when your reading has improved to the point where you might master *Candide*. Why, the best of all possible worlds!"

George Nelson wagged a finger in the air and laughed, tilting his head back. His nose quivered and the little black hairs protruding from his nostrils quivered, too. "Yes—that's what your face proclaims this morning, Mr. Weaver. The best of all possible worlds!" Then he leaned toward Shad, his enormous nose nearly touching Shad's shoulder. "But of course, it's satire, my boy. And when a student comes to appreciate satire, why, the world opens before him. For the teacher—well, there's nothing more satisfying to a teacher than opening worlds, one student at a time." He looked up at Miss Elizabeth. "Have you read *Candide*, Mrs. Perkinson?"

She smiled. "Yes, Mr. Nelson, of course. It was some years ago."

"Good, good, good. Now, Mr. Weaver, tell me why the

change of heart this morning? Caroline gave us your message, and, quite frankly, I don't understand it at all. I've heard from Rachel and Nathaniel that in only a month's time, you've made significant progress. You're a sharp lad. You have great potential."

Shad set the cup on the fine white saucer and it rattled. He had been Miss Jenny's dunce for years. He was an embarrassment to Jeremiah. A disappointment to Daddy. A frustration to Mama. Granddaddy's go-for boy. But here in this amazing house, this funny little man saw potential in him. He didn't know what to make of it.

He swallowed. He didn't think George Nelson had it right. The man didn't understand the ways of Virginia. Here firstborns had potential, not lackeys like Shad. "Sir, it's just— it's wrong, plumb wrong—me being in that colored school. I'm white." It irritated him that he had to state the obvious.

Miss Elizabeth sighed. "Mr. Weaver, I believe you made an arrangement. Tailoring lessons in exchange for reading lessons. When you have become an accomplished reader and those children fine tailors, then it will make sense to end the arrangement. But listen to you—to your misuse of the double negative, the lack of subject-verb agreement— why, you have tremendous potential, but you will need to continue lessons much longer than a month."

His eyes went back and forth between their faces. He didn't care a lick for Miss Elizabeth's grammar terms, but the fact that George Nelson saw potential in him gripped Shad through and through. This morning, he'd come to the house to quit lessons, and now he desperately wanted to stay.

"I have a proposition," said George Nelson. He stood and paced to the piano and back. "Once a week I shall work one-on-one with you alone, Mr. Weaver. One half an hour, every—what? You tell me, Mrs. Perkinson. Which morning might be available? I'd be honored to teach this lad while he, in turn, continues to instruct our young Negro charges in the fine art of tailoring."

"Well, I don't know," Miss Elizabeth began.

"Tuesdays!" shouted George Nelson. "Tuesdays here in the parlor. Seven o'clock in the morning. Sharp."

"But I—"

"A clock. Have you a clock, lad? I'm sure Mrs. Perkinson has a spare clock for you. Or a pocket watch—that would suit better, wouldn't it? Do you have your own pocket watch?"

"Uh, no, sir."

Miss Elizabeth cleared her throat. "Well, I suppose—"

"Marvelous!" shouted George Nelson. "Let's see here. Today is Wednesday. You've got instruction to give this morning and Thursday and Friday, and I'll see you bright and early Tuesday morning. Perfect."

Before Shad had quite grasped what he'd agreed to, he was down the back stairs and into the shed, and in his hand he held a fine little timepiece that had once belonged to Mr. Parks Randolph Perkinson.

The moment Rachel saw him, she threw her hands in the air. "Better late than never. Is that your motto, Mr. Lourdaud? What sort of school would this be if all of our students arrived whenever they pleased? What sort of teacher would I be ...?"

She went on and on about the value of timeliness, and Shad hung his head, rubbing his thumb up and down along the smooth glass face of the pocket watch, promising never to run late again.

24

Accidents Happen

FOR THE NEXT few days, Shad went through the motions, sounding out words as Rachel looked over his shoulder and teaching the children to set pockets hidden in the seams of jacket lining. But he was distracted. Anxious for the upcoming lesson with George Nelson, anxious over his brother's questions, anxious over coming and going through the Perkinsons' house and not warning Rachel that danger loomed, Shad's stomach twisted into a knot and he nearly stopped eating.

On Saturday night he went to another Klan meeting— a brotherly one full of song and backslaps and handshakes and one fellow telling stories in such a funny accent with such a lisp, why, Shad was sure it had to be Mr. O'Malley. He'd been right that day at the saloon when O'Malley hadn't taken the penny for the root beer—right that O'Malley was Klan, too. For much of the night, he wondered who else was under all the sheets.

Shad left the meeting with Jeremiah, Clifton, and Bubba, and after a spell, like so often happened, he and Bubba fell a few steps behind. They were near Venable Street when a fellow Klansman ran up. He looked at Bubba and Shad, then ran ahead and got Jeremiah and Clifton to stop. They talked quietly. Then Jeremiah and Clifton and the ghost turned around and headed back. Bubba and Shad waited. The night was extra dark, and the air was heavy like it was going to rain.

Shad watched from a distance as Jeremiah and Clifton met with some ghosts. One was the Grand Cyclops. Shad was beginning to understand how it worked. The meetings were crowded. A mob was easy to rile up, and nobody knew exactly who was under each sheet. The Grand Cyclops was careful about everything he said in an official meeting, and about making the meetings right brotherly and warm. Afterward, he would pull aside some boys and give out assignments.

When the Cyclops was finished talking with Jeremiah and had walked the other way, Jeremiah, Clifton, Bubba, and Shad headed up Venable Street. They pulled off their disguises, and whooee, it felt good to take in the fresh air, even if it was heavy with the damp.

It started drizzling and Shad's britches stuck to his thighs. When they got to the end of Venable, Clifton and Bubba peeled off, saying good night in hushed tones. Then Jeremiah and Shad headed for Nine Mile Road and it started to rain full-out.

"Hey," Shad whispered, "what did the Cyclops want you and Clifton doing?" He felt a tad disappointed that the Cyclops hadn't asked him and Bubba to handle something.

"Nothing," said Jeremiah.

Shad listened to the rain a spell. "Can Bubba and me come?"

"Shut up, Shad. We ain't doing nothing this week."

"Next week?"

"Geez, shut up."

"Okay, okay."

They walked some more. He saw Jeremiah pull on his goatee, and Shad knew it meant he was working out something in his head. After a time Jeremiah whispered, "Clifton and me told you to keep your ears to the ground and look around the Perkinsons' house. So did you look around or not?"

His question came at Shad like a blow. "What?"

"Don't gimme that, Shad. What do you know? The rumor about them maybe running a school for coloreds up Libby Hill—is it true or not?"

Shad stumbled. He scrambled to keep up. "How am I supposed to know?"

"You're the one what goes up there for tutoring."

"Yeah, well, I don't know. I'm in the front room, is all."

"When are you next going up there?"

Shad swallowed. "Monday morning."

"Yeah, well, good. We need to know what's going on *behind* the house, not in the front room."

The rain hit harder all of a sudden—pelting, driving sideways. Jeremiah picked up the pace. Shad felt rain stream down his cheeks and back. Jeremiah leaned in and put his mouth at Shad's ear. "How hard is it for you to see if there's a shed out back?"

"Well, I don't know. That—uh—it wouldn't be right for me to go around there."

"Ain't hard to walk around the block and see behind a house."

"I don't know. It's got, uh, a big hedge back there."

"It's a simple question, Shad. Miz Perkinson got a shed out back or don't she?"

Shad let his mouth fall open. Rain poured off him in sheets.

"Monday suppertime, I want a report, you hear me? Yes or no, a shed or no shed. I'm not asking for me, Shad. I'm asking for the brotherhood. The Cyclops needs to know."

"Yeah, okay."

"And if there is a shed, then we got to know if she's schooling coloreds there. 'Cause if it's true—Clifton and me, we're gonna torch it. And if there's coloreds in there when it goes up in smoke, well, all the better."

Shad's heart stopped. "J-Jeremiah, you can't do that."

"Assignment from the Cyclops."

"That's Church Hill. It ain't like some shack along the tracks. That's white folks up there."

"White folks schooling coloreds."

"That's Perkinson property."

"We ain't gonna touch the main house. Just the shed. It'll look like an accident, Shad. Accidents happen."

"You—you can't do that. You'll get arrested."

"Fat chance."

"You'll end up in jail again."

"And the Klan will get me out."

"Get you out? How they gonna get you out?"

The rain hit harder now, pelting Shad's back, carving

little streams in the dirt road, turning everything to mud. Jeremiah broke into an all-out run, and Shad let him get ahead. *Run,* Shad thought. *Go on and run!* Run so he wouldn't see Shad's face give him away.

I hate you, thought Shad. Burning a school? Not caring if children were inside? It was worse than not caring. The Klan—they wanted children inside—colored children. Wanted to make it look like an accident. Good Lord Almighty.

What if Rachel and the children were in there when it went up in flames? If Jeremiah carried through with this ... Shad shuddered.

He couldn't let the Klan do it. Lord, what had he gotten himself into? Was *this* what the Klan was really all about? He shook his head. He couldn't believe it. He wouldn't believe it. So much about the Klan was good. The brotherhood, the chickens. Men supporting one another, like Mr. Dabney buying a foot mat he didn't need.

The Klan was a good thing. And Daddy would rest easy knowing his family could survive without him, knowing Jeremiah and Shad were looking out for Mama. They were part of a brotherhood that cared for widows and Confederate orphans and the rest.

But this business about burning a colored school? Shad couldn't let the Klan do it.

But he couldn't stand up to them, either. They were too big. There were too many of them—they were everybody. Jeremiah. Clifton. Bubba. Mr. O'Malley. Mr. Dabney. Even his granddaddy.

He shuddered again. What if they burned the school and no one got out alive? The next day folks would shake their heads and say, "Shame. Did you hear about that school burning down with all them coloreds inside? Crying shame." Jeremiah and Clifton—they would strut up and down the streets of Shockoe, and men would mumble, "Shame," while patting the boys on their backs and offering cigars.

Now the rain hit so hard, it hurt. Shad stopped and turned. He held his face high and let it pound him—first one cheek, then the other. Let it hit him—he deserved it. *Lord, take me.* He didn't want to live to see them hurt Rachel and the children. A psalm came into his head and he whispered the words to the rain.

In my distress, I cried unto the Lord, and He heard me.
Deliver my soul, O Lord, from lying lips, from a de-
    ceitful tongue.

Then, as if the Lord had heard him, lightning lit the sky. Thunder boomed so loudly, Shad's heart leaped out of his chest. He ran.

When he got to the house, he tiptoed through and stripped off his FEED AND SEED shirt and Willy Johnson britches, leaving them in a heap in the corner of the room. Then he crawled into bed, his hair steaming like a wet dog. Jeremiah was already sound asleep.

25

Glory, Hallelujah

MONDAY MORNING, rain was still falling. On Friday afternoon Shad had sewn a pocket into his white silk shirt—sewn it low and on the left side, so it would be perfect for carrying a little timepiece. Then he'd washed the shirt and hung it to dry, but even after hanging near the cookstove for two days, the shirt was dead-bird limp. All that rain, and nothing in the house was dry.

He took Mama's black umbrella with the three broken wood ribs, but with the rain driving sideways and the wind popping his umbrella inside out, by the time he got to the Perkinsons', he was drenched through and through—a six-foot-tall puddle on the front step.

"Sorry," he told Caroline as she let him tiptoe down the hall to the back door.

"Get on! Quick, quick now."

Shad reached the kitchen and looked back to see her in the light of the kerosene lamp, mopping up the hallway, erasing any sign that he'd come through dripping wet.

He stepped outside and stood for a spell at the top of the stairs, setting his hand on the wooden banister. It had once been sanded smooth and painted, but the paint had worn in places, and today the banister was swollen from the rain. He rubbed his fingers lightly up and down the wood, thinking about the lesson he'd planned.

Kitty wanted to sew a dress, and she was ready for gathers. She was weeks ahead of the other children. It was plenty in a day for them to sew flat little sacks and remember to clip corners before turning a piece right-side out. But not for Kitty.

While the others practiced seams, he'd show Kitty how setting gathers meant running two lines of long basting stitches first, then pulling gently on the threads to arrange the fabric, then pinning the whole thing to another piece— like the skirt to the bodice or the sleeve to the shoulder— and running yet another line of basting stitches before settling in to do the fine work.

All the basting was akin to preparing wood for paint,

and with the rain, even with Kitty catching on fast, Shad didn't expect the lesson to go well—not on damp cloth.

He looked toward the shed, waiting for dawn to give it form. Then he thought about what he was doing, and the thought made him dizzy. What he was doing was wrong. It was exactly what the Klan feared. He was teaching skills to coloreds.

If Kitty learned to gather, and if he taught her collars and cuffs and buttonholes, her skills would be in demand. Some highfalutin lady might even hire Kitty—why, she'd only pay Kitty half what she'd pay Weaver's Fine Tailoring for a dress.

His fingers gripped the banister to keep him from toppling down the steps. He shouldn't have agreed to keep coming.

How long could he put off Jeremiah before he'd have to tell him what was what? Yes, a shed. Northwest corner of the property, away from the Twenty-eighth Street side, beside a hedgerow, just beyond the door to the icehouse, invisible from Twenty-eighth Street on account of the holly bushes. Jeremiah would have to get to it from the alley—from that little opening in the hedge.

Lord God Almighty, what the hell was he doing? He was

Klan—a KKK brother. He should have felt proud to serve the brotherhood—report to Jeremiah, make his assignment go smoothly. But no matter how much Shad talked to himself, he couldn't keep his head from shaking no.

The kitchen door opened and lantern light peeked out. Rachel stepped onto the landing. "Ha! Look at you—wet as an otter." She nudged his side and he held fast to the banister all the way down the stairs.

In the shed, rain pounded so loudly on the roof, it was nearly as loud as thunder. The roof leaked in four places, and the children pushed and shoved, trying to keep from standing under the drips. Even with the windows open, the air was thick with the stench of musty clothing and steaming bodies and smoke from the kerosene lantern. Shad didn't think a lesson on setting gathers would go over well, and he felt relieved when Rachel seemed to read his thoughts.

She declared, "Let's try something new today. We'll remain standing. Mr. Nelson has taught me the words to a wonderful song, and I'd like to teach it to you. It goes like this." She commenced to sing, and all the children turned her way.

Shad rested his eyes on her face and watched her glow in the lantern light. Darn if her rich singing voice didn't mesmerize him. It was deep and clear—as smooth as French satin.

> Mine eyes have seen the glory of the coming of the
> Lord:
> He is trampling out the vintage where the grapes of
> wrath are stored;
> He hath loosed the fateful lightning of His terrible
> swift sword:
> His truth is marching on.
> Glory, glory, hallelujah! Glory, glory, hallelujah! Glory,
> glory, hallelujah!
> His truth is marching on.

He watched her close her eyes as she sang, and when she got to the end of that verse, she opened them and started teaching the song, one line at a time.

As the children strained to hear over the pounding rain—to hear and follow the tune and the words—Shad was struck by an odd feeling of safety. It was like nothing he'd ever felt before—not in church, not at home, not in a brotherhood meeting. The pounding rain drowned out everything—the day, the threats, the Klan, Jeremiah. It was so loud, Shad was sure the neighbors couldn't hear the singing even though everyone was carrying on like there was no tomorrow.

And not only loud—but that rain was too *wet*. If it kept raining like this, rained for forty days and forty nights, Klansmen couldn't burn the shed if they tried. Not even a torch could take down the shed right now. Everyone would be safe as long as it kept raining.

Then a thunderclap made them jump. It sounded like a tree trunk had split in half, and Shad expected a great oak to crash down upon them. But nothing fell, and even if it had, well, that was the darnedest thing—the feeling of safety stayed with him. If the world had ended in that very moment with Shad singing "Glory, hallelujah" in a shed full of coloreds, he'd have gone to his Maker with a smile on his face. He sensed that he belonged like he hadn't ever belonged anywhere before.

He shook his head. *Stop,* he thought. He was losing his mind. *Leave, Shad—just get on home. Get out. You don't belong here.*

But his feet didn't budge.

Maggie inched her way through the children, around the drips from the leaky roof, and stopped at his side. She wrapped her wet arms around his waist, and her hands felt tense and tentative on his shirt. Shad cringed. He didn't want this little girl hanging on him. But then Maggie tilted her head and turned her face up and closed her eyes, and let her little-girl voice reach the rafters. Her hands and arms relaxed and settled into Shad's waist, and she gave herself over to the music. He felt her voice seep right through his shirt and into his chest, and the words to the song vibrated deep down in his soul.

Shad closed his eyes and for a second, he wasn't sure where to put his hand. Maggie hung on his waist and his hand hung in the air, looking for a resting place when nothing felt right. But after a spell, he set his hand on top of Maggie's shoulder—on that wet gingham dress with the crooked pocket she'd sewn on the front all by herself.

The next thing Shad knew, he felt a hand come down on his own shoulder—the shoulder on the side where Maggie wasn't. He turned, expecting—well, he wasn't sure what. Eloise, maybe? But the hand belonged to Nathaniel.

Shad frowned, irritated that the boy was keeping his eyes on him and Maggie, making sure Shad didn't do that little girl any harm. He glared in Nathaniel's direction, only to see the boy's eyes twinkle. Darn if that boy wasn't smiling as he sang. Darn if his hand on Shad's shoulder wasn't . . . friendly.

Then Shad couldn't stop his own smile from coming

up and erasing his frown. He tilted his head and took a deep breath and listened to the way Nathaniel's little-boy soprano voice blended right fine into all the other voices.

Glory, glory, hallelujah.

By the time Shad hit Nine Mile Road midmorning, the rain had slowed to a drizzle, then a mist. He opened the door to his family's little white house as a ray of sunshine cut through the clouds.

"Lord have mercy, a drowned rat—that's what you look like," said Mama.

Shad smiled. He knew she was right. "I'll throw on my nightshirt and put these clothes on the line."

"And hang these out there, too, would you?"

"Yes, ma'am," he said, picking up the basket beside the table where she was ironing. Later they'd sup at that table— the only table. Shad thought someday maybe he'd make Mama a board fashioned especially for ironing—maybe Christmas this year.

He changed his clothes and headed out to the line—a woven cotton rope running from the corner of the roof to the top of the outhouse. The rope hung low from the rain, and from the lowest spot of all—smack-dab in the middle—there was a slow drip that had made a little puddle in the dirt. He'd need to crank up the rope before he hung the shirts and pants and whatnot. But first he thought to check on the chickens, and he set down the basket.

"Hey there, Peep. Hey, Poke, how you doing?"

"Shad!"

He jumped. Shoot. Jeremiah was splitting logs near the outhouse. Shad's mouth went dry. The sun burned the top of his head, his shoulders, his back through the cotton nightshirt. He wasn't ready to see Jeremiah.

Shad watched his brother drop the ax and strut toward him. Shad could tell Jeremiah was going to bump his shoulder into Shad's. A brotherly bump. He saw it coming, and he moved with it and held his balance.

Jeremiah leaned into his ear. "They got a shed up there or not?"

Shad shrugged and kept his head down.

"Come on, boy. Shed or no shed?"

"I—uh, I don't know." Shad squatted and wrapped his fingers in the wire mesh around the chicken coop.

"What do you mean, *you don't know*?"

"I—like I told you—I'm in the front room. That's all."

Jeremiah slammed a fist on the wooden slats over the coop, and the mesh rattled. The chickens squawked.

"If you ain't gonna give me no report, I'll have to go up there myself."

Shad tried to steady the mesh—stop its rattling. He clenched his teeth and closed his eyes. The wire bent and he felt it cut into his hand. He opened his eyes to watch a drop of blood draw a line from the base of his middle finger straight down his palm. Shad looked at his hand like it wasn't even his.

"Worthless," Jeremiah mumbled. Then Shad heard him strut back to the ax. Heard him splinter a log and start whistling "God Save the South."

Peep came close, cocked her head, and cooed at Shad. He leaned toward her scruffy red-brown face, and went to whisper, "Hey there, Peep." But no sound came out.

26

Bad Boys

EARLY TUESDAY morning Shad sat in the chair by the front window and stitched a buttonhole. From time to time, he glanced at Mr. Perkinson's pocket watch, glad that he could now rely on it instead of wishful thinking that he'd get places on time. He ran his fingers over the watch, and it occurred to him that it was almost as fancy-pants as a brass door knocker. Owning a watch meant living a responsible life. It meant growing up and becoming a man and earning money that could buy fine things like armchairs and shoes and maybe even a pipe. Good dreams . . . maybe someday he'd buy himself a pipe.

He fussed with another buttonhole and rubbed his eyes. He hadn't slept well. He'd tossed and turned, trying to figure out a way to warn Rachel and Miss Elizabeth about

Jeremiah fixing to torch the shed. But if he dared say any-thing—no, he couldn't think about betraying the Klan.

By the time he needed to get going, dawn had long since given way to morning. Summer was coming and the days were growing longer. They'd eaten corn bread for breakfast and Jeremiah had left early, saying once again that he would get a day job up Richmond proper.

Shad set aside the sewing and pulled on his silk shirt—it was finally dry—and asked Mama if she needed anything in town.

"Nothing today, son. But you remember to watch your mouth around them Yankee-lovers, now."

"Yes, ma'am. I'm real careful and real respectful, Mama."

"That's my boy. If they ask about that dress—tell 'em I ain't done yet. Had to get Doc Moore's trousers done first, and then—"

"Yes, ma'am, I'm sure it's fine. And Mama, I been mean-ing to tell you . . ." He paused, searching for the right words.

Mama raised her eyebrows.

Shad swallowed. "My reading, Mama—it's gettin' better."

She tilted her head and the look on her face was kind, but at the same time, Shad saw a flicker of disbelief.

"Really, Mama. They got methods up there—methods Miss Jenny don't know."

Mama set aside her fabric, needle, and thread, and took a deep breath. She narrowed her already little eyes. "You pullin' my leg?"

"No, ma'am. Just you wait, Mama. One of these days, I'm-a show you what I can read. You got to give me a little more time, but I'm gettin' there, Mama. I am!"

Shad watched her tighten her lips and knew she was choosing her words carefully. He was so much like her— sometimes so much he couldn't stand it. A smile crept onto her face, and she said, "Okay, then, Shad, one of these days you gonna show me."

"Yes, ma'am."

"I'm proud of you, son."

"Thank you, Mama." Then he was off at a good clip, clocking exactly how long it would take to get from their little house to the overlook.

Mama's pride put a skip in his step. Twice he stopped briefly to snatch up bits of cloth and threads for weaving into another foot mat. When he turned off Twenty-eighth Street onto Franklin, he did his calculation. Thirty-one minutes and sixteen seconds. Whooee. And the time was now one minute before seven o'clock. He'd cut it awful close.

Caroline let him in to the warm smells of bacon and coffee, but she didn't offer him breakfast. She showed him to the front room where George Nelson was thumbing through a book. No sign of Miss Elizabeth at all.

"Ah, Mr. Weaver, yes," he said, checking his own watch and nodding in satisfaction. Then he gestured for Shad to sit on the crimson settee.

George Nelson had rolled up his white shirtsleeves, and also the bottoms of his brown trousers. Black suspenders held the trousers up—he was clearly in need of a tailor— and Shad imagined that Mr. Nelson might someday ask for his services. He liked to think so.

The man held up a book and pointed to each word as he read the title: *Harper's School and Family Series. The School and Family Primer: Introductory to the Series of School and Family Readers, by Marcius Willson.*

"Now, Mr. Weaver, we're going to skip part one, as it's the alphabet. Parts two and three cover two- and three-letter words. I believe you can handle them, as well. We're going to start on page thirty-nine. Here, see what you can make of it. I'd like you to read out loud, please."

Shad took the brown book, turning it over, feeling the

grain and smelling the musk scent of fine leather. The binding resisted as he opened to page thirty-nine, and when he got it full open, he felt the spine crack. Shad marveled at it. "Mr. Nelson, why—this book is new."

"Yes, my boy, I requested that Mrs. Perkinson order a set of these before my arrival. They're by far the best for beginners. Now, come, come. Please read."

Shad leaned over the page and began slowly. "*Do you see this man? He is . . .*" He paused, as he wasn't sure of the next word. It had some of the letters that gave him trouble. He looked at the picture of three men, hoping it would give him a clue. Then he silently scolded himself. No, he didn't want to guess. Didn't want to rely on pictures. He would focus on the letters themselves.

George Nelson said, "Look closely at that word. What are the four letters you see there?"

"*B* and, no—*d*, and, wait, that's a *b*. The letters *b* and *a* and *l*."

"Yes, and the fourth letter?"

"*D. Dal* . . . no, *ball* . . . it's *bald* . . . *He is bald.*"

"Perfect!"

Shad beamed. It was such a little word—*bald*—and once he'd said it, well, it was clear that the word was *bald*. He ran his fingers along the smooth paper. He liked this little book and wondered why no one had told Miss Jenny about primers like this one. It made so much sense, putting two-letter words together, then three-letter words, and so on. But that Bible—parts of it didn't make any sense at all.

He went on, slowing here and there, sorting out the letters and smiling at words he knew.

> Do you see this man? He is bald and he is old;
> but he is a *good* man.
> Do you ask how I . . .

Shad narrowed his eyes and set a finger under the word. "The *k* is silent," said George Nelson.

"Oh. All right, then," said Shad. "Now—uh, *know* . . ."

> . . . he is a good man? I know he is a good man,
> for I can see it in his face.
> Do you hear him talk to them? Do you know
> what he says?

When he got toward the end of the page, the word *bad* appeared, and he paused, hoping for a hint. But George

Nelson only waited patiently. The silence set Shad's mind to race. He became aware of everything around him. The smooth and rough textures in the fabric of the crimson brocade settee. The uneven widths of the floorboard planks. A bird chirping near the front window. The lingering scent of bacon.

Then Rachel came to mind—Rachel pointing out that whenever Shad hit a word he wasn't sure about—and there were many—instead of looking at the letters, Shad would look around the room. She'd been sitting beside him in the shed when she made that observation, and at the time Shad had thought her rather preachy. But today—here he was, doing exactly what she'd said.

He ground his teeth and set his eyes on the page. Again, Rachel came to mind. Rachel holding a slate before him and printing letters on it. Rachel telling him to make the same set of letters, each with a circle, and each with a little line attached.

He squeezed his eyes shut, opened them again, and forced himself to pay attention to George Nelson. He read.

He says, God made you. God is good. He can take care of you, and keep you from harm.

Here are two more men, but I do not know that they are good men. They may be bad.

They do not look much like good men. You must shun bad boys and bad men. Go not with them.

Shad froze. He didn't look up from the primer—didn't straighten or sit back in the chair. He remained hunched over the book, and he listened for George Nelson to move— to breathe—to react. Nothing.

He swallowed. Not only had he figured out the letters—the words—but along with them came the meaning. Why had Mr. Nelson chosen this page?

Shad felt George Nelson's eyes on him, and still he didn't look up. He wondered what his teacher knew about bad boys. About Shad's brother. About the . . . Shad stopped himself. He wouldn't let himself think about the Klan.

Seconds passed. A minute. Finally, George Nelson said, "Thank you. Now turn the page and continue."

And Shad breathed again.

Half an hour later, Shad had made it to page forty-two and the lesson was over. Caroline shooed him to the door. George Nelson called, "Before next week, pick up a newspaper and see what progress you can make with it. Bring it to the lesson."

"Thank you, sir."

Shad stepped out into the sunshine, thinking on how he was reading. *Reading.* Lordy, he'd read better today than ever before. He wasn't a dunce. He looked up at a cotton-ball cloud hanging in a pretty blue sky. *Daddy, did you see me today? Did you hear me?*

Shad leaped off the wide brick steps and skipped toward the overlook for one quick glimpse of the beautiful James River before he'd head to Granddaddy's for deliveries, then home to braid another foot mat. Today had been a good day. Tomorrow and the rest of the week he'd do tailoring lessons in the shed with the children, and at some point he'd be in town again and could pick up the *Daily Richmond Enquirer.* Thinking on reading the paper—why, it hadn't ever occurred to him to try. Not even try.

Shad beamed. Just one private lesson with George Nelson, and he was bursting with pride. How would he stand to wait a whole week until his next lesson?

He took in the sweet smell of honeysuckle and craned his neck down the hill to see where it grew. He lifted his face to catch the breeze, but darn if he didn't sense something funny. He felt eyes watching him. Felt the hairs on the back of his neck reach for the sky.

Shad turned. Shoot. Jeremiah was there—twenty paces off, leaning against a pine tree, squinting, with arms folded across his chest.

Shad's hands went into fists. He didn't tell them to fist up—they fisted up all by themselves. He relaxed his knees for balance in case Jeremiah marched his way and shoved him.

But Jeremiah surprised him. He started chuckling. He dropped his arms by his side. Then he laughed himself silly. He sauntered slowly in Shad's direction, and Shad moved toward him, and they met in the middle of the street.

Jeremiah spoke softly. "You wasn't lying."

Shad swallowed. He didn't say anything.

"I got to tell you, Shad. I had the strongest sense that you been lying to me. But you just came out of that house—out of some tutoring lesson, huh?"

"Yeah."

Jeremiah tilted his head a tad and got to pulling on his goatee. He glanced at the Perkinsons' front door, then back to Shad. He nodded. "I don't know, little brother. Something tells me you got something up your sleeve, and I ain't been able to figure out what it is, but you'd best know I'm watching you. You hear me?"

"What's your problem, Jeremiah? I ain't done nothing."

Shad headed toward Twenty-eighth Street and Jeremiah grabbed him by the shoulder. "You idiot." Shad tried to brush his hand away, but Jeremiah got a fistful of the silk shirt and held on tight. "You're a coward, is what you are."

"Get off-a me."

"Clifton and me—we gave you an assignment."

"What?"

"Don't *what* me." Jeremiah leaned into his ear, so close Shad smelled the whiskey—sharp like vinegar. He'd been to O'Malley's already—breakfast in a bottle. "A shed or no shed. Why's that so hard?" He let go of the shirt with a shove.

Shad fell sideways but managed to stay on his feet. He threw his hands in the air to show he wasn't a threat to Jeremiah. Not here, not now.

Jeremiah marched in close and put his mouth to Shad's ear. "I seen it, Shad. It's right there behind the Perkinsons' house. Ain't nothing mysterious about seeing that shed behind that hedge. Here. Lemme show you."

He grabbed Shad's forearm and pulled him down Twenty-eighth Street to the alley that separated the back-yards of the houses on Grace and Franklin Streets.

Shad's thoughts raced. Like a hound on a hunt, his ears perked up, and sure enough, when they got to the alley, he heard voices. Low, not loud, but they were there in the middle of Tuesday morning lessons, smack-dab on the other side of that enormous hedge. Rachel, Eloise, Maggie, Nathaniel, Kitty . . . The lessons would end soon and the children would slip through the opening in the hedge.

Please, not now, he screamed to Rachel inside his mind. *Keep quiet, stay put, don't move, and, for God's sake, no singing this morning.*

Shad strained to clear his face—keep it blank. Not show anything. Then he made to stumble and fell hard against the hedge. "Whoa!" he called out.

The voices stopped. Dead silence but for a bird twittering. A squirrel chattering. An orange tabby dashed across the alley and scrambled beneath the hedge.

Shad righted himself, rubbing at his face and arms where the holly leaves had scratched him.

"Shut up." Jeremiah grabbed the back of Shad's neck and thrust Shad's face into the opening in the hedge. He whispered, "There. Now do you see it?"

He held Shad for a second, then pulled him back into the alley.

A second. It was only a second, maybe two. But in that moment, Nathaniel appeared in the doorway of the shed. He saw Shad, and his face froze.

Then Jeremiah dragged Shad away, jerking his arm, marching with him down Twenty-eighth Street. They crossed over Grace, stopped at Broad while two carriages rattled by, then marched on. Shad felt Jeremiah's hand firmly around his upper arm, squeezing until the hustle-bustle of Church Hill was behind them.

"You don't get it, Shad."

Shad jerked his arm free.

"Now you listen here." Jeremiah's voice was guttural—not like Clifton's dying-man voice, but deep like a wild animal. "When Clifton and me tell you to do something, you do it."

Shad's arm throbbed from the pressure of Jeremiah's grip. He rubbed it, and darn if he didn't smear blood on the sleeve. The holly hedge had scratched his face and neck, and now he'd made brown-red marks on his fine silk shirt. Ugh! He couldn't run deliveries for Granddaddy with blood all over his shirt.

"The Klan ain't Sunday school, Shad. This is a brother-hood. And when the Cyclops asks me to do something, and when I go to you for help with that something, you don't do it if you *feel* like doing it. You do it."

Shad nodded. "Yeah, okay."

"You swore allegiance to the Klan, what means

you're part of a chain of command now. You got that?"

"Yeah, I got it."

Jeremiah shoved his shoulder. "Then you tell me—why was it so hard to report that Miz Perkinson had a shed behind her house?"

"Look, I didn't want to get seen in that alley."

"*Didn't want to get seen,*" Jeremiah whined, his voice high like a girl's. "Well, guess what? You got seen today. And you know what else got seen? A *Negro* in that shed." He leaned into the word *Negro* like it was long and heavy, weighing him down. "The Cyclops was right. There are *Negroes* in that shed."

27

The Golden Rule

"MAMA!" JEREMIAH CALLED as he banged open the door of their little house.

Shad followed him inside. Mama sat by the front window, up to her elbows in the pink flowered dress for Miss Abigail. She angled her thin eyebrows, and the skin on her pale forehead formed worry lines.

"Mama," declared Jeremiah, "that arrangement you let Shad make with Miz Perkinson—it ain't working."

Mama's shoulders fell. "I'm near finished this here dress, Jeremiah."

"I ain't talking about no tailoring, Mama."

She leaned forward, narrowing her beady eyes at Shad. "What in heaven's name happened to you, Shadrach?"

"I—uh, had a run-in with a holly hedge, is all."

"Lord, boy."

"Mama," said Jeremiah, "I'm talking about him going up there for lessons."

"Don't get into my business, Jeremiah."

"It don't look right—our family and them Yankee-lovers."

"You don't need extra reading lessons. But I do."

Mama pursed her lips, and it was a look Shad had seen on her face many times. He knew she was irritated but didn't yet have the words to see her through.

Shad rolled his eyes and marched out the back door. He didn't want to listen to the babble. Darn that Jeremiah. Darn the Klan. He was in a tight spot, and he had to get his thoughts running straight again.

He stripped off the silk shirt, worked the pump, and got a bucketful of cold water. He took a quick drink, then dunked the shirt and scrubbed at the blood spots, but many refused to scrub clean. He rubbed the fabric against itself and rubbed some more, rubbing until his muscles ached.

The sun beat down on him and his muscles throbbed, and after a time his body curved into itself, bending over the bucket like the branches of a weeping willow. He got

to thinking about other people working hard in the sun ...
about what it might have felt like to slave over someone
else's laundry ... about the lives the slaves had lived. He remembered a time when Daddy had lectured him over it.

Daddy.

His daddy.

He'd been gone a long, long time.

Daddy hadn't taken to owning slaves. Not that he'd ever
said as much in public because words like that riled people
up. But he'd told Shad—told him that day, why, it was right
out there in the cornfield. The memory washed over Shad,
and he let the shirt slip from his hands. He stepped away
from the bucket and looked over the weeds stretching two
acres up Nine Mile Road to the tree line.

Daddy. Shad and Daddy, hoeing up weeds together—
that's what he remembered. The dawn trying to glow. The
sun having a time of it, what with a heavy fog that morning.
The stink and steam of manure on the field. The little field
his family rented from Mr. Kechler—the field they thought
of as their own, not Kechler's. They'd always worked it like it
was theirs, and maybe they'd work it again someday, if only
they could set aside enough money for seed.

On that day in the field, Daddy was pushing a lump of

tobacco around inside his cheek, and every once in a while, he spat. Just like that—he spat into the row between the corn and the pole beans and the butter beans.

Shad said, "Sure would be nice to have us a slave for all this weeding." And Shad was on the ground before he knew what hit him.

"Don't you never say that again."

How old was he then? Eight? Nine? About the age Nathaniel was now. Shad rubbed his jaw—it stung more from the shock than Daddy's wallop.

"Promise me you'll never own no slave," said Daddy.

Shad opened his mouth, but he was still sitting in the beans, collecting his surprise, and he didn't say anything right off.

He heard Daddy growl. "Promise me, Shad."

"Yessir, Daddy, I promise." He stood up and brushed off his britches and wiped his chin against his shoulder. He watched Daddy go back to hoeing. Then he tugged on a morning glory vine that had climbed up the pole beans, and said, "Daddy, I heard of some what own 'em to give 'em a better life."

"Hogwash," said Daddy.

Shad rubbed his chin some more.

"Look, Shad—they're just trying to feel better 'bout doing wrong. Slavery is wrong. A *better* life?" Daddy spit again. "There ain't nothin' better than freedom, and don't you let them tell you otherwise." Daddy pulled off his cap and looked up to heaven. After a spell, he set the cap back on his head and said, "All things whatsoever ye would that men should do to you, do ye even so to them."

Shad smiled. He'd learned that line in Sunday school and knew it well. The Golden Rule. Daddy knew the Bible upside and down. But that day—Shad wouldn't ever forget it his whole life long—that day Daddy said, "Problem with the Bible, Shad, is it don't say slavery is wrong."

Shad remembered swallowing. He didn't know how it was after all those years that he could remember swallowing. But he did. Right there beside the pole beans, he had a good, long swallow and set his head to thinking hard. Shad hadn't ever heard anybody say there was a *problem* with the Bible.

Daddy stood there, shaking his head, nudging the toe of his boot into a thistledown plant. He pressed that weed harder and harder against the red soil until the stem of that plant wasn't but dust on the bottom of his boot. After a time, he whispered, "I don't want to go."

Shad said, "Don't go, Daddy."

He said, "I got to go."

And Shad let that sit because he knew it was true. Daddy had already told them he'd prepared to enlist. He'd put it off for a year and couldn't put it off any longer. Shad said, "Jeremiah and me gonna take good care of Mama." He knew Daddy wanted him to say that.

Then Shad thought he heard Daddy crying, but he wasn't ever sure because Daddy was hugging him. One of Shad's ears got smashed into Daddy's shirt and the other smothered by his big arm. Shad felt Daddy shudder all over. They stood that way until the fog lifted itself up and became a cloud and floated far, far away.

Shad pulled his silk shirt from the bucket, wrung out the water, and hung it on the line. He'd have to iron it later. Then he scrubbed his face and arms, and the holly hedge scratches stung like the dickens. The scratches were already red, and the water made them even redder. He looked a mess.

When he went back inside, Jeremiah was hunched over the table, slurping up soup. For a moment, Shad stood there in his Willy Johnson britches, hands on hips, water dripping down his face onto his bare chest, red splotches looking like he had the pox.

Jeremiah pointed his spoon. "Trouble. Nothing short of trouble—him running back and forth to the Perkinsons.'"

Shad let his head drop and bob a spell before he lifted it again. He could guess exactly what Jeremiah and Mama had been saying while he was out back. He stood fast, finding the gumption to make his case. "Granddaddy says not to hurt business, Jeremiah. You heard him."

"Yeah, well, *other people* will send tailoring our way."

The way he said "other people," Shad knew he meant the Klan—meant brothers would look after their own. Shad curled his lip. "If Daddy was here, he'd like the idea of me getting lessons. Of me learning to read."

"Oh, listen to you, now!" said Jeremiah. "Bringing Daddy into it."

"Geez, Jeremiah—"

"Boys, boys! Heavens." Mama set aside Abigail's dress.

Shad splayed his elbows wide. "Mama, I'm real careful when I'm up there. But I don't—Mama—I need them lessons. And anyhow, they're good people—the Perkinsons. They ain't bad. So, look—tell me this. I don't understand how, if our family didn't take to owning slaves and the Perkinsons didn't, neither, now why don't that make us friendly toward each other?"

"Ignoramus," said Jeremiah.

Mama sighed. "Shadrach, Lord knows slavery was wrong. But that war—it wasn't about slavery."

"Amen," said Jeremiah. "Did them Perkinsons put that idea in your head, Shad? That the war was all about slavery? Bullshit."

"Watch your mouth, son."

Shad set both fists on the top rung of a chair. "Daddy didn't ever want us ownin' slaves."

"And we never did, never will," said Jeremiah. "We ain't talking about slavery, Shad. We're talking about coloreds who don't belong here. If folks like Miz Perkinson give them reason to stay, well, it ain't right. Them working for pennies. Taking work Clifton and me ought to get."

Shad frowned. "The war wasn't about work."

Jeremiah arched his back and narrowed his eyes. "Yeah, well, Mr. Know-It-All. Tell me then. What was it about?"

Shad shifted his weight from one foot to the other. Scratched his scalp.

Jeremiah said, "Daddy didn't fight over no right to own slaves. He fought for Virginia."

Shad nodded. "Seceding. Pulling out and forming our own country. The Confederate States of America."

"That's right," said Mama.

"Amen," said Jeremiah, still squinting at Shad, "and when you talk about Daddy, you honor his good name and his good sacrifice. You don't smear him with no slavery bullshit."

"I said, *watch your mouth, son.*"

"Sorry, Mama."

"Now, Shad," said Mama, "no one thought slavery was right. We all agree on that. But what we don't agree on— what the war changed—was how things get decided. Now Washington has more power than it ought to have. And them Perkinsons—they're like all them Yankees—they're happy the war ended the way it did. When there's something men got to decide in Washington, the Perkinsons side with them Yankees."

Jeremiah pointed a finger at Shad. "And them Yankees gonna fix it to vote a colored into office."

"Boy!" Mama gasped.

"I hear you, Mama."

"I can't even think on it."

"Well, it ain't gonna happen if we can help it, Mama. But that's what they's fixing to do."

Shad frowned. "They's fixing the vote?"

"Sheesh! How did you get so stupid?" said Jeremiah.

Shad tightened his grip on the rungs of the chair. He kept down an urge to pick up the chair and swing it at Jeremiah—plumb smash it over his head.

"They's fixing to *give* coloreds the vote," he said like he was talking to a four-year-old. "What means a colored senator might-could get himself voted into office."

Mama shook her head. "Just thinking on coloreds ruling Virginia, why, it's enough to make George Washington cry."

"And schooling them coloreds," said Jeremiah, "well, darn if it don't get 'em ready to run for office."

Mama shook her head. "That Freedmen's Bureau setting up schools for coloreds? Ain't nothing good to come of it."

"Problem with coloreds," Jeremiah went on, "is they ain't smart enough to get elected, so there's no use wasting time tryin' to teach 'em. They're so stupid, they can't even read."

"Can, too," Shad mumbled.

Jeremiah leaned in close and put his beady brown eyes in Shad's face. "What was that?" His hot breath smelled like rotten fruit.

Shad bit the inside of his cheek.

"What are you saying?" asked Mama with a can't-believe-it hush.

Shad stared at the dirt floor.

Mama rapped her knuckles on the table. "You saying you know coloreds who can read?"

Shad shook his head. "Uh, no, ma'am."

"What're you saying, then?"

Shad's nostrils flared as he took a slow breath—a breath so deep he wished his lungs would carry him up to the ceiling, up and out and away from this little white house. He let out the air, shaking his head, then nodding, making up his mind what to say, what not to say. "Look. I think—I just think—well, thing is, I don't know."

Mama frowned.

"Spit it out," said Jeremiah.

Shad rubbed a hand over his mouth. His own mama couldn't read a lick, and he knew full well that nothing good would come of talk about coloreds and book-learning. Why, if he so much as hinted about a school for colored children? No, he dared not say a thing. His head throbbed. Seconds passed.

"Mama," said Jeremiah, "I told you he was an ignoramus."

"Now, son."

"Wasting his time trying to read." Jeremiah turned from Mama to Shad. "You know what you're doing? You're making a fool of yourself—doing chores for Miz Elizabeth. You ain't never gonna read."

Shad stood, knocking over his chair. "Shut up." He ducked into the bedroom for his FEED AND SEED shirt. He should show them—prove himself—find Daddy's book and read it out loud. He could do it!

But instead he ground his teeth. He slammed a fist into the wall. He wasn't ready. He could read some now—yes, he could! But not with his thoughts in a jumble. Not right now. He pulled on his shirt, stomped a foot, and stormed out of the house.

28

A Newspaper

ALL THE WAY up Nine Mile Road, Shad's heart thumped in his ears. He swung his fists, mad at himself for not getting his thoughts straight. Angry that he couldn't begin to explain how Mama and Jeremiah were wrong. Plumb wrong. Those colored children—why, even Nathaniel could read right good. And Rachel and Eloise with their Shakespeare and such? Shad could only dream that one day his reading might come close to theirs.

No, he couldn't talk at all about those children. Right now they were in such a heap of danger, it hurt to think about them. Jeremiah had seen Nathaniel in that shed. Now Shad needed to find a way to stitch everything straight—to rip out the seams of Jeremiah's story and start it all over again. But this fabric had gotten itself all tied up in knots, and Shad couldn't set a lick of it right.

He turned on Twenty-third Street, up the hill—always a hill. Lord, this town exhausted him. He walked, and his thoughts tore up his mind. What was it about everybody thinking coloreds were stupid as mules? Maybe it was the coloreds' fault. Like Rachel herself, putting on the ignorant Negress show when she went to market. Well, then, she had only herself to blame. But she wasn't stupid! Shad put both hands on his head and squeezed.

When he got to Venable Street, he flailed his arms at a gray tabby—boo!—and the cat darted up a tree. The sun was high and soon sweat was streaming down his face. The sky was clear, and try as he might, he couldn't feel Daddy looking down on him today. He wondered what Daddy would say—how Daddy would set things right—if only he'd come back from the war. If only . . .

At Seventeenth and Main, Shad ducked under the blue and white Weaver's Fine Tailoring sign and set his hand on the doorknob. He was just about to plunge inside when a vendor caught his eye. He'd seen the man a hundred times, but today he saw him anew. The newspaperman.

He stood across Main Street at the corner of the marketplace—a colored gentleman in a shabby gray vest and trousers, crumpled white sleeves, brown shoes with holes at the toes, a flat cap on his head. A man old enough to be Shad's father, but dark enough to be Rachel's. He stood by a bundle of papers, twine around them. In one arm he carried another bundle, and with his free hand, he held a paper in the air.

Shad froze at Granddaddy's door. The newspaper. George Nelson had told him to give it a go. Bring a copy to his next lesson. Shad swallowed. He had never tried to read the paper. No point in trying—the print was small and crowded, clearly a setup for failure. But if George Nelson had thought he was ready? Shad squinted, his hand on Granddaddy's doorknob, trying to get up the courage to cross the street.

The newspaperman handed a paper to a man in a top hat and pocketed a coin in return. Shad watched him glance about for new customers, and, seeing none, he sat on the bundle of tied-up papers and wiped his brow on a sleeve. The crowds had thinned—it was late morning—and Shad knew the man would leave soon. He'd walk toward Richmond proper, where he might sell another paper outside one of the popular lunch spots.

Shad watched him wipe his brow again, then drop his head over the papers in his lap. He sat there—just sat—and Shad stared, wondering if this man, too, could read.

The man must have felt Shad's eyes upon him, for he

lifted his head. Then he jerked his chin up at Shad. He stood with a smile and held a paper aloft. Did Shad want to buy?

Shad glanced left and right, waited for a carriage to rattle past, then strolled across.

"A paper today, son?" The man's voice was inviting—warm and in hope of a purchase.

"Uh, what are the headlines?" Shad slouched for a better look.

The man shrugged. "You tell me. I don't read 'em. Only sell 'em. And, uh, beg pardon, son, but if you don't mind my asking—you okay?"

Shad frowned.

"The spots there." He pointed to Shad's arms and face. "I know a good healer."

"Oh, uh, it's nothing. I ran into a holly hedge this morning."

The man chuckled. "Okay, then. A little salt will sting but keep 'em clean, son. You want a paper?" He lifted the newspaper higher.

Shad ran a finger across the large, fancy letters at the top. THE DAILY RICHMOND ENQUIRER. He glanced at the columns and his body tightened all over. Reading this would be hard. Too hard. The print was awfully small—more like the Bible than George Nelson's primer for beginners. His eyes settled on clear block type above the columns. TUESDAY MORNING, JUNE 18, 1867.

The man thrust a finger at the text and tapped impatiently on the third of six columns. "What about that one?"

Shad glanced at the man's face and in that split second, it was the oddest thing—his eyes dulled, his gaze dropped. "A nickel," he said with a vacant stare.

Shad rubbed the back of his neck, sure that this man could read. But clearly, he was set on hiding it. Did coloreds learn reading and hiding-their-reading at the same time? Letters and blank stares? Shad narrowed his eyes, and Rachel's words came into his head. *Those who survive in Richmond reinvent themselves as circumstances dictate.*

"Only a nickel," the man said again.

Shad felt for his pocket but had no coins. A week ago he'd gotten payment for the foot mat, but those coins were safely buried in a cubby under his bed.

"I'll ask my granddaddy." He turned to cross Main Street again, but in that moment a horse and buggy were coming toward him. He glanced at the handsome open carriage, mahogany with painted red trim. Then his eyes nearly popped out of his head. His mouth fell open. On a black leather-covered bench sat none other than George Nelson and Widow Perkinson.

The little man waved wildly, and Shad froze. Good Lord. It was hard enough for him to keep clearheaded over his lie about lessons from Miss Elizabeth. Did George Nelson understand how important it was to keep their arrangement secret? Shad didn't want to be seen in public with him.

Shad glanced around. There was the baker. The fishmonger. Farmers with late-season peas and early beans. The iceman chatting with the man in the top hat. The candle maker. Many of them knew Shad was a Weaver. He couldn't run from George Nelson. But he could steer the conversation toward tailoring.

George Nelson wore the dusty gray-green waistcoat and three-corner hat. Beside him, Mrs. Perkinson looked lovely as ever with her ginger-cinnamon hair curling out from beneath a pale yellow bonnet that matched her dress—one that Shad remembered Granddaddy stitching a year ago.

"Shadrach!" called George Nelson. The carriage stopped and he climbed down to the street, hopping over a puddle from yesterday's rain.

"Sir," said Shad, extending a hand and asking rather loudly, "did you want to be fitted for that suit today?"

George Nelson frowned. "A suit? Why, here's the newspaper. Have you read this issue? Good heavens, son, what are all these scratches?" The Yankee accent pegged the little man right away as a carpetbagger, and Shad cringed, fearing that every face in the market was now looking their way.

"I took a tumble," he muttered. "It's nothing. Really."

He heard Mrs. Perkinson call, "Mr. Nelson, we've already seen this morning's paper."

"Well, Shadrach," George Nelson said, "do you have your own copy? Have you read the front page?"

Shad coughed. "No, sir. I, uh—I haven't got a nickel, and—"

"Ah, of course. Here, here." George Nelson fumbled in his trouser pockets for a coin, and Shad felt his chest tighten. His throat. His fists. He wanted to run. Wanted George Nelson to run. Wanted everyone's eyes to turn away. Couldn't people mind their own business? His thoughts raced. What a shabby suit George Nelson wore—how poorly it fitted, how odd this leprechaun looked. How he wanted to steer the man across the street and into Weaver's Fine Tailoring and away from all these people.

He coughed and collected himself. "How about that fitting today, sir?"

George Nelson raised his eyebrows.

Mrs. Perkinson called from the carriage. "I have a

student coming to the house in half an hour, Mr. Nelson."

George Nelson turned toward her. "This boy has a fine idea, Mrs. Perkinson. I think I will get fitted for a new suit today." He exchanged a nickel for the newspaper and thrust the pages into Shad's hands.

"Can you do it next week?" called Mrs. Perkinson.

George Nelson ignored her and pointed to an article on the front page. "There, Shad. What does that say?"

Shad cleared his throat. The words blurred together, and he narrowed his eyes. He set a finger under a line and studied the letters. "Uh, *Letter from Wash-ing-ton*."

"Yes, that's exactly right."

"Sir," called Mrs. Perkinson again.

He glanced up. "Yes, Mrs. Perkinson? I'll walk back to the house from here. Don't worry about me."

"But it's straight uphill."

"No problem. Shadrach can point me in the proper direction. I haven't had a good walk since I arrived."

"Really, Mr. Nelson, I think—"

She stopped abruptly. Shad turned. A figure had appeared between the carriage and the market. A tall boy who sauntered toward Shad and George Nelson, blocking Mrs. Perkinson's view.

Clifton.

Shad felt his muscles turn to jelly. His knees sagged. He didn't know if his ears filled with fuzz or the marketplace went quiet, but in that moment all he saw—all he heard— was the sound of Clifton's boots coming toward him. *Thud. Thud. Thud.*

"Who is your acquaintance?" Clifton asked, and his tone was dark and menacing.

George Nelson looked up. Way up. Clifton was a few inches taller than Shad. Today Clifton needed a bath and a shave. His pimply skin was even blotchier than Shad's holly-hedge scratches, his blond hair unkempt.

"Well, hello there, young man," said George Nelson, the little hairs in his nostrils quivering. "My, you grow them tall in this town, don't you?"

Shad said, "We're busy, Clifton. See you later."

But Clifton leaned over, thrusting his hand toward George Nelson. "Clifton Day, sir. Day like the sunshine. Howdy-do, there. Don't believe we've met."

"Mister—"

"Busy," said Shad, cutting off George Nelson. "We're busy right now, Clifton. He needs a new suit."

"Yes," said George Nelson, gesturing toward the carriage, "Mrs. Perkinson and I will be opening the Colored Normal School shortly and I do need a better suit for the opening."

"You don't say," said Clifton. "You gonna be teaching there?"

"Why, yes, young man. Yes, I am."

Then Mrs. Perkinson was at George Nelson's elbow. Shad hadn't seen her climb out of the carriage—but there she was, whispering in his ear, tugging at his arm.

"I see," George Nelson said to her. "Uh, yes, all right." Then he turned to Shad. "I'm so sorry, but the fitting will have to be another day. Apparently I have an engagement of which I was unaware."

He and Mrs. Perkinson avoided the puddle and climbed back into the carriage, and Shad let his arms fall to his sides, let his breath whoosh out. The newspaper dropped from his hand, and he stooped to pick up the pieces before they sucked up the wet ground. The carriage clattered away and he heard Clifton chuckle. He stood to see Clifton rub his chin hairs, see his eyes turn to slits.

"The Colored Normal School," said Clifton. A smirk came halfway up one side of his pimply face. "You don't say."

29

A New Recruit

FOR THE NEXT couple of days, Shad avoided Jeremiah as best he could. With every step up Church Hill, he looked over his shoulder, watching for signs of the Klan, dreading what Clifton and his brother might do. At mealtimes he kept his mouth shut. After meals, he kept busy with mending jobs. The days passed, the lessons went on, and he made deliveries around town. All the while, he kept an ear to the ground. No news was good news.

On Thursday, June 20, the Klan called another meeting, and Shad headed out the window with Jeremiah. The night was warm and clear, and Shad kept his guard up, expecting his brother to turn on him, but Jeremiah didn't. He seemed in good spirits.

When they went over the ridge and the Mechanicsville road stretched long and straight before them, they caught a glimpse of Clifton up ahead, ducking behind a tree. The moon was no more than an eyelash, and the night was mighty dark, but it was something how Shad's eyes adjusted, letting him make out shadows and shapes. The glimpse he got of a too-tall ghost—no question, it was Clifton.

Jeremiah elbowed Shad and whispered, "Let's play a trick on him," and the two of them crept into the piney woods. Shad smiled, enjoying this little trick, liking the way Klan membership could be good. Sometimes brotherhood was good.

Shad and Jeremiah waited. Sure enough, after a while, Clifton came out from behind the tree and peered this way and that. Then he turned his back and sauntered away, up the Mechanicsville road.

"Let's go," said Jeremiah.

Shad ran beside him, crouching through the pine trees. When they neared Clifton, they darted onto the road, breaking into the rebel yell.

Clifton jumped sky-high.

Shad laughed.

"Get on!" said Clifton.

Jeremiah slapped his back. "Gotcha!"

In his dying-man voice, Clifton said, "I am the ghost of Cold Harbor." Then he laughed. He gave Jeremiah a bear hug. "Put your sheets on, boys. You crazy?"

"Aw, we'll get there," said Jeremiah, unrolling the bundle under his arm. "What's on for tonight?"

"New recruit," said Clifton, but he didn't say it like he meant it. He said "recruit" like he was wink-winking under that sheet. He laughed again, then Jeremiah laughed, and Shad felt stupid because these boys clearly had a joke going and Shad didn't get it.

From the pocket of his burlap-sack shirt, Shad pulled out the piece of muslin with the two cutout eyeholes. He threw it over his head.

Then he felt Clifton's punch on his shoulder. "Well, if that ain't a god-awful disguise. For a family of tailors, you Weavers got the sorriest sheets."

Shad pushed his arm away.

Jeremiah said, "Shut up, Clifton."

"Can't your Mr. Fine Tailoring granddaddy sew you something?"

"Yeah, Shad," said Jeremiah. "You got to do better 'n that."

"Yeah, yeah, yeah," mumbled Shad. "I'll get on it."

"Get to the meeting now," said Clifton. "Bubba's up there already."

Shad and Jeremiah found their way to the house, stepping clear around a good-size pond, then up a hill. The house looked haunted. Even in the dark Shad could tell the bushes needed pruning and some windows were boarded up. Ever since the war, the countryside had right many abandoned farmhouses with fields gone to weed.

Inside, ghosts lined the walls like sardines. A lantern sat in the middle of the room. It smelled dank—stale breath and body odor.

"M-m-make room, m-make room," said one. Had to be Bubba. Good old stuttering Bubba. Shad was glad to know his buddy was there.

Everyone shuffled, and Shad found a place against the wall.

"So I was saying," came a strong voice. "We got to be *extra* welcoming to our newest recruit tonight."

Shad picked up on a wink-winking all around, and it set him on edge.

"Why we bringing him *here?*" said a ghost on Shad's left.

The strong voice said, "What's it matter?"

"What if he tells on us?"

"When we're done with him, he won't be able to tattle."

Then there was all manner of chuckling, and Shad looked from disguise to disguise and wondered who all these boys were.

After a spell Shad heard a ruckus outside and the door burst open. Somebody grabbed the lantern, and light swung around the room. An awful stench came in. It was worse than body odor. Shadows jumped and people bumped, and Shad couldn't make out much for all the commotion.

Shad saw one of the ghosts shove a boy to the middle of the room. The boy wore a blindfold and his face was hidden. His sleeve was torn and his shoes were gone. He fell to all fours, kicking like an animal. He howled, "Get your hands off me!" and it wasn't like any voice Shad had ever heard. It was high and scared.

Shad tightened all over. He understood how a voice got high when it got scared. Shad's voice got high sometimes.

He saw the boy kick, and the room broke out laughing. Then the boy ripped off his blindfold. He wheeled around, and Shad nearly swallowed his tongue. He couldn't believe his eyes.

Shad knew that kicking animal—knew it wasn't a boy.

It was a man. A little man. The new recruit—he—*oh, God.* It was Mr. George Nelson.

Shad watched three ghosts tackle George Nelson and hold him down while they got the blindfold in place again. A funny thought popped into Shad's head—he'd tell George Nelson that they'd tickled him with a feather and put a baby bird down his back and into his britches. *It wasn't so bad,* he wanted to say. *Just good old boys having a good old time. You'll laugh about it tomorrow, Mr. Nelson.*

But on the heels of that thought came another: George Nelson might not have been recruited at all.

"State your name for the record," said a ghost. The voice came from one of the officers who had been introduced his first night. What were all those titles? The Grand Cyclops. A Grand Scribe. A Grand Turk . . .

He heard George Nelson grunt.

"Where'd you get that nose?" somebody jeered.

The whole room howled. This time Shad laughed, too. Here, laughing was all right. They were just boys with cloths on their faces. Shad liked how no one could tell who he was.

George Nelson stood and ran his hands over his gray-green britches as if to brush them off, but Shad didn't think there was much point in trying. He was badly scuffed up.

His hat was gone. His oily hair was plastered to his head. Come to think on it, Shad realized his hair wasn't oily. George Nelson had something *in* his hair, and the something smelled foul.

Why, these boys had rubbed chicken shit on George Nelson. Nothing stank worse than chicken shit.

Shad watched as George Nelson put hands on hips and got a little pout on his mouth like he meant to lecture the room. He bent one leg at the knee and poked out his other hip like he had had enough, thank you. He was a schoolteacher all right.

Somebody yelled, "Pip-squeak!"

The room howled with laughter again. Shad bit the inside of his cheek.

"Your name," said the Grand Scribe again. "State your name for the record."

George Nelson refused to say his name. Somebody shoved him. Then another shoved him.

A voice said, "Get the barrel."

"The barrel! The barrel!" Now all manner of ghosts shouted and hooted and hollered and rough-handled George Nelson.

Shad saw a ghost come through the door with a large

wooden barrel. He put it down with a thunk and pried off the lid. A stench hit the room so hard, Shad's hand went to his nose. It was worse than chicken shit. They must have gotten the barrel from the docks. Rotten fish. The only stench worse than rotten fish was skunk.

Next thing Shad knew, boys had picked up George Nelson and were cramming him into the barrel. He wasn't going to fit. He was little, but he wasn't *that* little.

George Nelson thrashed to beat all.

Shad inched around the ghosts so he could see better.

George Nelson cursed up a storm. He flailed his arms and pulled off his blindfold again.

Before Shad could say "Dixie," George Nelson's hand flew at Shad. He got hold of the muslin cloth over Shad's face. Shad's disguise flew into the air. It happened so fast. George Nelson's eyes locked on his.

He saw Shad and Shad saw him.

George Nelson knew Shad and Shad knew George Nelson.

It was a second. A split second. Then Shad saw a ghost wallop George Nelson on the head. He got him right in that big nose, and George Nelson went limp. Somebody shoved the cloth back over Shad's head, and Shad couldn't see a thing.

The room erupted. Boys roared. Shad struggled to find his eyeholes. He twisted the cloth around. He couldn't see. He was in the mob and it was moving. Boys shouted and jeered. Shad heard a clatter. Something metal fell over. Was that the lantern? Where were his eyeholes?

Shad lifted the cloth and saw a ghost in front of him, a ghost beside him, ghosts all around. They were moving. He was moving. They squeezed together, through the door, out the door, onto the porch. Cool wooden planks under Shad's feet. What were they doing with George Nelson?

An awful thought came to Shad and it made his stomach lurch. It brought bile to his mouth. Lord God Almighty. George Nelson wasn't a recruit. They meant to kill him.

Shad heard a cheer go up and he looked down the hill. Was that the barrel there—rolling down the hill? The mob cheered and the barrel rolled, and it was getting away in the dark. Shad stood on the farmhouse porch, wanting to scream, to tell them, *No, stop the barrel*—but he froze with one hand over his mouth.

Fast as the cheer came up, it died down. A hush came over the mob. Shad heard a splash. The mob cheered. The barrel hit the pond. Holy, moly. It was going to fill with water. George Nelson wouldn't be able to breathe.

Then Shad heard someone yell, "Fire!"

And all hell broke loose.

Shad was pushed off the porch. Hands shoved the muslin cloth back over Shad's head. Then someone grabbed his arm. Someone was pulling him. The cloth was crooked and he couldn't find the eyeholes. He couldn't see! The grip tightened on his arm. He ran with the mob down the hill. The ground went from grass to damp and mucky and up to grass again. Then it was packed dirt and he thought they were on the Mechanicsville road.

The ghost at his arm kept pulling him. He heard boys shout and call to one another. The night crackled and roared like thunder.

"D-d-don't stop. K-keep running," said the ghost at his ear, and Shad knew it was Bubba.

"But we can't leave him in the pond!"

"C-come on!"

Bubba pulled him across the road. Now Shad's feet stuck to pine needles. He was out of breath. He smelled smoke. He tasted smoke. He felt stupid—so unbelievably stupid for not seeing right away that the boys had planned to kill George Nelson.

Slow down, Bubba, thought Shad, but Bubba kept pulling. Shad could hear him panting hard, and Shad panted, too.

Then Bubba stopped. He put a hand on Shad's shoulder and snatched the cloth from his head. "Look b-b-back now. Real quick. L-look. Then we g-g-got, we got to run."

Shad turned. The farmhouse was a brilliant ball of fire. Ghosts ran every which way like a flock of sheep from a wolf. Flames licked the sky. The fire roared and crackled. A beam crashed deep inside the farmhouse and sparks raced to the stars like fireworks.

"C-c-come on!"

"We can't leave George Nelson in that barrel."

"Who?"

"He—I—uh." The words caught in Shad's throat. *Oh, God.* Bubba didn't know him. George Nelson had never said his name.

"C-c-come on!"

"Bubba, I—I came with Jeremiah. I need to find him."

"J-Jeremiah don't n-n-need nobody. He c-can take c-c-care of himself." Bubba put two hands on Shad's arm and pulled him into the woods.

"But the fire—"

"S-s-somebody kn-n-nocked that la-lantern."

"The man will die!"

"He was g-gonna d-die anyway."

"But, Bubba—"

"Now he'll d-die faster. C-c-come on."

Shad wanted to go back for George Nelson. They'd meant to kill him! He had to get him out of that barrel. Shad was sure that he and Bubba could pull George Nelson out. He planted his feet. But Bubba was strong. He nearly yanked Shad's arm off.

"Bubba, I got to—"

"No!"

"But he—"

"You g-g-go back and you b-b-betray the b-b-brotherhood."

"Dad blame it, Bubba."

"C-c-come on!"

Bubba pulled and Shad couldn't stop him. He didn't stop him. He ran. He hated himself for running. He hated himself for leaving George Nelson.

Please, please, he begged, *please somebody save him.* Maybe word would travel fast and people would come. The fire wagons would come. He prayed, *Please, Lord God Almighty, save George Nelson. Please.*

30

A Standoff

BAM. BAM. "MA'AM? Mrs. Weaver? Official business of the government of the United States. Open up!" The voice was flat and nasal—not Virginia-born.

In a wink, the Yankees were inside the house and Shad was on the floor. In two winks' time, they had wrestled Jeremiah onto a horse and galloped off toward Richmond proper. Shad stood bruised and confused, Mama in tears.

A half hour later, Shad was on Broad Street and he ran into Rachel.

Rachel? She didn't belong there at that hour, wearing such mismatched clothes. She said something that made him angry. It was the sass in her voice—the tone when she said "sir." It was the way she said, "George Nelson saw 'the Weaver boy'" before he up and died.

George Nelson had seen "the Weaver boy" shove him in a barrel. Lord have mercy.

Shad grabbed Rachel by the wrists. Grabbed her and twisted her wrists. And then he hated himself. Hated himself for hurting her.

Then he was at Granddaddy's.

Then they were rushing through Richmond proper.

They got Sheriff Parker and the sheriff got Mr. O'Malley, and the bunch of them were headed for the Yankee jail with a lie so big, their noses would outgrow George Nelson's before tomorrow morning. *Lordy,* thought Shad, *how has it come to this?*

If Shad went along with Granddaddy and Sheriff Parker and Mr. O'Malley, and lied to the Yankees with the gin rummy story, and if they managed to spring Jeremiah from jail—Good Lord Almighty, Jeremiah would come after him. It was Shad's fault Jeremiah had been arrested. Shad's fault because he'd been too lazy to get a decent ghost disguise. Shad's fault because he'd let George Nelson see his face.

Now he marched toward the Yankee jail knowing full well that he had to make a decision and he didn't have much time. Would he go along with Granddaddy and these men and lie so they could spring Jeremiah from jail?

Or not?

How could he lie?

But how could he not?

Granddaddy was right there beside him. And Mama needed Jeremiah back—needed Jeremiah bad. But no, Shad didn't think he could lie without his face giving him away. The gin rummy story? What a cock and bull story.

Shad glanced at Granddaddy marching there on his right. In front of him marched Sheriff Parker and Mr. O'Malley. The four of them strutted smack-dab down Marshall Street toward that big brick house that the Yankees had taken over and turned into a jail. With every step, Shad's head hurt like the dickens.

They crossed over Second Street, and lookee there. Yankees on patrol half a block toward Broad. A whole slew of them. Sheriff Parker shortened his stride, and darn if Shad didn't walk right into him.

"Watch where you're going!" barked the sheriff, shoving Shad backward.

Shad lost his balance. He stepped on a sharp stone and next thing he knew, he was hopping on one foot and grabbing Granddaddy's shirt to stay upright. His ribs cried out in pain all over again. The spot where his head had hit the windowsill started throbbing.

Every pair of eyes turned his way.

Shad saw Sheriff Parker's hand go to his holster.

The Yankees' hands went to their muskets.

"Leth keep on walking," said Mr. O'Malley real quiet.

Sheriff Parker's chest puffed up and his shoulders arched back.

One of the Yankees made his chest big, too, but he was a boy—not much older than Shad. He coughed and took two steps forward. He and Sheriff Parker squinted at each other. People on foot who had thought to turn down Second Street saw the standoff and turned back.

O'Malley whispered, "Leth not do nothing here, thir."

Seconds passed. Maybe a whole minute. Shad thought back to the time Jeremiah had held a staring contest with a bunch of Yankees, and now, here was Sheriff Parker doing the same. The sheriff didn't move, so Granddaddy and Mr. O'Malley didn't move, either.

Shad fingered his sore ribs.

The Yankees shifted their feet, hands on their muskets.

Granddaddy whispered, "We got more important business than fussing with these trigger-happy boys."

Sheriff Parker nodded. He took his hand off his holster and waved it in the air. Then he folded all of his fingers but one into a fist. When Shad saw that one finger—his middle one—hanging over the street, puffing itself up for all the world to see, he felt proud all of a sudden. Proud to be one of the sheriff's people. Proud to stand up to those damn Yankees. Proud to show them they didn't belong on the streets of Richmond.

Then the sheriff picked up his pace. Shad and Mr. O'Malley and Granddaddy scurried to catch up, and Shad heard the Yankees break into jeers and laughter.

How he hated them! Mama was right about Yankees kicking the South when it was already down. Hadn't that man kicked Shad this morning when Shad was already down? He'd kicked Shad square in the ribs, which wasn't what Mama had meant, but yes, he had, and now Shad wished he'd knocked that man flat.

Those Yankees didn't belong in Richmond. Their presence here—why, they were the cause of his brother getting riled up. The cause of the Klan forming in the first place.

If the Yankees hadn't stationed themselves down here—if they had gone home and left Virginia alone after that war ended—why, Virginia would be fine. Virginia would have taken care of her own and handled her own problems. But instead, the Yankees stayed on, marching through the streets, wreaking havoc. Richmond didn't need them. Virginia had paid a heavy price, and the war was over, and she did not deserve to be under martial law.

Shad was proud to be part of the sheriff's posse. As he marched along, he heard the Yankees laugh and felt their sneers on his back, and the more he thought about them, the angrier he got. Shad fingered the bruises on his ribs and the lump on his head, and after a spell, the decision he had to make wasn't such a tough decision, after all.

Yes, he'd played gin rummy last night. He'd had quite a night—had beat all those fine men and his brother to boot. Yes, Shadrach Alfriend Weaver could play a mean hand of gin rummy.

Way on ahead up Nine Mile Road, Shad thought he could see Mama. Sure enough—that was Mama all right. She was barefoot, but even from this distance he could see a lightness in her step.

Jeremiah picked up his pace. When Mama got close, Jeremiah opened his arms and she ran straight into them. He lifted her off the ground, and she cried happy tears.

"It's okay, Mama," Jeremiah said, stroking her back. "It's okay. They didn't hurt me bad."

Mama's face was filthy, and Shad stood there, watching as Jeremiah tried to rub off some of the dirt. He was tender with her, touching her slowly, but the smudges ran deep and refused to come off.

"Baby," said Mama. "My baby. They feed you?"

"Naw."

"Come on, let's get you some supper."

Shad watched Jeremiah slip an arm around Mama's waist, half holding her up. He settled in behind them, Mama's worn blue dress rubbing against Jeremiah's britches, her mousy-brown hair hanging long and tangled, frayed thin like old silk.

Shad breathed slowly now. The sun was hot overhead, and he felt tired. It was only early afternoon, but today had already been a long day. He'd done what Mama had wanted—he'd brought his brother home. The Yankees hadn't had anything on Jeremiah other than the last words of a dying man, and they knew it. Pure hearsay. Those words couldn't hold a candle to the alibis of so many fine, white, upstanding citizens.

Shad pulled a long blade of grass and set it in his mouth. He kept his eyes peeled for threads, and sure enough, that blue piece of cloth was there—still caught in the brambles. He untangled it and slipped it into his pocket. He'd done a good job sewing the pocket. His FEED AND SEED shirt bulged there, chock-full of threads and cloth bits. With these and the pile of scrap cotton back at the house, even with all the pieces he'd taken to the Perkinsons' shed, he still had enough to braid a new foot mat. He wished he'd stayed home working on a mat last night. Wished he could go back and do yesterday all over again.

He had never meant to kill anybody, never meant to get caught up in something so wrong.

"Thank you, Shad," Mama called over her shoulder. "Thank you for bringing your brother home."

Shad sighed. He was an afterthought to Mama. It was always "Jeremiah this" and "Jeremiah that." His brother, the favorite son. "Yes, ma'am."

"Damn Yankees never would've fingered me if it wasn't for *him*," Jeremiah said with a snarl.

Mama planted her feet in the dirt road and Shad stopped on a dime, sending another jolt of pain through his ribs.

"What? You tellin' me *Shad* got you arrested?"

"No, Mama, no—I didn't mean that. Meant he was just stupid."

"Well, what then? What did they charge you with?"

"Wasn't exactly a *charge*, Mama. Not exactly. They said it was an arrest, but, really, they done brought me in for questioning."

"Questioning about *what?*"

"Well, seems there was a murder, Mama."

"Jeremiah Bradford Weaver! Murder? Lord!"

"I didn't do it, Mama. They questioned me and thought they had the right fellow, but I didn't do it."

"Shad did it?"

"No, ma'am."

"Then who did?"

"KKK, Mama. It was the Klan. But Shad and me—we wasn't there. We was at O'Malley's."

"Oh, my. My, my. I don't know, boys. I just don't know. Mercy!"

"Look, Mama," Jeremiah went on, "Shad ain't got a good enough disguise."

"Well, then, we'll get him a better one! Shadrach, why didn't you tell me you needed a better disguise?"

Shad opened his mouth, but nothing came out.

Mama stared. "Shad?"

"I—uh . . ."

"Tsk, tsk, tsk," she scolded.

Mama started walking again, and Shad watched Jeremiah lean into her ear, telling her about his ordeal with the Yankees.

Shad slowed his pace and let them get a good distance ahead. It hit him that Mama hadn't even flinched over him needing a disguise to run with the KKK.

Shad's head spun and he couldn't get his thoughts to line up. The damn Yankees. The barrel. The fire. The gin rummy lie. George Nelson—he'd been murdered last night. His teacher had died, for crying out loud! He was a funny little man, sure. But a good man. A little white man with a big nose.

Would it have mattered if he'd been Negro? Well, no. Nobody would have batted an eye if he'd been Negro. Even Rachel had understood that it was more wrong that he'd been white.

Rachel. For a spell there, he'd forgotten about Rachel. About her school. About Jeremiah's plans to burn down the shed. Good Lord, Shad was so stupid! He'd gone and helped spring Jeremiah from jail, and now he wanted to kick himself. Everything was such a mess.

Maybe Jeremiah would decide not to burn that shed. Now that the Klan had managed to kill the Yankee teacher, well, Jeremiah would leave the shed alone, wouldn't he?

A nightmare. That was it. Had to be a nightmare. Shad rattled his head. *Wake me up, nightmare.* Where had it all started? When he'd met Rachel? When he'd started those reading lessons? He'd wanted those lessons so badly.

Dern it all. This town—Shad hated this town. There wasn't anything right anymore. He hated Jeremiah and his friends. He hated the damn Yankees. He hated the Klan. He hated all the people who'd owned slaves and made Virginia fight over them. He hated the war.

He hated thinking on all the boys who grew up here and died. That big old war took Daddy away and Mama's daddy and cousin Willy Johnson and Jimmy Turner's brother, Bobby, and Miss Jenny's daddy and three sons, Abel, Nate, and Thomas, and Mr. Hanson's brother and his two boys and Mr. Kechler's boys and Harrison Woodman and Custis Peabody and Eustace Turnbull and Elijah Wallace, and Shad thought if he kept naming names, the list would never end.

31

Keep the Cause Alive

WHEN MAMA and Jeremiah got to the house, they stopped and turned and waited for Shad to catch up. Mama said, "Well, what in heaven's name did you have on last night, Shadrach?"

He looked at his feet. He didn't know how to talk to her just now.

"It was a little cloth with eyeholes," said Jeremiah. "And that Yankee pip-squeak snatched the cloth off him. He saw Shad's face and told people 'the Weaver boy' did it. That's what he said. 'The Weaver boy.' Then he died, and good riddance to him. Of course them damn Yankees thought he meant *me*, not Shad."

"Shad?"

He felt Mama's eyes pierce his heart, but he had no words for her. He let his face go blank. Dumb and happy—

was that what they called it? What good ol' boys wanted everybody to think? Screw up the face. Shrug the shoulders. Let the world think he was dumb and happy when he knew full well he wasn't either. But this way, Mama might leave him alone. Right now, all he wanted was to be left alone.

Then he saw a bit of light come into Mama's face, and it was odd the way her frown and the light crossed each other. Something had occurred to Mama, and she was trying to put two and two together. She turned to Jeremiah and said, "You told me you was at O'Malley's."

"Yeah, well. Yes, ma'am. O'Malley's."

"Now, look-a here. Your story don't stack up."

Jeremiah wrapped an arm around her shoulders. "Mama, you just remember the part about O'Malley's, you hear?"

"And what Yankee pip-squeak y'all talking about?"

"The one Miz Perkinson brought down here to teach the coloreds," said Jeremiah. "Ignorant carpetbagger."

"Oh, my, goodness gracious. I don't know," said Mama. "We certainly don't need his kind here. But I just don't know about you boys getting caught up in this. This ain't right at all. I wish your daddy was here."

When she said "daddy," her voice trembled. Next thing Shad knew, she was sniffling. Then she was all-out crying.

"It's too hard," she said. Now she was bawling. She crumpled against Jeremiah's chest. "Too hard raising you boys without your daddy."

"It's okay, Mama," said Jeremiah softly.

"Murder ain't okay. My boy getting arrested—it ain't okay." She choked on the words.

"It's okay, Mama," Jeremiah said again. "I didn't do it. Even Sheriff Parker spoke up for me. And Daddy—he'd be proud, Mama."

"Daddy," she said faintly.

"Proud we're doing right by Virginia, Mama."

"Proud." Her voice sounded to Shad like it was far, far away.

"Yes, ma'am," said Jeremiah, stroking her back. "And you know, Daddy would be Klan, too, if he was here. He sacrificed himself for Virginia, didn't he, Mama? We honor his sacrifice. We keep the cause alive. The Yankees are doing Virginia wrong, Mama. That pip-squeak—he didn't belong here. Never should've come."

"Never should have," agreed Mama. She sniffled and tried to get ahold of herself. "Daddy died a noble death, didn't he?"

"Yes, ma'am."

"And he'd turn over in his grave thinking on coloreds

running for office and getting themselves elected." Mama started bawling all over again.

"It's okay, Mama. Don't you worry yourself on it. Klan ain't gonna let that happen."

"Thank you, son. Thank you." Mama breathed deep, and each breath brought a shudder. Shad watched her pull away from Jeremiah and wipe her face in her skirt.

Then she turned to Shad with eyes so red and swollen, they looked like open wounds. "Shad," she whispered. "Shadrach, I didn't know you was Klan, son. You been growing into a man faster than I been keeping up."

Shad nodded.

Mama reached up to his shoulder and patted him. "My, my, but you've grown. Thank you, Shad, for bringing Jeremiah home. I was beside myself all day thinking on you boys. Just beside myself. Come on. Let's get you some supper. Then I'll see what fabric I've got. Shad, if you're gonna go running with them boys in the night, you need a disguise what covers you head to toe."

She gave Shad a final pat and went inside, mumbling, "Let's get us some supper."

Shad watched the door slam shut behind her, and he listened to it rattle in the frame.

Jeremiah went around back and Shad sat in the dirt,

stewing over last night's ugliness. Granddaddy had lied. And Sheriff Parker. And Shad. And Mr. O'Malley—Shad heard him say it. He'd told that roomful of blue uniforms, "Yes, sir, the boys was at my place." And because of his lisp it came out, "Yethir, the boyth wath at my plathe."

Then Shad felt the ground rumble. He got a rush in his heart like this morning when the Yankees had come bang-bang-banging their way into the house. He heard galloping. He hopped up and looked down the road. Sure enough—it was a horse. But not a posse, thank God.

Shad put up a hand to shield the sun. Was that Mr. Kechler? Well, shoot. It was. Since when did Mr. Kechler come out their way? He had to want something. Why didn't he send his colored girl, Loretta, if he wanted something?

Jeremiah came around the side of the house. Mama stepped out front.

"Well, hello there!" called Mr. Kechler as he rode up.

Shad hadn't seen him in months, and didn't remember him as friendly. Mr. Kechler was a stern man. A serious man—a businessman who had lost so much in the war, well, nobody had lost more than Mr. Kechler. Before the war he'd owned sixty-seven slaves and hundreds of acres of fields. He'd produced as much tobacco as France could buy and as much cotton as England and Massachusetts could spin. Then the war started and of course his two boys signed up. Then one of them died at Chancellorsville and the other at Fredericksburg. And if that wasn't enough, why, the Yankees came through and made off with his horses and fed his cows to their army. All his cows. Imagine that. Then his slaves went free and his beard and mustache turned from dark brown to ice gray.

Today he rode up on a fine white stallion, and that meant he had to be making money again. He patted the horse's neck and slid down his flank. He reached out a hand to Jeremiah, and when Jeremiah went to shake it, Mr. Kechler pulled him into a hug. They were both tall—both over six feet—but Jeremiah was thin and Mr. Kechler was not. His fine brown tweed vest curved over a paunch. A gold chain looped out of one vest pocket.

"So good to see you, my boy. I heard you'd been arrested and released, and I just wanted to stop by and check on you and your family."

"Yes, sir. Thank you, sir. I'm fine."

Mr. Kechler nodded toward Shad and Mama. "Mrs. Weaver, I'm so sorry there was some sort of misunderstanding about your son. I'll make sure that doesn't happen again."

His voice was deep and rich. He was the best-educated man this side of town. Shad had heard tell he'd been first in his class at the College of William & Mary.

Mama nodded. "It's right kind of you to stop by."

"Shadrach—you have grown a heap this year. You're the spitting image of your father, do you know that?"

"So I'm told, sir."

"Your mama is lucky to have you boys looking after her. The greatest blessings in the world are sons like you. I know your mother is proud."

Shad saw his mama blush. Her eyes got wet and he thought she was going to bawl again. But she didn't. She sniffled the tears back and a smile came up. She said, "As proud as the day is long."

"Amen, Mrs. Weaver. And the days are long this time of year. Amen. Sometimes our responsibilities are hard to bear." He went on like a politician throwing words at a crowd. "And it pains me to think of you and women like you, widowed by Northern aggression, living at the mercy of Yankee militias who storm our streets and terrorize our citizens. I rejoice in the commitment these fine boys feel to Virginia, and I'm honored the Weaver family is living on my property."

Shad felt a calm come over him as Mr. Kechler spoke. Shad's knees got soft and his feet held tight to the packed dirt. His heart stilled. Mr. Kechler was not going to ask for rent they couldn't pay. He wasn't asking for anything. He'd come with glad tidings—with blessings like Shad had never heard from him before.

Suddenly Shad knew something more than the calm he felt. Something about the voice. Shad had heard that rich, educated voice in the middle of other voices. In the middle of commotion and sweaty bodies. In the middle of a room, coming out from under a sheet.

Shad's eyes caught Mr. Kechler's and the man grinned. He didn't say anything because he didn't need to—the grin said it all. Mr. Kechler knew Shad knew that Mr. Kechler was the Grand Cyclops.

32

A New Disguise

EARLY ON SATURDAY, Shad stopped by the chicken coop and found the first egg. "Peep, you have no idea how long we been waiting for this!"

Peep cooed, and Shad rushed into the house, cupping the egg in both hands as if he'd found gold. Mama kissed it, then cracked the egg into a bowl and mixed it with flour and a pinch of salt and a handful of sugar and some milk that Kechler's girl, Loretta, had dropped off yesterday. She'd dropped off bacon, too. Lord, what a feast!

Mama cooked up the best griddle cakes they'd had since the war. When that bacon fat popped, darn if it didn't make little grease spots on Mama's blue sleeve. But she just pulled up quick on her apron and dabbed away the spots, all the while whistling "Dixie."

After they ate, Mama went to the outhouse. The second she was out the door, Jeremiah shoved Shad up against a wall and growled, "You owe me."

"What?"

"Don't you never again mess up so bad them Yankees nab me, hear?"

"Let go o' me. You and Clifton—you the ones what tipped off the Klan 'bout that Yankee."

"I need a report by midweek, you hear?"

"What are you talkin' about?"

"I said, *you hear?*"

"You think I'm deaf? I helped spring you from jail, didn't I? You're the hero. The Klan loves you. You ain't got to prove yourself no more. After last night, we can all lay low for a little while."

Jeremiah slammed a palm flat on the table.

Shad jumped.

"Lay low?" Jeremiah bellowed. "That's what them damn Yankees want—that we back off. You siding with them now, Shad? You a Yankee-lover?"

"No—come on. I just meant—"

"If they think a little jail time can slow us down, they got no clue. No clue how many of us there are. We gonna get 'em good. Now I said I want a head count. You *hear me?*"

Shad shook his head. "You're crazy, Jeremiah. Plumb crazy. What has got into you? What did them Yankees say to you?"

Jeremiah made a twisted sort of laugh. He opened his mouth to speak, then closed it and opened it again, as if he couldn't make up his mind whether to answer Shad's question. Seconds passed before he finally let it out slowly . . . very slowly. "Poor white trash."

Shad narrowed his eyes. "What?"

"The whole time I was in there, Shad—that's what I had to listen to. 'Poor white trash. Ignorant fool. Bigoted idiot.' If my hands hadn't been tied, I'd have flattened every one of them."

Shad swallowed.

Jeremiah put his face so close to Shad's, their noses nearly touched. He smelled of rancid grease. "Let me tell you, Shad—they messed with the wrong boy. Now, I need to know—how many coloreds are in the Perkinsons' shed?"

"You already killed the teacher. They ain't got no school without a teacher."

"They got a shed. And when I'm finished, they ain't gonna have no shed. Now I want to know exactly what time them coloreds go into that shed. What time in, and what time out, and how many of them."

Shad threw his hands in the air—backing away— washing his hands of this chore. But Jeremiah came at him, tilting his head and grabbing the front of Shad's silk shirt, pulling him in so close, so fast, Shad's nose slammed into Jeremiah's forehead.

"Wednesday," said Jeremiah with a growl. "You get me answers by Wednesday." With a shove he let go of the shirt, and Shad fell against the wall.

The back door opened and Mama came in. Shad froze. Mama looked from him to Jeremiah.

To Shad.

To Jeremiah.

"What the dickens," said Mama. "What's going on?"

"Nothing," said Shad, turning away. The words "poor white trash" throbbed in his ears, and he bit his tongue so as not to let them slip.

"Jeremiah," said Mama, "if you're staying home this morning, that front window's jammed up. Ever since that heavy rain, I ain't been able to close it proper. Can you fix that for me, son? Sand it down and whitewash it. Shad and me— we're gonna work on a disguise. Ain't that right, Shadrach?"

"Uh, yes, ma'am."

Mama rummaged through a basket of fabric pieces. "I got some heavy gray cotton in here. Been meaning to sew you some new britches. You done outgrown those Willy Johnson hand-me-downs. They're too short. And your bare feet—why, Granddaddy wants you to see Mr. Hanson this Thursday to fit you for a pair of boots."

"Yes, ma'am."

Jeremiah ran a finger along the windowsill. "Mama, you finish that dress for the Perkinson girl yet?"

"Just about, son. Got to add the lace trim. Then it needs ironing. Shad can deliver it up there Tuesday or Wednesday."

"Good," said Jeremiah. "Good thing Weaver's Fine Tailoring is keeping on good terms with the Perkinsons."

Mama folded her arms across her chest and tilted her head. "Well, now, you know your granddaddy and I ain't seen eye to eye over the Perkinson business. And what with you telling me Miz Perkinson brought that carpetbagger to Richmond, well, I don't know, son."

"I'm just saying, Mama. Just saying she's got lots of connections. Lots of friends, and we don't want to be on her bad side."

Shad bit his tongue.

Mama said, "Well, Jeremiah—you said it—that woman looks down on me and I get to grinding my teeth every time she gives us a tailoring job. Shad—you gonna handle that delivery careful, now, ain't you?"

"Yes, ma'am, he sure is," said Jeremiah.

Shad felt numb. He looked back and forth from Mama to Jeremiah. Then Mama got him to sit. She put a tin can on his head and began to take measurements.

"Lord, Mama, I don't need no rust in my hair. Got enough problems with lice."

"I'll sew fabric around the can. You ain't got to worry 'bout no rust. Now sit still. We'll do some nitpicking later on today." She threw the sheet over the can and Shad felt her measure for eyeholes. "I'm gonna sew the fake eyes up high, all right? How do you like that idea?"

"Okay, mama," he said. He didn't have the strength to argue. The one thing he knew for sure was that with Mama doing the thread work, he was going to have one of the finest-made disguises in the whole Ku Klux Klan.

Over the next few days, Shad was so beside himself, Mama kept him in bed. He ached all over—head pounding, innards rumbling. By Wednesday, he told Mama he felt better and could handle the delivery fine, but the truth was that over those days of lying in bed and trying to settle his stomach, he'd decided that he needed to warn Rachel. He didn't know how he'd go about doing it, but he knew it had to be done.

Mama asked him to pick up another bolt of fabric from Granddaddy, and he set out with the dress folded nicely in a clean burlap bag. He knew he should go to the Perkinsons' first and unload the dress—it made sense to do the delivery before the pickup—but he was still working out what to say.

Not only that, but the last thing he wanted was to run into the children—Maggie and Nathaniel and Kitty and the rest. He didn't want to get anywhere near the Perkinsons' house until long after morning lessons were done.

When he pushed open the door to Weaver's Fine Tailoring, it squeaked like always, and the little bell tinkled. He heard the start of the familiar *clip-thunk, clip-thunk* across the floorboards overhead, and he was upstairs before Granddaddy reached the top step. The room smelled of pine sap and yesterday's fish.

"Well, good morning, there, Shad. How's your mother?"

"Fine, she's fine, sir."

"You okay?"

Shad looked away. "Yeah. I mean, yessir, I'm okay."

"Shadrach, when are you and your mama and Jeremiah gonna move—" He stopped his regular litany and frowned. "Something on your mind, son?"

Shoot. How did he know? Shad shook his head. Jeremiah had made Shad swear not to tell anybody anything.

Granddaddy went back to his sewing machine, and Shad's breath started up again. He looked around the room. Looked for signs of the Klan. Looked for something— anything—that would tell him Granddaddy wasn't easy with the Klan. Something that would tell him he could spill the beans on Jeremiah.

He watched as Granddaddy pressed a foot pedal, making a wheel turn on the devil machine. He listened to the spool of thread rattle and went in close to see the needle zoom up and down. Tiny stitches appeared in the fabric. Like magic.

"Best investment I ever made," said Granddaddy. "Now, what's in that sack there, son?"

"The dress Mama sewed for Miss Abigail. I'm headed up that way to deliver it, and I just stopped by here for a new bolt of cloth. Mama said you had a new one?"

Granddaddy jerked his chin toward a bolt by the back wall.

"Sir, uh, you got anything else you need delivered to the Perkinsons?"

Granddaddy shook his head. He pumped the foot pedal and the machine whirred. Then he mumbled, "Don't know why Miz Perkinson needed no Yankee teacher up there."

Shad chewed on the inside of his mouth, wondering what Granddaddy knew and didn't know about everything the Klan had planned.

"Shadrach, what ever happened with you and that tutoring business?"

"Uh, well, I ain't been up there since that man died."

"Crying shame."

"Yes, sir, crying shame."

Granddaddy lifted his foot from the pedal, and Shad listened as the wheel stopped turning, the machine stopped whirring, the spool stopped rattling, the needle stopped its frantic up-down-up. Granddaddy pushed his chair back and it screeched on the floorboards. He sighed and crossed his arms over his black vest. "Schooling coloreds. Ain't nothing good to come of it."

"Yes, sir—them coloreds. Jeremiah was asking where Miz Perkinson schools 'em."

"Jeremiah?"

"Uh, yes, sir." There—he'd done it. He'd found a way to sneak Jeremiah into his words, and now he waited. He watched Granddaddy closely. Sure enough, Granddaddy tensed up. It was a tension nobody else would notice. But Shad was looking for it. And it was there. A flutter across his face. A twitch of his arm.

"What's Jeremiah want?"

Now Shad was tongue-tied.

"Shad?"

"Uh, yes, sir. Jeremiah—he . . . uh."

He watched Granddaddy lean forward, hands on knees—watched him push himself up. Granddaddy came in close to Shad's ear and lowered his voice. "Is the Klan planning something?"

Shad nodded slowly.

Granddaddy started pacing the room. *Clip-thunk, clip-thunk.* He took both hands to his head and sent his fingers through his hair. He rubbed his face. Dropped his head into his hands. Picked his head up. Dropped it again.

"Lord, have mercy," he said. "Miz Perkinson and her

kind keep our family in business. Don't Kechler know that?" He slammed a hand on the sewing table.

Shad waited. He knew Granddaddy wasn't really asking a question. He was just talking.

Shad felt tight all over. He'd come today with a hunch that his granddaddy wasn't easy about Klan business, and he was right. He needed Granddaddy to know that things were going on, but he was getting good at keeping his mouth shut.

33

A Warning

ALL THE WAY up Church Hill, Shad worked out in his mind what he'd say. The last time he'd seen Rachel—Friday—shoot, he felt sick thinking about what he'd done.

He didn't know what had come over him that day. He shouldn't have hurt her, and he needed to apologize again, and lordy, what a mess this was.

But right now, even more important than an apology, Shad needed to warn her. If Jeremiah found out what Shad planned, he would kill Shad. If Jeremiah and Clifton and Mr. Kechler and Sheriff Parker found out, they would— Shad rattled his head. He couldn't think about them. No, he couldn't let them make decisions for him. Not anymore.

When he got to the Perkinsons', Shad heard piano

music and knew that Rachel was home. He set the bolt of fabric on the steps and paused to take in the letters on the brown wrapping. He looked slowly at them and sounded them out. *Calico, blue, one hundred percent cotton, Frederick & Sons, Atlanta, Georgia.*

Shad breathed deeply. He could read. He wasn't quick, but he knew how to try. He could sort out letters that used to befuddle him. He smiled. *Thank you, Mr. Nelson,* he thought. *Thank you ever so much.*

Shad left the fabric on the step, straightened his long legs and skinny torso, and looked at the knocker—the molded brass lion's head. He reached for it and stopped. He remembered George Nelson rat-a-tat-tatting and couldn't bring himself to touch it.

He turned and sat on the top step. Then he put his elbows on his knees and his head in his hands. If he walked to the overlook, he'd be able to see down the hill to the James River and the canal and the train tracks. For a moment, he thought maybe everything would be easier if he threw himself in front of a train. Maybe he should—

Shad heard the door open behind him and he jumped. The music grew louder.

"Mr. Weaver," said Caroline. Her heavy eyes fell on his

silk shirt and went down his new gray britches to his bare feet. Without moving her head, she glanced from side to side. Then her eyes paused on the burlap sack. After a moment they lifted to his face. "I didn't think we'd see you here again."

Shad held up the sack and cleared his throat. "Uh, the dress for Miss Abigail."

"Ah, yes. Of course."

He waited for her to take the sack, but she didn't. She stared. The piano went on and on. After a spell, she said, "I don't think it's right for you to be here."

Shad coughed. She was right—it wasn't *right* for him to be there. Wasn't anything *right* in Richmond anymore. If he started talking about all the things that weren't right, he might never stop. *Don't get me started*, he thought.

He looked at his feet. Then he picked up his head and said, "I'm real sorry about everything what's happened."

"Just a minute," she said. And she closed the door.

Shad twisted the top of the sack into a knot. He was sure Caroline was getting Miss Elizabeth. As much as he wanted to run away, he knew he had to face her. Had to get it over with—had to let Miss Elizabeth scold him up one side and down the other.

A few minutes later, Caroline returned, and she was alone. Shad let out his breath. The piano kept playing and playing, and Shad knew Rachel was there in the front room.

He and Caroline exchanged goods—the dress for a sack of foodstuffs. He nodded and she nodded, and she went to close the door, but he said, "May I have a word with Miz Rachel, please?"

"Humph." Caroline closed the door in his face and the music got soft again. Then in the middle of a song, he heard the piano stop—just stop. Shad's ears strained to finish the tune, but he didn't know it. He couldn't end it.

The door opened.

He saw Rachel's bare feet—brown on top and lighter around the edges. He slowly lifted his head. She wore a black cotton dress, gathered at the waist. A mourning dress. Her mouth was a flat line. She didn't invite him in.

"Mr. . . . . *Lourdaud*, you have some gall to show your face on this property." She crossed her arms over her chest. "Why did you need to see *me*? My mother said you asked for me."

"Your mother?"

"Caroline."

"Oh, I didn't—"

"Why would you? Why should my family be together

when every other colored family is scattered across the South?"

"Look, I'm sorry. I just—"

Shad saw her hand move to the doorknob, ready to slam the door in his face. But she didn't slam it. She stared. "Your brother got away with it, didn't he? George Nelson was *my* teacher. *Mine*. And Eloise's."

"I'm sorry, Rachel." He felt her eyes bore a hole in his heart.

"And the irony of it is that the school—the children—they asked for *you* this morning. And yesterday. And the day before that. And Friday, too. All those days of tailoring lessons they were looking forward to, and you didn't come."

Shad shifted his weight from one leg to the other.

"Look, Mr. . . . . *Lourdaud*. I don't know as I'll ever forgive and I certainly won't forget, but let me tell you something. I am going to move on. I have a duty to my students, and they are asking about the tailoring. They don't feel Mr. Nelson's absence. They feel *yours*."

Shad kept his eyes on his feet. He deserved this tongue-lashing. Deserved every word.

"All of my students have known worse to happen to

their own Negro brothers and fathers and mothers and cousins than what happened to George Nelson."

"Look, I—Rachel—" Shad brought his head up and for the first time let his eyes settle on hers. "I came here to warn you. You got to leave town. Go. Just go."

"What? Speak up, for heaven's sake."

Shad took a step backward so as not to stand too close. Then he leaned forward and whispered. "They plan to torch the shed."

"What about the shed? I can't hear you."

His throat tightened and wouldn't let him get the words out. He came in close and swallowed. He whispered, "The Klan means to torch your school. You got to warn the children. Leave town for a few days. It ain't safe for you here."

She whispered back. "The Freedmen's Bureau supports schools for Negroes. The Klan can't burn our schools."

"Oh, yes, they can, Miz Rachel."

"They'll be arrested."

"They vouch for each other. If the Yankees take 'em to court, they got—what did he call it? *Alibis*, what means they lie for each other."

"We have support in this town."

"You got enemies. Every shop owner and ironworker

and glassblower. Every lawmaker. The sheriff. They're all KKK."

"And just exactly when do they plan to burn it?"

"Tonight. Well—first thing in the morning. Once all the children get inside."

Rachel got quiet. It wasn't like her to be quiet. The only time he'd seen her quiet was the time he'd twisted her wrists. He looked at her—looked at the sun shining into her eyes—and his thinking got scattered. He didn't know what to think anymore. He was in trouble, that's what he was thinking. He had betrayed the Klan and they would shove him in a barrel and roll him into a pond.

34

A Torn Skirt

"ARE YOU WILLING to disclose to Mrs. Perkinson what you have told me?"

Shad shook his head no.

But she said, "I'll get her. Stay there." And she was gone. Just like that. The door closed in his face.

The last person in the world he wanted to see was Miss Elizabeth. He couldn't tell her any of this. He'd come to deliver Abigail's dress and warn Rachel. That was all. When Jeremiah and Clifton came to torch the shed, he prayed that the colored children would be home safe in their beds. School temporarily closed on account of the teacher out of town for a spell. That was all.

He knew Rachel was telling Miss Elizabeth everything right now, and he knew he should run. But he couldn't bring himself to move.

"Mr. Weaver?" announced Caroline. "Mrs. Perkinson will see you now."

Shad left the bolt of fabric on the front step and slunk into the house. Miss Elizabeth stood in a simple black dress, arms folded across her chest. It occurred to him that Rachel had stood just like her, arms folded across her chest. Rachel had learned all of her ways from Miss Elizabeth.

"Mr. Weaver. Well, well, well. I'm surprised you have the gall to show your face in my house."

He made his face blank. "Ma'am?"

"Don't pretend, Mr. Weaver. And don't intimidate my girls. If you have something to say, say it to me."

Shad wrung his hands. He looked at his feet. He coughed. He knew he deserved her anger, but he hadn't come here to admit anything. What had happened, happened. George Nelson had died. But that wasn't the end of it. More was going to happen.

He watched her pace the room. She pointed at the crimson brocade settee and Shad sat.

She paced. With one hand to her brow, she said, "In this house, we are grieving the death of George Nelson."

"Yes, ma'am. I'm sorry he died."

"When you so ruthlessly *murdered* George Nelson—"

"No! No, ma'am, I didn't."

"Don't lie to me."

"I didn't kill him!"

"I know Sheriff Parker better than you might imagine, Shadrach. That man pulls strings all over town, but he doesn't fool me, and neither do you."

"I swear, ma'am. I swear on—" Shad jumped from the settee and ran to the bookshelves.

"A Bible—is that what you're looking for, Shadrach? So that your sworn statement will be as believable as John Parker's statements? Or David Kechler's? Ha."

Shad didn't move. His back was to her, so she couldn't see his face in that moment, and he was glad she couldn't. He didn't know what Miss Elizabeth knew.

He straightened slowly and turned around. "Ma'am, I came here today to deliver Miss Abigail's dress. That's all."

She tilted her head to one side and squinted at him. "I hear that the Klan means to burn our school at first light."

"You ain't heard nothing from me, ma'am. I came with a delivery from Weaver's Fine Tailoring. That's all, ma'am."

Shad thought she was going to smack his face. He got ready for her little repeat-after-me business.

But instead, she said, "I see." She sucked in her cheeks and stared at him for a long time. She paced some more.

"All right, then, Shadrach. I understand. And I appreciate your coming today." Miss Elizabeth turned toward the hallway. "Caroline! Would you please bring me that sage skirt?" Then she pointed at the settee and addressed him like a dog. "Sit."

Shad went back to the settee.

Caroline brought the skirt, and Miss Elizabeth held it up and out. She turned it this way and that until she found a straight seam. Then Miss Elizabeth clenched her fists around the seam and yanked.

Shad nearly jumped out of his seat. She was ruining that skirt!

Miss Elizabeth smiled. "Here," she said, handing it to him. "Please bring it back the next time you need to warn us. Do you understand? You need not say a thing. Just return the skirt on a day that *suits you*."

Shad didn't know what to say. He looked down, taking in the fact that Miss Elizabeth understood. *She understood!*

"Uh, ma'am?" Shad stood. "Miz Elizabeth, if it's a straight, simple seam what's ripped like this, well, your coloreds can fix a straight seam. Anybody can fix a simple, straight seam. You don't need no tailor for this."

He saw her face go into a funny, crooked smile. "How

bright you are, Shadrach." She took the skirt, looked it over, and yanked again. This time a ragged tear ripped sideways, fraying the cotton.

Shad ground his teeth.

"There. How's that? Have I torn it enough for your grandfather to mend? Or your mother? Or you, Shadrach? Perhaps you can mend it yourself. You're quite the tailor now, aren't you?"

"Uh, yes, ma'am."

"Be sure to return it on a day you need to warn us, do you understand? We won't *need* it until then."

"Yes, ma'am."

"And Shadrach, before you go today, the proper English is: *You haven't heard anything from me*, and *You don't need a tailor.* The double negative is improper."

"Beg pardon, ma'am?"

"*You haven't heard anything from me.* Say that one first, please—*you haven't heard anything from me.*"

Shad walked slowly down Twenty-eighth Street toward Nine Mile Road. He carried a sack of food and a bolt of blue calico fabric wrapped in brown paper. Under his shirt, he held a sage skirt, rolled up as small as he could get it, and tucked beneath an arm. As he walked, it rubbed against bruised ribs, and he thought to shift the bolt, sack, and skirt into different positions so that nothing would rub, but he didn't make the shift. He let the rub hurt. He deserved to hurt.

Way up ahead he saw the break in the tree line where his family's little house sat. He slowed his pace and a shudder went through him. So much was so wrong.

He had up and befriended a colored girl. Rachel. Was that where it had all started to go wrong? He'd let himself get sucked into that crazy world of hers—that Perkinson household—that amazing place. And she had dared to let him sit in her classroom. She'd opened her school to him, and now her school would go up in flames tonight.

Because of him.

Shad went inside. Mama was running an iron over a damp linen skirt, and steam was billowing up. *Pssst. Pssst.* The fabric sizzled. Her hand and the handle of the iron were wrapped in rags. Something simmered at the cookstove. Smells of pork fat and butter beans. Shad set down the sack and the bolt of fabric.

Mama's eyes went to the sack. "That from Miz Elizabeth?"

"Yes, ma'am."

He watched her pull the cloth strips from the iron's handle and set the iron in the cookstove fire. Then she unwrapped the cloth strips that protected her skin from the heat. She opened the sack and laid out the foodstuffs—cornmeal and sugar and a pouch of tobacco—turning each one over as if looking for a reason to return it.

Shad fingered his shirt with the sage skirt folded underneath. He didn't want to talk to Mama right now. He said, "I'm gonna check on the chickens," and he went out.

He needed to hide the sage skirt. Breathing was easier away from Mama, but the deeper he breathed, the tighter his fists. He wore a thin coat of sweat.

He couldn't keep his mind off Jeremiah. He'd have to report to his brother tonight. Eight children. They'd arrive just before the crack of dawn, stay about an hour and a half, maybe two. That was all. There. He'd make his report after supper tonight, and early tomorrow morning, Jeremiah and Clifton would torch the shed.

The bed tilted when Jeremiah got up in the night. Shad heard the sound of straw crunching. Feet sliding into boots.

A boot hook dropping to the dirt floor. Cool, damp air slipping through the window. The sweet smell of chestnut blossoms. Creepers singing by the pond.

Shad pretended he was asleep, curled in a ball. He heard Jeremiah's britches brush the windowsill. Heard his body drop to the ground. Funny how he kept going out the window now that Mama knew full well they were Klan. He might as well walk straight out the front door.

Jeremiah ran into the night, and Shad rolled onto his back. His thoughts were a jumble. He wanted to know what Jeremiah was doing each minute. How far up Nine Mile Road was he now? How long would it take him and Clifton to get to that shed and send it up in flames? Where was Rachel? Where were Miss Elizabeth and Caroline and Eloise right now? Nathaniel and Maggie and Kitty?

Shad wanted to follow Jeremiah. But no, he didn't dare. One look at his face and everyone in the Klan would know he'd warned Rachel.

35

Lord Have Mercy

SHAD HEARD BIRDS chirping and opened his eyes to sunlight coming in at a slant. He'd fallen asleep. He jerked his head to see Jeremiah's side of the bed. Empty. His brother hadn't returned.

Shad slipped to the outhouse, sure to see Jeremiah coming or going. But no. He wasn't at the outhouse. Or the well. Or the chicken coop.

Shad gathered eggs—one each from Peep and Poke—and found Mama at the cookstove. "Look, Mama. Two eggs today."

"Where's your brother?"

"I don't know," he said, cringing over yet another lie. He knew full well where Jeremiah had gone. He just didn't know what had happened when he got there.

Mama fried the eggs and set them on plates with last night's leftover corn bread. Shad wasn't hungry. He stared at his egg and Mama stared at hers, too. He remembered days with nothing to eat, and that made him put a bite to his mouth.

After a time he said, "I'll save this corn bread for later, Mama."

She nodded and wrapped it in a piece of cheesecloth. Then she took her place in the chair by the window and hemmed a fancy shirt for Doc Moore. She put in two stitches, looked out the window, two more stitches, craned her neck.

Shad picked up the scraps of fabric and threads for braiding into a foot mat. His fingers shook. "You want me to find him?"

Mama shook her head. "Near the death of me the day they arrested him. Both you boys was gone, and I cried the day long. No, Shad, you stay right here. Give me peace of mind."

"Okay, Mama."

At the sound of a horse, Shad and Mama jumped up. But it wasn't Jeremiah. Wasn't anybody they knew. They sat down again—Mama by the window, Shad by the table. They didn't talk. They waited. And stitched. And waited.

After a spell, Shad heard a *clip-thud, clip-thud*. Granddaddy. It wasn't like him to come out their way in the morning.

They met him in front of the house, and Granddaddy didn't get two words out of his mouth before Mama started crying. "Oh, no. No, no, no."

Granddaddy hugged her. "He's okay, Adeline. Just beat up, is all."

"Where is he? Where's my baby?"

Granddaddy closed his eyes and buried his face in her shoulder. "Libby."

"No!" Mama wailed. She pushed away from Granddaddy. She threw her hands in the air, let out a scream, and would have collapsed on the ground if Shad hadn't caught her. He patted her back gently like patting a baby, and her tears wet the front of his shirt. "He's just a *boy*," she mumbled.

Shad set his head on top of Mama's. Libby Prison. Good Lord. During the war, Union prisoners had been locked up there, and, ever since, the Yankees had controlled it. They held former Confederates there—men who'd refused to relinquish their arms, men who'd attacked the roaming Yankee militias, men who'd stood up for the South long after the war had ended. Granddaddy had called them political prisoners. Said they never got a fair trial. Lots of men who went into Libby Prison never came out. Some got a trial and a walk to the gallows. Many died of dysentery.

"Not Libby. Lord, not Libby," whispered Mama.

Shad walked her into the house. She slumped into a chair and buried her head in her hands. "I knew something was wrong this morning. I just knew it."

"We'll get him back, Mama," Shad told her, trying his best to sound strong.

"Jeremiah. My baby," she mumbled. "What'd they get him for?"

"Taking a torch to a shed," said Granddaddy.

"W-why on earth? Where?"

"Perkinson house."

"No! Why would he burn her shed?"

"School for coloreds."

Mama gasped.

"Word is that some Yankee friends of Miz Elizabeth were staying at the house. They caught the boys in the act."

"Them Yankees have it in for Jeremiah," cried Mama. "Last time they thought he'd murdered a man, and they questioned him—"

"We ain't just talking about questioning, Adeline."

"But why *Libby?*"

"Caught 'em red-handed, is what I'm telling you."

"Lord, help us."

Granddaddy ran a hand through his silvery hair. His mustache hung limp. He was in sore need of a shave. "An offense against a colored school is an offense against the Freedmen's Bureau, and that's a government agency."

"How we gonna get him out?"

"We'll see."

Shad listened and didn't say a thing. If he talked, he might give away how he'd betrayed the Klan.

Mama shuffled to the cookstove and mumbled something about last night's butter beans. "I got to feed him."

Granddaddy paced. *Clip-thud, clip-thud.*

"I want to see him," Mama announced.

"They might not let you see him."

"Then I'll stand outside and Jeremiah can wave to me from the window," said Mama.

"Boys get shot if they lean out windows."

"Not no more! That was during the war."

"Just saying, Adeline. Just saying."

"Well, I mean to see him," said Mama with resolve.

"Lord," whispered Granddaddy, shaking his head. "Lord have mercy."

By the time Shad, Granddaddy, and Mama got to the curve in Nine Mile Road, Mama was limping so hard, Shad needed to hold her up at the waist. Her scuffed shoes had rubbed her ankle raw, and Shad doubted she'd make it all the way to Libby—all the way across Shockoe to Cary Street.

Around the curve came a horse pulling a rickety farm cart.

"Well, if it ain't Bertram Dabney!" shouted Granddaddy.

"Henry Weaver! How you been?"

"Been better."

Mr. Dabney's face was long and narrow, with a dusty beard that pulled it even longer. Shad watched him tip his beat-up cap at Mama as he leaned over the neck of his horse—a spotted gray mare, flea-bitten with one ear lopped off. Shad thought she was a sad-looking horse, but something about the way her big black eyes took him in made her seem a thoughtful and intelligent animal. She reminded him of Daddy's horse, old Mindy-girl, who had enlisted with Daddy and never come back.

"Listen, Henry," said Mr. Dabney quietly, but not so softly that Shad couldn't hear. "Word is your grandson got picked up last night."

Mama burst into tears, and Shad wrapped his arm tighter around her.

"Oh, ma'am, I'm so sorry. Adeline? I didn't recognize you."

Mama whimpered.

Granddaddy said, "Say, Bert, we're heading to Libby right now. You wouldn't by chance be able to give us a lift, now, would you?"

"Libby?" gasped Mr. Dabney.

"So we've heard."

"Climb on in. I just unloaded kale and collards down Shockoe. Y'all don't mind riding in the cart?"

"Much obliged."

This was a stroke of good luck. Shad held the pot of butter beans Mama had brought for Jeremiah, and the men lifted her into the farm cart. Granddaddy sat up front with Mr. Dabney, and Shad and Mama rocked and bumped along in the back. As they rode, Mama and Shad peeled up scraps of kale and collards from the floorboards. They wiped off the dirt and added the hearty greens to the pot, making a fine little feast for Jeremiah. The whole ride, Shad heard Granddaddy and Mr. Dabney talking up a storm, but it was politics and government and taxes, and Shad couldn't keep it straight.

When Mr. Dabney stopped at the Cary Street corner, he and Shad helped Mama from the cart. Mr. Dabney made a show of acting particularly careful, leaning in close to Mama, then straightening up tall, preening with pride over the opportunity to help a Confederate widow.

Before he rode away, Shad shook his hand and said, "Thank you for the ride, sir. And, uh, thanks for the chickens, too."

"Don't mention it, son. Glad y'all could use 'em. They laying eggs yet?"

"Yes, sir. One each this morning."

"Good to hear, son. You take care o' your mama now."

"Yes, sir."

Mr. Dabney nodded toward the prison. "Good luck," he whispered in a tone that said they'd surely need it.

Shad watched the rickety cart clatter away, then turned to take in the desolate brick building. It sat on the south side of Cary, stretching a whole block east from Twentieth Street. The prison had once been a tobacco warehouse, then a dry goods supply warehouse, then a warehouse for people—Yankee prisoners first, and now whomever the damn Yankees wanted to lock up. The canal ran along its far side and the James River beyond that.

Shad put a hand to his stomach, wishing for a privy

right now, wishing he'd never tipped off the Perkinsons, wishing he'd never met Rachel, never come to care about those colored children, never joined the Klan.

The heavy wooden door creaked as Granddaddy pulled it open. Three boys in blue uniforms looked up from plates of biscuits and bacon, grits and gravy, and Shad's mouth watered. His nose hadn't smelled gravy this good since—he didn't know. He couldn't remember the last time.

The oldest-looking boy stood but didn't offer a hand. "What can we do for you?" His voice was flat and tight, his upper lip fuzzy. A clump of dirty blond hair fell over one eye.

Granddaddy nodded. "This is the mother of one of the boys you arrested last night. She's brought him some breakfast." Shad was struck by how soft and warm Granddaddy's voice sounded, not threatening in any way. He seemed older here in front of these Yankees, and in an odd way, even pitiable. An old man helping a poor woman plead her case.

The Yankees chuckled. The standing one sat down and ate some grits.

Shad, Mama, and Granddaddy waited.

The Yankees kept eating.

After a spell, Granddaddy said, "We'd be much obliged

if you'd give this boy's mother a moment with her son."

One of the Yankees pushed his empty plate aside and pulled out a pouch of tobacco and a square of paper, and rolled up the dried leaves. Another Yankee sauntered toward Mama to stick his nose in her pot. Shad tensed up, ready to slug that boy if he so much as touched Mama. But he didn't touch her.

The door behind Shad swung open and a burly, squat Yankee came in. The other three saluted him.

"At ease. What do we have here?" said the burly one. He was older than the boys and had a scar across his nose, running down into a thick brown mustache.

"Family of the accused," said one.

"Which one?"

"Weaver," said Granddaddy proudly.

The boy with the tobacco smirked. "Wants to *see* her son." He said "see" so oddly, Shad couldn't catch his meaning.

He saw the burly one raise his eyebrows as he came around the table, and the others shuffled out of the way to let him sit. The body odor shuffled, too.

"Did they tell you what your son did, Mrs. Weaver?" the burly one asked.

344 • A. B. WESTRICK

Mama shook her head.

"Let me put the situation in perspective, ma'am. He's charged with arson, attempted murder, and destruction of property belonging to a federal agency."

Mama shook her head faster now.

"He lay in wait at a schoolhouse on the property of Mr. Parks Randolph Perkinson, deceased. Widow Perkinson was at home, as were four servants. Children arrived at sunup to commence lessons. Your son was seen barricading the door to the schoolhouse, then setting fire to the building."

"No!" Mama cried. Granddaddy put an arm at her waist.

"There were eight students and two teachers inside at the time."

Shad's knees buckled.

"My men arrested your son, and he—well, ma'am—your son put up quite a fight."

Mama was crying now.

Attempted murder, was that what he'd said? *Attempted.* So did that mean Rachel hadn't died? The children hadn't died?

"Ma'am, why don't you leave that breakfast here with my men, and we'll be sure to get it to your boy? You don't want to see him this morning."

Mama snorted and threw her head high. "I came here

to see my Jeremiah, and I ain't leaving till I see him."

The burly Yankee rolled his eyes. He nodded at the others. "I don't suppose it will hurt to show this woman the monster she created."

Mama raised the pot of beans to throw it, but Granddaddy snatched it away. Shad grabbed her elbow, and Mama hissed like an angry cat.

Two of the Yankees crossed the wide, dusty floor planks and went out the back door.

Shad tried to picture the shed—the schoolhouse. Eight inside. He wanted to know more, but he didn't dare ask.

They waited. And waited. Shad shifted his feet. Finally, he heard scuffling. Dragging. Rattling noises toward the back. Then the door opened, and he saw a blue uniform. A Yankee came through the door sideways, pulling Jeremiah by an arm.

Jeremiah looked bad. Shackles on his ankles—Shad saw them first because Jeremiah was bent over and had trouble walking. His brother's boots were gone, his britches muddy. His shirt wasn't white anymore. It was torn and bloodsoaked. His arms were tied behind his back. His face—*God help him.*

Mama slumped and Shad caught her.

Jeremiah's face—Lord, his face was plum and watermelon pulp. His mouth hung open. His lips and one eye were swollen purple.

Mama pulled away from Shad and flailed her arms. "What did you do to him?"

Granddaddy growled. "This is a travesty."

The burly Yankee shrugged. "You demanded to see him. We obliged. If your boy hadn't resisted arrest, I promise you he wouldn't be in this condition this morning."

"He needs a doctor," said Mama.

"Doc Moore stopped by first thing today. He checks on our inmates every day, ma'am."

Jeremiah coughed. Shad watched a thin line of red-tinged drool fall from his split lip and go all the way to a little puddle on the floor. "Mama," Jeremiah whispered.

The room went silent.

"Mama, I'll be okay."

Mama reached her arms toward him.

Granddaddy held her back.

The Yankees held Jeremiah. They weren't going to let Mama hug him, and it was just as well. Jeremiah had to be aching all over. It hurt to look at him.

"I don't think he can eat yet, ma'am," said a Yankee.

"Maybe in another day or two. But we sure as hell don't want that gruel. You leave it here, and we'll get it to him when he's ready."

Shad saw Mama's nostrils flare.

Granddaddy said, "Come on, Adeline." To Jeremiah he said, "We'll be back, son. You get some rest. I'll meet with Sheriff Parker today, and you just hold on there. We'll get you out of here."

Jeremiah nodded.

Granddaddy guided Mama to the front door, and the Yankees opened the back to drag Jeremiah away. As Granddaddy and Mama stepped out front, Shad heard Jeremiah whisper his name. He turned.

"Shad," Jeremiah said again, and it seemed to take all his strength. He opened his mouth to talk, then paused to watch Mama and Granddaddy get all the way outside.

A Yankee pulled Jeremiah's arm. Shad saw a flash of anger cross his brother's beat-up face, and Jeremiah shoved his shoulder into the Yankee, forcing the boy to let go. The Yankee let go all right, but he laughed. The other Yankees laughed, too. They knew Jeremiah couldn't go anywhere.

"Shad," whispered Jeremiah. His voice cracked and his face winced in pain. "It'll be a while 'fore I get home.

You take care of Mama, you hear me? Whatever happens to me—don't you never let nothing happen to Mama. You hear?"

Shad nodded. "I hear you."

Then the Yankees dragged Jeremiah through the back door.

36

The Next Time

AS THEY WALKED up Twentieth Street toward Main, Shad could smell the James River and was glad for it. This Shockoe smell—it was nothing after that stench in Libby Prison.

Mama limped so badly, Shad and Granddaddy had to work together to hold her up. After a bit Granddaddy said, "Adeline, stay the night in Shockoe."

"Lord, no. Take me home."

"It's too much to get you all the way out Nine Mile."

Thank you, Granddaddy, Shad thought. Weaver's Fine Tailoring was so close—just another half block to Main Street, then three blocks west.

They shuffled along in silence, and when they got to Main, Mama took a deep breath. "All right, then. But only for one night."

Over her head, Shad's eyes caught Granddaddy's and they shared a look of relief. Shad knew Granddaddy would talk her into staying longer. Not just staying, but moving to the shop. With Jeremiah locked up in Libby, it made sense. Mama could visit him easier. Shad could fetch the chickens. He could put in more tailoring time instead of running deliveries from Nine Mile Road and back.

When they turned on Main, they could see that a crowd had gathered ahead. People were there for market, of course, but also because Weaver's Fine Tailoring sat on the corner, and word was out that the Weaver boy had been arrested.

Shad felt Mama tighten. Then she wiggled for him to let her go, and he watched her brace herself for the walk toward the crowd. Mama picked up her head, made a funny little laugh, and wiped her face with the back of a hand.

Then she and Granddaddy and Shad walked forward.

When they got to the Union Hotel at the corner of Eighteenth and Main, a flat-faced woman with curly dark hair saw them and called up the street. "Adeline Weaver!" She rushed toward Mama, and other ladies followed. Soon a slew of bonnets circled around her.

"How is your boy, Adeline?" asked the flat-faced woman.

"He's fine," said Mama, and Shad marveled at the way she lied without pause or even so much as a blink. "Doing fine," she went on. "We just come from Libby. Took him a nice breakfast."

"Libby? Lord, Adeline!"

"What are they charging him with?"

"There must be some mistake."

The voices of the ladies blended, one into another, until Shad couldn't hear them or Mama anymore.

Granddaddy tugged at Shad's sleeve and nodded toward Weaver's Fine Tailoring—one more block down Main Street. "Might have some customers today, Shad. You bring your mother along soon now, will you?"

"Yes, sir," he said, watching as Granddaddy limped toward the shop.

Shad took in the sights past Granddaddy—the hustle of people going to and from the farmer's market. Stovepipe hats, kepis, forage, and flat caps. Print skirts, aprons, and bonnets. Men puffing on pipes. Farmers wrapping onions and rutabaga in newsprint, and pocketing pennies in return. Chickens, flowers, fish, cornmeal. When Mama was ready, they'd stop at their choice of the tables that stretched the entire block from Seventeenth to Sixteenth Streets.

He rubbed his eyes. It had been a long day already, and the sun wasn't quite overhead. He tried to remember when he'd last eaten. It had been early—a fried egg. He and Mama needed a bite of something more. Shad would find the baker's stand first—a biscuit might settle his innards.

Then Shad's eyes caught a black kerchief, and he froze. He stared.

She was there, bending over a child. Not just one, but a group of children—four, five, six, seven of them. She was dressed in mourning clothes and putting something into each little outstretched hand. The children were putting the somethings into their mouths. Rock candy, perhaps?

One by one, delight came across their faces. Kitty twirled with outstretched arms. A boy bounced up and down. Gabriel.

Shad watched Rachel put a hand on Maggie's head, then give her a hug. She rubbed her nose against Maggie's and kissed her little cheek, and Maggie skipped away and back again. Then Shad saw Eloise, too. She was coming up Main Street with Nathaniel, and they were carrying brown sacks.

Shad glanced beside him at Mama and the ladies who were chattering like squirrels beneath the wrought-iron fire ladders of the Union Hotel. Then he looked back down the block at Rachel and Eloise and the little ones. The Yankees had said the shed was full—eight children and two teachers—when Jeremiah set that fire. That meant someone had gotten them out, all of them, safe and sound. And now they were here.

It was just like Miss Elizabeth to send them to market for a treat after such a fright. Send them out to hold their heads high. Show the Klan they weren't going to be intimidated. No, the Perkinsons didn't run from trouble.

Shad turned to check that Mama wasn't watching him watch Rachel. She wasn't. The ladies were tipping their foreheads into Mama's. Rubbing her sleeve, patting her back.

Then Shad's eyes were back at Main Street. At the colored children. Lookee there at them, sucking on that candy as if they could suck away all the hatred coming their way.

Shad's head spun. Back and forth he turned. Mama beside him. Rachel and the children down the block. And past them another half block was Granddaddy. He'd made it to the front of Weaver's Fine Tailoring at Seventeenth Street, and a group of men were talking with him. They stood in their dark vests and trousers, smoking pipes and gesturing this way and that.

Shad couldn't hear a thing they said. Something told

him he didn't want to hear, anyway. Something else told him he'd heard it all before. And he'd hear it all again.

He was one of them. A good old boy. A Confederate son. He'd sworn allegiance. The next time the Klan called a meeting, it wouldn't be Jeremiah or Clifton telling him to put on his sheet. It would be Granddaddy.

His very own granddaddy would tell him when they were heading out and where they were going. Shad would wear his disguise—the best tailored ghost disguise in all of Richmond. He'd go and listen well. He'd keep his ears to the ground and catch wind of whatever the Klan was planning, and he'd . . .

A shiver went through him. Shad looked at his feet. Rubbed his eyes. Ran both of his hands through his hair. He stood that way for a minute or two, scratching at his scalp. Staring at his dirty toes. Whatever the Klan planned, if it had anything to do with Rachel or the Perkinsons, Shad would deliver that sage skirt. He'd make a quick delivery, and wouldn't say a thing. Not one word.

A funny feeling came over him. A feeling like someone's eyes were on him. Shad brought his head up, and there they were. Right there.

Rachel's eyes.

Still half a block down, but fixed cold on him, her head tilted to one side—face blank, mouth flat. He looked at her, and she at him, and they stood like that, half a block apart while the hustle-bustle swirled around them.

He wanted to tell her how relieved he was to see her. How he knew he'd be able to sleep tonight because he'd seen her safe. How he would make her proud—he knew he would! He would keep reading—keep focusing when letters flipped and blurred together. Keep trying. And he hoped the children would keep stitching—even if he couldn't be their teacher anymore.

Rachel. He wanted to tell her all of that. Wanted to shout *Amen!* that she and the children were still alive. But he didn't dare say anything. Didn't dare approach her. Didn't smile. Didn't even move. He just looked at her and held his face still.

AUTHOR'S NOTE

Shad and Rachel's story is fiction. Scattered newspaper articles hint at the presence of the Ku Klux Klan in Virginia during the post–Civil War years (Reconstruction), but little if anything has been written about Klan activity in the Richmond area. Books about Reconstruction tend to focus on the political history of the time, especially the Thirteenth, Fourteenth, and Fifteenth Amendments to the United States Constitution—amendments that abolished slavery, provided civil rights for all, and gave African American men the right to vote.

Much of our modern understanding of the South comes from books like *Gone with the Wind*, but historical documents reveal that, unlike the main characters in that novel, the vast majority of white Southerners were not landowners or slave owners. Most were small-time farmers and tradesmen, and many were illiterate. Those who opposed slavery refrained from speaking up against the landowners. The boys and men who fought for the Confederacy were a diverse group whose motives ranged from love of their birthplace and dreams of glory, loyalty, and honor to defense of property and legal arm-twisting (they were drafted). Many of those fortunate enough to survive the war returned home to cities ruled by Northern militias.

In this novel, I tried to depict the tensions ordinary, impoverished, and poorly educated white Southerners might have felt during the period of Reconstruction. They were grieving massive losses of property, friends, and family members while struggling to understand and adjust to enormous political and economic changes.

My research led me to interview descendants of Southern soldiers, many of whom have remained staunchly anti-Yankee to this day. When I asked why such sentiments linger despite the fact that the war ended in 1865, some said the anger stems from a feeling that Northerners had belittled them. The war was over and the South had been defeated, and yet "Yankee aggressors" patrolled the streets. "The North kept kicking us even though we were already down. The United States treated Japan and Germany after World War II better than the North treated the South after the War Between the States." Anger over defeat, humiliation over postwar treatment, and fears about the political power African Americans might yield at the voting booth together fueled the rise of the group that came to call itself the Ku Klux Klan.

In late 1865 or early 1866, a group of young men in Pulaski, Tennessee, started the Klan as something of a social club—a brotherhood for soldiers who had returned from the war without jobs, without money, and often without homes, as the Northern army had burned much of the South during the war. The founders came up with odd rituals and titles (like the Grand Cyclops), and maintained an air of secrecy as a way for bored, disaffected men to entertain themselves.

As the Klan grew and new chapters formed, some members began to commit crimes while wearing their ghostly garb. Soon a group that had formed as a brotherhood became defined by lawless acts of violence. The organization became known for terrorizing blacks, Jews, immigrants, and anyone they didn't like. Although many white Southerners spoke out against the Klan, many also supported it, and the KKK flourished (1867–1871) until the government cracked down on it. The Klan disappeared for a while, and in the 1920s and 1930s reemerged with a vengeance, establishing chapters throughout the United States. Even today, some chapters remain active.

For young readers interested in looking further into the period of Reconstruction and the origins of the Ku Klux Klan, I recommend *They Called Themselves the K.K.K.: The Birth of an American Terrorist Group* by Susan Campbell Bartoletti (Houghton Mifflin, 2010), and *Reconstruction: Binding the Wounds*, edited by Cheryl Edwards (Perspectives on History Series, Discovery Enterprises, Ltd. 1995).

QUESTIONS FOR FURTHER RESEARCH, DISCUSSION, AND CONVERSATION

1. The Thirteenth Amendment to the United States Constitution, adopted in 1865, prohibits slavery and involuntary servitude. Although Shad's family never owned slaves, they still felt the effects of the amendment. Find evidence in the text of their feelings. Do you think their behavior was typical of the time? Why or why not? (Refer to pages 257–63.)

2. After the Civil War, many white Southerners began to describe the Confederacy as "a noble lost cause," and in *Brotherhood*, Mama says Daddy "died a noble death" (page 302). In the context of the story, define the word *noble*. Why does she use this word in this situation? Why did Southerners come to describe their part in the war this way?

3. Granddaddy says, "Schooling coloreds. Ain't nothing good to come of it" (page 316). What is the Weaver family's general feeling toward schooling? What disturbs Granddaddy about allowing people of color to get an education?

4. Mama tells Shad, "Some is meant for schooling and some not" (page 112). What effect does Mama's low expectation of Shad have on him? What is Shad's learning disability, and what motivates him to want to read?

5. The Fourteenth Amendment to the United States Constitution, adopted in 1868, grants citizenship to all people born in the United States and guarantees them equal protection under the law. The Fifteenth Amendment, adopted in 1870, grants all adult male citizens the right to vote. Although the story in *Brotherhood* takes place before the passage of these two amendments, Southerners were aware that politicians were arguing over the issues. Mama says, "And them Perkinsons—they're like all them

Yankees—they're happy the war ended the way it did. When there's something men got to decide in Washington, the Perkinsons side with them Yankees" (page 263). How did Southerners think these two amendments would affect the balance of power in the South? What changes were hardest for white Southerners like Mama to accept?

6. Mama says, "Just thinking on coloreds ruling Virginia, why, it's enough to make George Washington cry" (page 264). What does this statement tell you about Mama? How do you think the Weaver family would react to the news that an African American man would one day be elected president of the United States? How might Miss Elizabeth have reacted to such news? Find statements in the text to support your opinions.

7. Although Granddaddy is a member of the KKK, he fears that the brotherhood is "overstepping boundaries" (page 18), and Shad notes that Granddaddy isn't "easy about Klan business" (page 318). Why would a

man like Granddaddy join the Klan and go along with them even though he questions some of their actions?

8. What does Rachel mean by the comment that "every other colored family is scattered across the South" (page 323)? How did the institution of slavery affect the structure of African American families?

9. Shad thinks that Jeremiah has "too much pride to stand on a street corner and wait for a day job from a stupid carpetbagger" (page 73). What is a carpetbagger? Do you agree or disagree with Mr. O'Malley (page 53) and Jeremiah (page 301) that George Nelson is a carpetbagger? Why?

10. Rachel tells Shad that "the Freedmen's Bureau is giving food to everyone who needs it" (page 65), and Miss Elizabeth says that "we're all grateful for support from the Freedmen's Bureau" (page 97). What was the Freedmen's Bureau? Can you think of organizations today (either government or nongovern-

ment agencies) that provide help similar to that provided by the Freedmen's Bureau?

11. There are two instances in *Brotherhood* in which boys set out "to have a little fun" with the freedmen. Describe them. *Brotherhood* gives us a glimpse of the boys' side of the story, but not the victims' point of view. How do you think the freedmen might have felt, and what might the impact of these "fun" pranks have been on them? (Refer to pages 143–48, and 174–83.)

12. The reader does not hear Miss Elizabeth ask Rachel to let Shad attend her school (see pages 103–05). Imagine their conversation and write it from Rachel's point of view. How might the final scene at the marketplace (pages 352–55) have been different if written from Rachel's point of view?

13. Shad's relationship with the schoolchildren changes throughout the novel. How is his initial attitude toward them (pages 127–36) different from his attitude

later, when he wants to shout "Amen!" that Rachel and the children are still alive (page 355). Identify scenes when you see Shad's attitude begin to change. What do you think is the most significant turning point in his relationship with the children?

14. How would you feel about Jeremiah if he were your older brother? Identify passages where Shad (A) admires Jeremiah, (B) fears him, (C) stands up to him, and (D) fails to stand up to him. Take one of those passages and explain whether you would have handled it the same way Shad did, or differently.

15. How did you feel about Jeremiah when he was arrested the second time? In the scene at Libby Prison, did you believe the Yankee's statement that Jeremiah had resisted arrest (page 346)? If Jeremiah were to tell his side of the story, how might he describe what happened the night the Perkinsons' shed burned? Now rewrite that scene from Rachel's point of view.

16. How does Shad justify the rise of the Ku Klux Klan (page 293)? What do you think of his justification?

What could Virginians and other Southerners have done after the war to prove to the Yankees that they could and would handle their own problems? Why did Northerners think that martial law was necessary? In what foreign countries today do American soldiers patrol the streets, and how are today's situations the same as or different from the American South after the Civil War?

ACKNOWLEDGMENTS

I am grateful to numerous friends, relatives, and organizations whose knowledge, exhibits, and archived documents helped me write this novel: my aunt Mary Bryan Harms, Tom Robinson of Richmond's Gallery 5 (formerly the Virginia Fire and Police Museum and Steamer Company No. 5), the White House and Museum of the Confederacy, the American Civil War Center at Historic Tredegar, the Edgar Allan Poe House and Museum, the Virginia Historical Society, the Valentine Richmond History Center, the Library of Virginia, the Black History Museum and Cultural Center of Virginia, and Sally Craymer for her expertise in teaching children with dyslexia and other learning disabilities.

I am indebted to Susan Hankla for offering classes where fledgling writers find encouragement, to Deirdra McAfee for her editorial eye, and to readers who critiqued early drafts: Gigi Amateau, Claudia Brookman, Dick Davis, Ann McMillan, Meg Medina, Nylce Prada Myers, Jan Tarasovic, and Penelope Carrington Wallace. Special thanks to the supportive community within James River Writers, and particularly to the faculty and students at Vermont College of Fine Arts, notably my advisers Ellen Howard, Louise Hawes, Uma Krishnaswami, and Kathi Appelt, whose suggestion to restructure the story was nothing less than brilliant.

A huge thank-you to my agent, Leigh Feldman, and editor, Regina Hayes, who saw promise in this novel and provided insightful suggestions that guided me in making valuable revisions for clarity, depth, and polish. And finally, to my amazingly talented husband and children: your creative passions inspired me to find my own. Thank you, all.